In The Sanctity
of Revenge

By Brian Schnoor

For Mom, Dad, Kelli, and Tim

Dedicated to my beautiful wife and children. You
are my home and my everything

PART ONE

JUST BECAUSE THE SUN IS SHINING,
DOESN'T MEAN THERE ISN'T A STORM JUST OVER
THE HORIZON

I have set before you life and death, the blessing and the curse...

- Moses, Deuteronomy

CHAPTER ONE

Skeletal arms trembled, struggling to lift the old steel revolver. Blue and purple veins popped through celluloid skin. Shaking hands with frail fingers and rusted joints fought with the trigger to pull the heavy hammer back. Jack Hanlon smiled at the sight.

SATURDAY JUNE 5, 2010

The sun hung high in the cloudless afternoon sky, drying the sidewalks and baking away the evidence of the viscous storm of the night before. Small branches and twigs littered the lawns and gutters of the sleepy Chicago side street. The two opposing rows of brick bungalows, most redbrick, some yellow-brick, that lined either side of Mobile Street had weathered the storm as they had done for close to a century now. There was no major damage. A few basements had taken in water, but just enough to make a mess before receding back into the floor drains.

Saturday morning was uneventful at the Hanlon home. Amy had gotten up with the boys and made them blueberry pancakes for breakfast while Jack slept in. Around noon, dressed in the gym shorts he'd slept in, cheap slippers, and an old softball shirt that read "Mad Dogs" in script across the front and bore the logo of Windy Ray's Tavern – "Proud Sponsor of 16" Softball Since 1972" - on the shirt's back. Jack lifted the lid to the black, iron mailbox hanging on the wall just outside his front door. It was empty. He stood on the front porch, and peered up and down the quiet street in hopes of seeing the mailman walking his cart down the block. No luck.

Across the street Mrs. Kelly watered her flowerbed despite the heavy rains that had doused them overnight. When she saw Jack, she waved. Jack waved back and tried to duck back into the house before the old lady could trap him into a conversation but it was too late. She'd already dropped her hose and was heading across her small patch of perfect lawn calling his name, "Jack, oh Jack. I want to talk to you."

It's not that Jack disliked Mrs. Kelly. In fact, he liked her very much. She reminded him of his grandmother, and he felt a sort of responsibility toward her since her husband passed. Jack would spend weekend days doing little jobs around Mrs. Kelly's house, fixing this, patching that. Amy would take her shopping if the weather was bad and the buses were running slow. But lonely widows can talk an awfully long time, and make a big deal about things of no consequence, and frankly today Jack wasn't up for one of those conversations. His mind was elsewhere.

"Jack," she called hustling across the street. "Jack, I want to talk to you. Don't go anywhere." She hurried as quickly as a seventy-eight year old woman in Walgreen's sneakers can. Jack stepped off his porch and met her on the sidewalk.

"Hi Mrs. Kelly, how are you?"

"Oh, I could complain, but who would listen," she replied.

'Apparently, this morning, it's going to be me,' Jack thought, but held his smile.

"Anyway, did you hear that storm last night? It woke me from a sound sleep. I thought lightening hit that big tree and that it was going to fall in on my head. Thank the Lord it was just a clap of thunder. Did it wake the children? You look like you missed a good night sleep."

"Yeah, Timmy woke up a couple of times, but went back to bed pretty quick. Once I was up though, I had a hard time falling back to sleep. I wish I was more like Amy, she gets up with the kids, and as soon as her head hits the pillow again, she's out cold." Truth was, Jack was already up. He hadn't been sleeping well lately.

"That's because women work harder than men," Mrs. Kelly gave a wink and a smile.

"In my house, that is certainly the case. I won the lottery when I married Amy. She's one of a kind."

"Don't you forget that Jack Hanlon," she said, her eyes narrowing, then flashed him a wink and a smile. Jack had often thought that Mrs. Kelly had probably been a very beautiful woman in her youth, and now and then a flash of that girl would appear in that wink and smile she often gave to let you know she was teasing. "Ah, she coulda done worse herself too ya know," Mrs. Kelly continued, "Anyhow, the reason I stopped you is because I was wondering if you could do me a favor."

"Sure Mrs. Kelly, what do you need?"

"Well, the storm last night did knock a huge branch off the neighbor's tree into my backyard. I've been telling them for months now that the tree needs to be pruned, but that good for nothin' bum sits on his backside all day doing nothing, and you know she's not much of a housekeeper. I've never been inside, but from what I hear there is crusted food all over the kitchen and dust bunnies everywhere. How people could live like that is beyond me. Anyhow, I know he'd never move it from my yard, or at least I'd be waiting till my last breath for him to do it, so if you wouldn't mind just stopping by - when you have time of course, no hurry - and just put it out in the alley for me?"

"Of course Mrs. Kelly. Give me a minute to put on a decent pair of shoes and grab a saw and I'll be right over."

"You're a doll Jack, thank you. You know, since Harold died I've really come to realize how nice it was to have a man in the house. I am certainly for women's equality and what not, but there's no denying that there are some things men are better at taking care of. Maybe I'm just an old woman, I don't know. And don't you dare tell a soul I said that or so help me God I'll shoot you right in the face," she smiled and winked at him again with that twinkle in her warm blue eyes. That's when Jack had the vision of those skinny little arms struggling to raise a pistol to eye level and fighting to pull the trigger. The thought had made him smile and he wondered if she noticed. Of course, if he knew what would eventually come of them all, he never would have found such a scene amusing.

"Okay, see you in a few minutes." Jack turned to go inside, then stopped and turned back toward Mrs. Kelly who was about to cross the street back to her house. "Mrs. Kelly, did you happen to get your mail yet?"

"No, he hasn't been by yet Jack. It's that new fella. I don't like him very much. He's slow. When we had the black fella..." she said the word 'black' a little quieter than the rest, almost a whisper but not quite, "... we always got our mail by ten o'clock, even on Saturdays. This guy though, you never know when he's gonna decide to show up. I've complained several times."

"I'm sure you have. Thank you Mrs. Kelly." Jack took another look up the street for the mailman, then dropped his head and went in the house to fetch his shoes and chainsaw.

It didn't take long for Jack to cut up the branch and move it to the alley for Mrs. Kelly.

The mail finally arrived a little after two. Jack was beginning to hate the new mailman as much as Mrs. Kelly did. Of course, the mailman can't control what comes and doesn't come in the mail, but that didn't ease Jack's disdain for the man when, after having waited all day, the envelope containing the settlement papers from GS wasn't in the bundle of ads and coupons and bills the chubby, pink-cheeked man handed him that Saturday afternoon.

"How can a man who walks the neighborhood for a living be that fat?" Jack thought.
Jack wanted to call his lawyer to find out what the hold up was with the papers, but knew he'd get the voicemail. Seth had gone on vacation and wasn't due back in the office until Monday. It would have to wait.

Frustrated, Jack tossed the bundle of ads and bills on the dining room table and went out to the yard to pull some weeds and have a cigarette. Quitting hadn't been easy and he was furious with himself for retreating back to his nicotine addiction, but he promised himself he'd quit again once this whole mess was resolved.

5

As Jack tugged up the dandelions from the lawn and yanked at the weeds around the rose bush, he thought about work. He didn't want to. He wanted a respite from it, but for months now, it was all he could think about.

Before everything had gone wrong, Jack had liked getting lost in his thoughts. Often, he got his best ideas when he was pulling weeds or mowing the lawn or jogging through the neighborhood. Nowadays, the dark recesses of his mind were like a quicksand, pulling him down into a suffocating place with no bottom, no resolution and no escape. There were times when he'd be so lost in his thoughts, he'd catch himself talking aloud to no one and hoped the neighbors hadn't heard him. He had a new-found empathy for the crazy homeless people who wandered the streets and bus terminals talking to themselves, lost in their own world, absent from the here-and-now to live only inside their own head where the voices reside.

He had one of these moments in the yard as he was digging a stubborn prickly weed from the garden and was brought out of his trance by his ten year old son Sean.

"Daddy... daddy," Sean called. Jack looked over his shoulder at the boy. "Daddy, who are you talking to?"

Jack cleared his throat and replied, "No one, Seany. Just thinking out loud, I guess. What's up?"

"Wanna play catch?"

Jack stabbed his hand shovel into the dirt and stood up. Blood rushed back to his legs. He was grateful for the distraction. His boy had pulled him out of the quicksand, at least for the moment.

Sean tossed the football to Jack then ran about eight feet across the small, city yard and waited for the pass, his back foot nearly up against the chain link fence dividing the Hanlon yard from the Dumbrowski's next door. Jack tossed a lazy spiral to the boy and Sean caught it, set a perfect quarterback position and fired it back. Father and son repeated this back and forth several times before Jack broke the silence.

"How's school, Sean?"

"Okay. Only one week left. I can't wait 'til summer vacation starts."

"What've you been learning?"

"Nothing."

"Nothing? All that time and you don't learn nothing?" Jack said with a smile.

"Anything, Dad. Don't learn *anything*."

"Well it sounds like you've learned *something*."

"That's English. I like English. I hate math."

"Everyone hates math, son. It's just one of those things you have to learn. You won't get anywhere in life without math. What are you learning in English?"

"We had to read this story about a fox that ate the farmer's chickens, so the farmer lit the fox's tail on fire as payback…"

"I don't think I've heard this one," Jack said as he tossed the ball back to his son.

"… and guess what happened."

"I don't know, what?"

Sean held onto the ball for a moment. "The fox ran through the farmer's field with his tail on fire cause it was hot and it hurt his butt and his tail lit all the farmer's wheat and stuff on fire on accident and the farmer wound up with nothin' at all cause it all burned down. Crazy, huh?"

"Wow, you're tellin' me. That's a good story. What's the moral, Sean?"

"The farmer made his own crops to burn down 'cause he was mad at the fox and lit the fox on fire. If he didn't do that, he would've lost some chickens but not all his wheat too and then have nothing left at all."

"You got it, kiddo."

"Yeah, pretty easy stuff. I got an A on that quiz."

"So what did you wanna do this summer?"

"Me and Devin Reilly are gonna spend the whole summer at the Jeff Park pool."

"Sounds like a fun-filled summer. Think you'll be able to break away from the pool long enough to go fishing with me down at Northerly Island?"

"I think I can pencil ya in for that, Dad," Sean replied with a smile.

"Gee thanks Sean. Can you pencil in an afternoon at Montrose Beach and maybe a Cub game with the family?"

"Yes, I can definitely find time for those. But, not the weekend of June 23, that's when the old Jeff Park Theater is having a Star Wars movie marathon! They're showing episode one through three in order!"

"They are? Boy, I woulda loved that when I was your age."

"Dad, you liked Star Wars?"

"Are you kidding? I saw Return of the Jedi like six times at the Gateway that summer it came out. I used to run around the neighborhood pretending I was a Jedi knight."

In his best impersonation of Yoda, Sean growled out, "The Force is all around you young Jedi, but beware the dark side."

"Sean," Jack said in an attempt to sound like James Earl Jones, "I am your father!"

"There's still good in you Father, I can feel it!" Sean giggled as he recited that line. His giggling threw him off balance as he threw the football.

Jack ran up and caught Sean's wobbling pass, tucked the ball under his arm and ran toward his son as if he were running for a touchdown. He juked left, ran right and when Sean grabbed hold of his hips, Jack dropped to the ground.

"Got ya Dad!" Sean yelled.

"Oh, you got me did ya?" Jack started tickling the boy just below the ribs where he knew his son was the most ticklish. Sean laughed so hard it was a struggle to breath. Jack beamed. His son's contagious laughter rang out into the summer breeze.

That night Jack found himself sitting at his kitchen table, smoking cigarettes, and unable to sleep again. He ran the whole thing over in his head for the millionth time. He wanted to stop thinking about it, he really did. But he couldn't. Thinking about it got his stomach churning and his heart rate up. His temper rose, and he had to walk, but he couldn't escape it, so he sat and it drove him crazy and he'd get up and walk again. He'd begun wearing a hole in the carpet between the kitchen and the front room. He'd walked the neighborhood countless nights, meandering aimlessly up one block then down the next, unable to escape his thoughts. Television was no help either. He would find something he thought would be interesting, then ten minutes later realize he hadn't been paying attention, so he'd flip through the channels uselessly. It was the channel in his head he was trying to turn off and it wasn't working. No song held his attention long enough to subdue him, no book was able to grab his mind long enough to be more than a series of meaningless squiggles forming no words or thoughts.

He had finally given up and sat at the kitchen table smoking his cigarettes, something Amy had never allowed him to do in the house before. She'd relented when she was awakened night after night by the constant opening and shutting of the screen door as he'd go out and come back in from the back porch.

Jack reached in his shirt pocket for his cigarette pack, but it wasn't there. As if snapping out of a dream, he was suddenly aware of his surroundings. It was nearly four a.m. His kitchen was dark except for the lights under the cabinets at the far end of the room that shed just enough glow to cast faint shadows on the opposite wall and door. Jack looked around and found the cigarette box on the table in front of him. He picked it up. It was empty. He got his shoes, reached in his pocket and found a balled up ten-dollar bill, grabbed his keys and went out the back door toward the gas station at the corner.

The morning air was humid with a slight chill. Fog hung high in the alley, gathering around the lamplight like a swarm of mosquitoes. Though it was six miles east of his alley, Jack could smell the lake in the air, a mix of fresh water and stale fish. He liked it.

The city was quiet on Sunday mornings. The four o'clock bars were just emptying out and a few muffler-less cars roared by down Montrose Avenue, but for the most part, everything was still. Jack breathed in the Lake Michigan air as deep as he could and exhaled slowly.

At the gas station, the store area was closed and locked. Jack had to make his transaction through an aluminum drawer and a tin speaker. From behind the glass, the muffled voice of the attendant reverberated through the speaker in a thick accent. Jack assumed he'd said something along the lines of 'how may I help you' or 'what the fuck do you want'.

"Box of Marlboro Lights," Jack pulled the ten out of his pocket and placed it in the waiting drawer. The drawer closed then opened again. The sawbuck was gone, a box of cigarettes and some change left in its place. Jack walked off smacking the pack against the palm of his hand.

When he got back home, he sat on the back steps smoking and admiring the peacefulness of the pre-dawn, the sky dark as night but on the verge of daybreak. Jack teetered between the peaceful city around him and the clanging clatter in his mind.

CHAPTER TWO

The bedroom was still dark, but the first morning birds were already chirping to life when Amy heard the back door close and lock. Downstairs the floorboards creaked as Jack stepped through the kitchen and into the front room. She checked the alarm clock on the nightstand and saw that it was almost a quarter to five in the morning. She figured he must have run out of cigarettes and went out to get more. He'd been going through them quite rapidly as of late, frighteningly so.

She lie there in the dark for about half an hour before she gave up trying to fall back to sleep. She felt her way through the black hallway to the stairs. Holding on to the wall as she went, she carefully descended the staircase to the first floor.

The Eastern sky was beginning to show just a hint of the bright morning to come.

10

She found Jack asleep in the La-Z-Boy, curled under his flannel shirt, jeans still on, shoes tossed beside the chair. Amy grabbed the throw from the back of the couch and laid it atop her husband, tucking it in around his shoulders and under his chin. She watched him lie there in what she imagined must be a most uncomfortable position. His cigarette pack and lighter had fallen to the floor. Amy brushed the hair back from his forehead and kissed Jack gently, careful not to wake him.

They had met in college. Jack was in his third year studying Business Administration and Amy was in her second year, still an Undeclared Liberal Arts student. Amy was working in the school bookstore to help defray the costs of tuition. Money was tight back home, but Amy worked hard and saved as much as she could, got some loans and convinced her family to send her downstate for school. She had aspirations of becoming a doctor, but didn't quite know if she had what it took to make it that far. So for the time being, she was happy just to be in school and was fighting hard to stay there.

In the fall of that year, Amy met a rugby player named Dan. He was California blonde, with blue eyes, and a gym-rat build, wide shoulders, thick pecs, big biceps. Dan had an okay sense of humor and was fairly intelligent. They met at a party when he and his Rugby friends had shown up and put some arrogant frat boys in their place. So far Dan was the best thing Amy had encountered at school, so she figured why not give it a shot.

It didn't take long for her to grow tired of him. He had an antique mentality about a woman's place and he spent too much time speaking about himself. She'd never caught him cheating, but figured he probably had. He was a flirt and there was no shortage of girls paying him attention. His friends had hit on her too many times to count, and he seemed to either not notice, or not care. In any event, by March she was done with him and she told him so. He did not take it well. It occurred to Amy that maybe she was the first girl to ever break up with Dan.

He went from virtually ignoring her while they were dating to practically stalking her after the break-up. He would call her at all hours of the night. He would be waiting outside the lecture hall for her when she came out of class. He would slide notes beneath her dorm-room door, at first sweet and nostalgic, but after going ignored, they quickly became mean and threatening. Nothing so blatant that she felt she could or even should go to the police, but still it was enough to make her uneasy.

Then one afternoon while she was working at the bookstore, she noticed a cute guy perusing the magazine section. She'd seen him in there a few times before, but he always seemed to disappear without buying anything.

"Hi," she said, "Can I help you find something?"

The boy smiled back at her. He had a kind smile. A warm smile. A safe smile. The kind of smile you want your baby to look up at one day.

"Um," the boy replied, "Ah, I was just kinda looking." He placed the copy of Men's Health he'd been reading back on the rack.

"For anything in particular?"

"Actually," he said with a nervous smile, "I was looking for a book called 'How to Ask the Pretty Girl Who Works at the Bookstore Out On a Date Without Looking Like A Complete and Total Ass'. I checked the self-help section already and now here, but I can't seem to find it anywhere and I could really use it right now."

This made her smile. "I'm not sure we carry that one."

"I see. I didn't think you did. Maybe the Library has it."

"Yeah, maybe they do," she answered, "but honestly, I don't think you need it as bad as you think you do.'

"No?"

"No. I think you're doing pretty fine without it. Of course there's only one way to find out."

"How's that?" he asked.

She gave him a look that said 'seriously, are you really that stupid?'

"Oh yeah," he caught on, "I guess there is only one way to find out." He cleared his throat. "Um, pretty girl who works in the bookstore…"

"Amy"

"Sorry, um pretty girl named Amy who works in the bookstore, I'm Jack, would you like to…"

The anger and jealousy in the voice that interrupted them was all too familiar to her. "Hey! Amy!"

Dan's face was beat red, his blood vessels were pulsing, his fists clenched at his sides. He wedged himself between them, putting his back to Jack. "What the fuck? You just stop returning my calls? What's going on?" He stepped towards her. She backed away. Still, he was too close. His breath was hot and gross. "I mean, really, what the fuck? Are you too good for me now? Is that it? I love you. I put it all out there for you! Why don't you call me back? Huh? I want an answer!"

"Dan, I told you, it's over. I don't want to see you anymore. You've got to let it go. Leave me alone." She stepped away again. He followed.

"Is that how it is?" he took another step towards her, she took another step back but he hovered scary-close to her. Others in the store had noticed and were now watching. "Who the fuck do you think you are bitch? You think you can leave me? Fuck you. You think you're too good for me?"

"*I* think she's too good for you." Jack's voice was steady, matter-of-fact.

Dan turned to look at Jack. "Who asked you?" Turning back to Amy he asked, "Is this the reason you dumped me? This fuckin' dweeb? You bangin' him now?"

"No you asshole, I dumped you 'cause you're a self-centered, boring idiot. You treated me like shit and the only reason you want me back is because I broke up with you and it bruised your ego. So now I'm telling you in no uncertain terms to fuck off!"

Dan raised his hand and began the motion to smack Amy across the face when his arm was stopped and pulled back. In one motion he was turned around where Jack met him with a sharp, quick shot to the nose, then, before Dan could react, Jack took him facedown to the floor and tangled his legs. Dan's head bounced hard off the thin layer of commercial carpet when Jack took him down causing his vision to blur and nausea to set in. Jack wrapped his left arm under Dan's left armpit in a half nelson, while his right arm repeatedly swung a meaty fist into the side of Dan's neck fast and efficient and hard. Dan let out a roar of pain as a crowd gathered around. Dan turned his head so it was no longer on its side, resting his chin on the floor. He struggled trying to get up on his hands and knees. Each time he raised up some on a straight arm, Jack would buckled the elbow and Dan would drop chin first back onto the unforgiving floor. Then Jack reached over the top of Dan's head, took the index and middle fingers of his right hand and shoved them hard up Dan's nostrils and yanked Dan's head back by the nose. There was nowhere for Dan to go. If he pushed forward, the pain was excruciating. If he tried to go backwards, Jack would pull his head further back and drive his knee into Dan's spine.

"Apologize to the lady," Jack said.

"Fuck you," Dan spit out.

Using Dan's nostrils as a handle, Jack yanked Dan's head back further. Dan let out an agonized yell.

"Apologize to the lady," Jack repeated himself. Dan felt the hard meaning behind the quiet words, but spit out again, "Fuck you and fuck her."

With his left hand, Jack pressured Dan's head down so his chin dug into the floor again. Then, with the two fingers of his right hand still firmly shoved up Dan's nostrils, he gave a quick, forceful twist of his right hand and forearm. Dan's nose gave a sharp 'crack' as it bent sideways, then a small pop as Jack's fingers exited the nostrils, which now faced westward instead of south.

Blood poured from Dan's nose.

Jack gave him two hard blows to the ribs and kidney, then two more punches to the side of the neck. Jack grabbed Dan by the hair and pulled his head back. He gave him a sturdy shot to his exposed throat, whispered something into

14

Dan's ear, then calmly rose off of Dan and straightened his shirt. Dan remained on the ground holding his nose and coughing.

Amy stood frozen with her hands to her mouth. Jack turned to her and asked if she was all right. She nodded yes. She couldn't believe what she'd just seen. She had thought he was cute before and was going to say yes to his request for a date, but now, he seemed more ruggedly handsome than cute. He had the warm brown eyes of a puppy dog and the fierce protector's instinct of a German Shepard all wrapped up in the body of a collegiate wrestler. She was smitten.

The crowd dispersed. Having seen how the whole thing had started, the bystanders held no sympathy for the bleeding man on the ground.

"Where was I?" Jack asked smiling and a little out of breath. "Oh yeah, pretty girl named Amy who works in the bookstore, would you like to go out with me sometime?"

Amy felt the strange urge to cry, but instead she smiled an enormous smile and nodded. "Yes," she said, "I would like to go out with you sometime. How about tonight? I get out of here around six. Does eight thirty sound good?"

"Sounds perfect," Jack answered.

Amy gave Jack her address and a hug and he left. On his way out, he passed two campus police officers running in response to a call about a fight in the bookstore. When they got there, they found an angry bleeding man with a severely busted nose, and no witnesses.

At 8:30 that night, the Resident Assistant on duty called up to Amy's dorm room to tell her Jack Hanlon was in the lobby for her. They'd been together ever since.

The man in the La-Z-Boy now, twenty some odd years later, was a little softer, a little rounder in the belly. He wasn't horribly out of shape, but time and work and age and the turmoil of the past several months had sculpted him into something softer than the collegiate wrestler she'd met that day on campus. Still, he was cute. She watched him sleep and, for the first time in a long time, saw the patient and peaceful-natured man she'd married. The harsh lines of age and of time seemed to have evaporated from his face as he lie sleeping and she thought of him again as a boy. She thought of the passionate period between those first few dates and the first few years of marriage, when they simply could not keep their hands off each other. That passion had lasted longer for them than it had for most of the other couples they knew. It took becoming parents for that passion to subside a bit, and even then, it was only a bit. By the time the second one came around, it was energy that was lacking more than passion, and by the third, well, they were just hanging on for dear life.

They were now outnumbered, outwitted, and out of breath, but they did their best to keep the romance alive. He did his part. He'd stop off for a dozen roses at the corner store on his way home when they were on sale for $12.99 a dozen. When they weren't, he'd buy one from the panhandler at the exit ramp of the expressway who sold single roses for a buck out of an old five gallon bucket.

Jack adored her. He wore it on his face, showed it in his eyes. Everything he did, he did for her and their children. No amount of paunch around the belly or lines around the eyes could diminish that.

But he seemed so unhappy lately. What she wanted most was to see him happy again.

CHAPTER THREE

Mrs. Kelly shuffled to the door as quickly as she could. It was early and she was still in her slippers and housecoat. She couldn't imagine who would be ringing the doorbell at this hour on a Monday.

She pulled back the small, yellowed curtain on the window of her front door to see who was on her porch. It was a large man, about thirty-five years old or so. He had a potbelly and a receding hairline. He wore a polo type shirt with a company logo over the left breast. The logo read simply: 'Home improvement and Remodeling' and beneath is in script the word 'Owner'. He had a tape measure clipped to his belt beside his cell phone and he held a clipboard in his hand. Behind his ear was a pencil. Mrs. Kelly cracked the door, leaving the chain in place.

"Yeah?" she answered in her grouchiest old lady voice.

"Hello ma'am, sorry to bother you at this early hour." The man's voice was softer and kinder than she thought it'd be.

"What do ya want?" she barked.

"Well we're going through the neighborhood as a service to our neighbors to inspect their roof and look for damage from this past week's storm. There's no obligation to buy anything from us, and there is no fee for us to take a look, do a quick inspection and give you a report on what we find. We're doing this as a free service for our fellow neighbors because this was one heck of a storm and it produced a lot of damage. The last thing you want is a damaged roof over your house. So do you mind if I take a look and make sure everything is A-OK up there?"

Mrs. Kelly's yellow-brick bungalow was built in 1919 and, as was the case with many of the classic Chicago bungalows of the time, it still boasted the original green clay tile roof. It was this roof, along with the front bay lead-glass windows, that had made her fall in love with the place when she and Harold were house hunting as a young couple.

Harold liked the clay tile roof too. "Barely any maintenance and this puppy will out-live us both, and maybe even the kids. Just gotta keep the gutters clean and the mortar strong and it will withstand anything, including the passage of time," he'd told her.

As a result, she'd never thought twice about the roof. She'd never had anyone out to look at it since Harold passed. He said it would last forever, so why worry about it? Of course, nothing lasts forever, does it? The thought that her beautiful, indestructible roof might be compromised sent shivers through her.

He seemed harmless, and what would it hurt to let him take a look? An inspection is something she'd probably been neglecting out of ignorance for years now. If he said he found something and wanted to sell her a roof, she could always say no. He said the inspection was free… why not let him take a look around. Besides, he had a wedding band on his left hand bearing the Irish cladagh and he wore a crucifix around his neck. 'He couldn't be all-bad,' she thought.

"Okay, have a look around if you want, but I'm not buying anything," she snarled.

"Of course ma'am. My associate and I will be up there for a little while. We'll try not to disturb you."

With that the man turned and gave his partner in the nondescript pickup truck the high sign and hustled down the stairs. Mrs. Kelly shut and bolted the front door, but continued to watch the men as they took a ladder off their truck and leaned it against her house. For the next half hour, she heard footsteps and scraping and various 'workman's' noises above her head. When it stopped, she looked out the window again to see the man she had spoken to, helping his partner put the ladder in the bed of the pickup again. Then he made his way to her door.

"Well Mrs. …"

"Kelly," she answered.

"Thank you. Well Mrs. Kelly, is Mr. Kelly home?"

"No… he's," she almost told him the truth, but decided against it, "he's out at the moment. But he's due back very soon." She threw that in there just in case they had planned on raping her.

"Well, perhaps you'd like to have your husband call us…"

"No. No, that won't be necessary. If you tell me what you found, I'll be sure to pass the message along."

"Well Ma'am, we found significant damage. When was the last time you've had this roof looked at?"

She made up a number and lied, "It was twelve years ago or so. I thought these clay roofs were indestructible."

"They are tough, ma'am," the man explained, "but like anything else, they don't last forever, and a tough enough storm on an almost hundred year old roof will cause its share of damage." He reminded her of her grandson now. "Ma'am, I hate to tell you this, but you need a new roof. Desperately. I almost don't feel comfortable leaving you

18

here under it for the night. That storm did a number on it. You have to fix it or when winter comes, you will be laying under a bed of snow and a pile of clay shingles. We have to get this done soon. Because this is such an emergency, and because we're doing other roofs in the neighborhood already, I'm going to quote you half of what I quote most people. Usually, a job like yours here would run about forty thousand dollars, clay tiles aren't all that easy to come by these days, but I happen to have some from a tear down that will lessen your cost. I'll give you the clay tile shingles, and immediate instillation for just twenty-five thousand. I would go lower if I could, but that just barely covers my materials and labor costs, and I do have some little ones at home..."

"Maybe I should call my insurance company. This should be covered by my homeowner's policy."

"You could do that ma'am if you'd like, but your premiums will skyrocket if you make a claim this big," he warned her, "They may even drop you. Then if you have a fire or some other catastrophe, you'll be up the creek."

"Well why the hell do I have insurance for then?" the old lady was close to tears.

"Well Mrs. Kelly, you know insurance companies aren't in business to lose money after all. They make it up somewhere, and that somewhere is your premiums. The other problem is that it is going to take them a week, maybe two, just to get a man out here to look at the job. Then he has to go back and run the paperwork through different channels. It'll be a month or more before you're approved. By then, you could be walking on your roof because it will be in your basement."

"Oh dear." Mrs. Kelly folded her arms and bit her lip. She'd missed her husband terribly since he passed, but never as much as in moments like this. He would know exactly what to do. God how she wished he were there with her to talk to this man at the door, or push the insurance company along quicker, or at least whisper in her ear, "do this Dear" or "do that, Honey". She listened for a moment hoping to hear his voice, but all she heard was silence.

A meaty hand reached for her through the open door. She nearly jumped out of her skin. The man at the door softly rested a reassuring hand on her shoulder and gave it a gentle squeeze.

"Mrs. Kelly. I know this is overwhelming ma'am. If you'd like to think about it, please go ahead. I'm not trying to push you into anything. But I do want to tell you, I am a father of three young children, I go to church every Sunday morning, I have been fixing roofs for over fifteen years now, I wouldn't steer you wrong. How about you think about it for a day or two and I'll come back and you can tell me what you've decided. In the meantime though, I'd like to put a tarp up there for you, just to be on the safe side. Once water gets in the walls ma'am, the damage becomes much more expensive to fix."

Mrs. Kelly looked into his eyes. "What parish do you belong to?" she asked.

The man smiled at her. There was a slight hesitation before he replied, "What parish do I belong to? Oh, I'm a long time parishioner over at Our Lady's."

"Our Lady's what?" Mrs. Kelly interrogated.

"I'm sorry?"

"You said the parish you belong to is Our Lady's. Our Lady's what? Our Lady of the Resurrection? ... of Perpetual Help? ... of Angles? ... of Hope? ... of Victory? ... of Mercy?"

"Our Lady of the Rosary," he answered, "It's on Ogden Avenue just passed..."

"I'm familiar."

Mrs. Kelly studied the man.

"Would you like to see pictures of my little ones?" he asked. Before she could answer, he was holding up a wallet sized-photo of three darling girls. She thought of those girls running up and hugging 'Daddy' after he'd come home from a hard day's work. She thought of Harold. She thought of her own Daddy.

"I won't pay a penny over twenty thousand," she stated with a newfound confidence, her decision having been made. "When can you start?"

"The end of the week soon enough?"

"Oh, that sounds just fine. Lord knows I don't want to go through the winter wondering when the roof is going to fall in on me. Do you take Visa?"

"I'm sorry ma'am, it's really just a small family business. We take personal checks or cash."

"Well, okay. Let me get my checkbook."

"Great."

"I'm not paying the whole thing upfront, mind you. I'll give you half now and the other half when you're finished."

"Sounds fair," he said. Then he checked his watch and took a quick look over his shoulder.

"So, a check for ten thousand will..." Mrs. Kelly had the pen on the check ready to write.

"Hold on. Now, we did agree on twenty, so half of that *is* ten thousand, but then these clay roofs really do need some extra care, expensive supplies, extra help. Why don't we say an even twelve grand, and we'll be able to start by Thursday."

Mrs. Kelly considered that for a moment. She had no idea what was standard. She knew not to give him the whole thing, but if another two grand would get the ball rolling faster, then so be it. The price was the same in the end; it was just a little bit more up front.

"Okay. Twelve thousand." Mrs. Kelly scribbled out a twelve thousand dollar check and handed it to the balding man on the porch. She looked up at her ceiling and swore she saw cracks where there weren't any last week. She was terrified her roof was going to fall in on her. That was not the way she wanted to die.

"Now don't cash that until tomorrow. I have to get to the bank first."

"Not a problem ma'am. You have a nice day now." The man had a spring in his step as he glided down the steps and practically skipped to his van. In a heartbeat he was gone. Mrs. Kelly hoped she'd done the right thing. There was nothing left to do but worry and call the bank to transfer the money. She did both.

CHAPTER FOUR

Two Years Earlier
AUGUST 8, 2008

It could be a year before he saw a dime, but the money was coming, and it would be good money. When all would be said and done, Jack would look back on this as having been the worst day of his life, the beginning of the end. But he didn't know that at the time. No, on this hot August day, Jack Hanlon felt the need to celebrate. He stopped off at a cigar shop and bought himself one of the good, eight-dollar ones, then went to the florist for a dozen yellow roses for Amy, and finally the liquor store for a bottle of red and a lottery ticket. It had, after all, been a lucky day, hadn't it?

They ordered carryout from the Gale Street Inn and celebrated as a family at home. Amy listened attentively as Jack told her about the old man in the Denny's parking lot, the flat tire, and everything that happened from there. She was amazed. Even the boys listened without interruption, though it helped that they were busy gnawing away at their barbeque ribs.

After the table had been cleared and the kids sent to bed, Amy curled up on the couch next to Jack and poured the last of the wine into his glass.

"Are you sure you figured it right? Jack, that's incredible." She wore a pink nightshirt from Victoria's Secret that was made to look like a football jersey with the word 'PINK' written in block letters across the back. It fell at about mid-thigh. The neckline was generous. It fell off to the right revealing her bare shoulder. It was Jack's favorite.

"Eh, give or take a little." Jack ran his hand from her knee to mid-thigh and back to her knee again. "Don't get too excited yet though. It's a long process. We have to convince the doctors that our equipment is right for them. Even with the agreement I secured today, a staff-doctor can nix the deal if he's leery about using our machines. Then we have to send out project planners to figure out delivery and installation, determine if any re-wiring or updates to the building's cooling system need to be done. Once all of that is squared away and we have a delivery date, the hospital still has ninety days to use the machines before payment is due. Once the ninety days are up and they've made their payment, *then* I can expect my commission. It's a lengthy process, but we're talkin' about 36 hospitals in the Midwest, and they have to come to me first. And this Mr. Hornsby, he says most of them are ready for new equipment and if he puts in the word that he's buying one for the Elk Grove location, most will follow his lead. With the incentives in this new sales associate contract General Systems gave us, even with the lowered commission, it's more money than I've ever made, Amy."

"And you had no idea who he was when you changed his tire?"

"None. I had a meeting with him at ten. I'd never seen the guy in my life. I was early and stopped off for breakfast and noticed the old man next to me getting into his car had a flat, so I told him. He was older and dressed nice so I offered to fix it for him. He asked what I do for a living, I told him, said I had a meeting with Advanta, next thing you know, he tells me who he is and we hit it off. I have breakfast, head to his office for the meeting, walk out of there with a preferred sales agreement for the entire Midwest. God was shining on me today."

"You did a good thing, and God was rewarding you." She scratched her nails lightly on his head in a casual manner. "You know what we could do with that money, Jack?" Her voice was just slightly above a whisper.

"I know exactly what we're going to do with that money Amy dear. First, we are going to pay off the credit cards. There isn't too much there, but any is too much for my peace of mind. Then, we're going to buy a new hot water heater and a washing machine, braces for Trevor of course, and then, we'll start a college fund for each of the kids. Pay a few thousand off of the mortgage, and whatever we have left, we'll put into savings." He didn't mention the romantic vacation he'd budgeted for, he wanted that to be a surprise.

"All very practical, Jack. That is exactly why I love you."

"You wouldn't rather I spend it on a bigger diamond than that little thing I bought you when we got engaged?"

"The most precious gems you could give me are sleeping soundly upstairs."

"Awwww," he teased.

"Awwww," she met his mocking and for a moment they teased in harmony. She wrinkled her nose and rubbed the tip of it against Jack's, then backed off again. "Seriously though," she continued, "if we could give our boys a college education without saddling them or ourselves with debt, that would be a dream come true. So few people get to do that these days. Besides, a big diamond would get in the way when I'm showing you how I want you to load the new dishwasher you're going to buy." She poked him playfully in the ribs and smiled a smile that made his heart leap.

"Of course, how could I forget the dishwasher?" Jack was running his hand a little higher up her thigh now with each stroke, "So you like my plan?"

"Mmm. You had me at 'hot water heater'," she smiled as she said this and her fingers gripped his hair and she pulled him to her. They kissed like they did when they were dating, deep and passionate and meaningful.

Amy fell backward on the couch, Jack on top of her. She loosened the buttons on his shirt and slid it off his shoulders. Despite his sedentary occupation, he still retained most of the musculature definition of the collegiate wrestler he'd been when they met. Strong shoulders, sinuous muscle fibers stretching down to his biceps where they heaped high and firm and wrapped around to an equally tight bulge on the back of the upper arm. She ran her hands along the ridges of his strength and felt the old fires inside her flare again.

Jack pulled her nightshirt up above her navel and ran his hand high along the smooth, tight skin of her leg. She fumbled with his belt, his button and his fly until she held him firmly in her grasp.

They tumbled off the couch to the floor. He pulled her nightshirt over her head and she wiggled free of it. He kicked his legs free of his pants. His mouth moved from her lips to her neck and he kissed her where her nape met her soft freckled shoulder. She responded as she always had to that with a purr and a deep inhalation.

Their hips moved in syncopation. Every nerve ending was lit. Every move, every touch delivered tiny, electrified jolts of pleasure. Beads of sweat formed on Jack's forehead. He lifted his upper body high taking his weight off her chest and looked down at her, into her warm familiar eyes and across her beautiful face that only seemed to get prettier with age and he was overcome with love for her. She, for her part, looked up at him, feeling him inside her, she felt safe and loved and desirable. In his eyes she saw the fulfillment of her every wish, the father of her children, the strong protecting body, the gentle soul and generous heart and it drove her deeper into love and rapturous delight.

Their tempo quickened. They were sprinting now. Sprinting toward the finish line. Amy's face contorted and turned beat red as she let out a cry of joy, her fingers scraping Jack's back, her thighs squeezing him tight.

Then with a final thrust of the hips, a joyful squeal from Amy and a bear-like growl from Jack, they broke the finish-line tape in a giddy, breathless, exhilarating tie. Her eyes bore the delicious sensuality and brightness of a woman satisfied and he loved her more than ever in that moment.

They collapsed onto each other and laughed. Sweaty and out of breath they basked in the heat of the good fortune that had befallen them.

CHAPTER FIVE

JULY 4, 2009

That summer, Jack, Amy, and the boys spent the Fourth of July at Charlie Schiffer's annual bar-b-que on Eddy Street. Charlie and Jack had grown up in the same neighborhood, and wrestled together in high school. Charlie was also captain of Jack's softball team. Charlie's annual shindig was always a big event. Old familiar faces from the old neighborhood would assemble in Schiffer's massive yard beside the brick two-flat on a double-lot. Chicken and burgers and Italian sausages and hot dogs and sautéing onions filled the air with an aroma that traveled upwards towards the near-by 'L' platform. Those waiting for the train would peer down over the railing in ravenous envy. Various salads lined a stars-and-stripes-plastic-tablecloth-donned folding table.

And of course, the beer flowed freely. The party would begin at 1:00pm and last until close to midnight. It was not unusual for Charlie to go through every drop of the four kegs of beer he provided.

Jack didn't drink often, and rarely drank to excess, but Amy knew that Charlie's party on the Fourth meant she'd be driving home. She didn't mind. Jack so rarely got to see his old friends these days, and he so enjoyed the party. He was never a bad drunk. In fact, he was a very happy drunk. He took on a childlike humor, and became very loving and affectionate towards her. It was his one time each year to really let loose and enjoy himself, and she didn't begrudge him that.

It was at Charlie's party that summer of 2009 when Jack found himself sitting at a round iron picnic table sharing a beer with Ricky Jimenez, a solid but squat man with more hair sprouting up from the back of his Hanes tank top than he had left on his head. Ricky and Jack grew up as neighbors in the same two flat, Ricky and his family on the second floor, Jack and his family on the first. They'd been friends since they could crawl.

Ricky Jimenez was an electrician with a knack for finance. Since as far back as Jack could remember, Ricky always had money. He didn't come from money, he worked for it, and he scammed for it, but he could always sniff it out, and once he had it, he knew what to do with it. He was the first of Jack's circle of friends to have a regular job. Every Saturday night and Sunday morning you could find Ricky Jimenez outside the church steps selling the thick Sunday editions of the Times and the Trib. But even at twelve years old, Ricky figured out a way to squeeze extra income out of his little weekend job.

Between masses, when the ushers weren't looking, Ricky would grab a stack of the weekly church Bulletin, the leaflet handed out by the ushers when you entered the church. The weekly Bulletin was full of all the pertinent information regarding the parish for the week: a letter from the Pastor, school events, who was sick, who had died, and wedding announcements. Parents who sent their children off to Mass did so with the instructions to 'bring the Bulletin back'. This had two purposes, first they wanted to read the news within, and second it was proof that their little angel actually went to Mass and turned in the envelope containing the weekly offering.

Kids would line up at Ricky Jimenez's newspaper stand, open the little envelope with the weekly offering, and split the money inside with Ricky in exchange for a Bulletin. Then they would run off to the arcade or the hot dog stand or Walgreens with money in their pocket and a free hour to do as they pleased rather than sitting through the doldrums of Father Mac droning on in his Homily about the pleasure of the generous spirit that would give of his or her time, talents, and most importantly, money. No standing, then sitting then kneeling then standing again. No almost falling asleep in the pew. Instead, freedom. And it really didn't cost them a dime because the money they gave Ricky was their parents' money and it was going to go to the Church anyhow, so why not buy an hour of prayer-free liberty, and pocket half the cash for themselves? It was a brilliant scheme and it soon bought Ricky Jimenez the best bike in the neighborhood.

Whatever his job, Ricky found a way to earn extra money on the side. At sixteen, Ricky Jimenez was talking about compound interest and the benefits of municipal bonds. His financial shrewdness grew as he did. He was the most money savvy guy Jack knew. It was only natural for a slightly buzzed Jack Hanlon to ask his old pal Ricky Jimenez for advice on how to handle the impending windfall.

"So what kind of money we talkin' here Jackie-boy?" Ricky asked with mustard smeared across the corner of his mouth, his jaw working on a big bite of Italian sausage.

"Pretty good, Rick. Very good actually."

"And you're thinking of this Illinois Brilliant Beginnings 529 for your boys' college?"

"Yeah. You know, tax-free growth, safe investment. This kind of payday doesn't fall out of the trees. I need to jump at the opportunity to give them a future with no student loans and a good education, ya know?"

Jack had heard of the Brilliant Beginnings college savings fund on TV while in a hotel room in St. Louis. Sponsored by the State of Illinois, the fund promised a safe and lucrative investment vehicle for college savings with plenty of tax benefits.

"Well hermano, the fund isn't backed by the state, it's just offered by the state. Illinois hires some firm to run it for them, certainly a firm with political ties, there's big money in fees associated with a fund this big. But the tax-free growth is a good deal. You're going to save for college somewhere, right? So why not in a plan that the state is offering you to be able to withdraw tax-free?"

"That's what I thought too. I'm due to get the first check in early August. I think I'll buy into the fund then. You can deposit money slowly, a little here, a little there, over time, but like I said, this kind of payday ain't gonna last forever. I don't wanna end up down the road with less in there than I could have had. I think I want to put a solid amount in right off the bat so I'm sure it's there and isn't going toward buying paint for the front room or car repairs or shit like that. I want to know it's taken care of."

"Well, there's nothing wrong with putting in a large sum off the bat. The more time you have your money in there, the more it'll grow. I say, do your due diligence and if you're satisfied that it's a good investment, go with your instinct. Just don't neglect your retirement, man. Kids can take out loans for school, you can't take out a loan for your retirement."

"Thanks Ricky. I figured it was the right thing to do, I feel better now though knowing that you agree. Ready for another beer?"

"If you're goin', sure I'll take an Old Style."

Jack got up and fetched two beers from the keg feeling confident and at ease about his plan to invest in the State of Illinois Brilliant Beginnings 529 Fund.

Jack whistled a Dean Martin tune. Amy drove all of her tuckered-out boys home. It was nearing midnight and the Fourth of July was fading. Sulfuric bursts of color periodically lit the sky above distant rooftops. Jack whistled the happy tune, tapping his fingers against the armrest of the front passenger seat and looking out the window like a puppy out for a ride. Amy glanced at him and smiled. He didn't notice.

Once home, Amy hustled all three boys off to bed then hit the sack herself. Jack grabbed a beer from the fridge and, still whistling that same tune, went straight to his computer.

He logged on to the State of Illinois Brilliant Beginnings website and established an account. He transferred twenty-five thousand dollars from his savings and checking accounts into the 529 plan, wiping out the totality of the family savings and then some, the money to be replaced in short order once the big paychecks from the Advanta sales arrived.

Then he polished off the can of beer, shut down his computer, and went to bed next to Amy, no longer whistling, but that happy tune still playing in his head. *"How lucky can one guy be, I kissed her and she kissed me. Like the fella once said, ain't that a kick in the head..."*

He fell asleep still grinning.

CHAPTER SIX

AUGUST - NOVEMBER 2009

The first pay cycle of August came and went without a commission in his check. "Typical," he thought. GS was famous for late payment. That extra day's interest meant more towards the bottom line. General Systems is one of the five largest corporations in the world, and yet they will not pay a bill to any of their suppliers or vendors on time no matter how big or small the amount. It is against corporate policy to pay an invoice within forty-five days. Several small vendors have gone belly-up waiting for a GS invoice to be paid. Jack knew all of this, so he also knew he was at the bottom of their list of people to be paid.

He continued getting his small salary, and he continued to work on selling to more Advanta hospitals. Every now and then he'd inquire as to the status of his most recent commission. Each time he was told that it was still processing.

August came and went. September came and went. October came and went with no commission added to his check, and no explanation as to why other than "it's still processing". Jack was seven sizeable commission checks behind, four from the March sales and three from the May sales, with two more coming due in November from sales in Wichita and Chicago.

In addition to that, payment had been made the first week of November from hospitals in Cincinnati, Kansas City, Paducah, and Madison, the commission from which Jack was expecting by Thanksgiving. With those four sales added to the others he'd secured over the course of 2009, Jack had surpassed the first incentive level and was well on his way to the second, which he hoped to reach in December when the ninety days were up and payment was made by four Illinois hospitals: Murphysboro, Kankakee, Joliet, and Effingham.

Jack went to payroll again and asked to speak to the supervisor. A tall lanky man told Jack in monotone that the matter had been transferred to another department and that he would need to speak to his immediate supervisor regarding the matter. His immediate supervisor was unavailable. Jack sent an appointment request via e-mail.

Two days later, Jack was summoned to the branch manager's office. Upon entering he noticed his H.R. rep, the Regional Vice President, and two men in expensive suits. One of the suits he recognized as Gerald Fitzsimmons, the Vice President of Legal Affairs, the other, he'd never seen before. In the corner of the office was a small black suitcase, the kind that rolls on wheels with a telescoping handle. 'Time for the thieving to begin,' thought Jack.

"Jack, we've been looking over your numbers here, very impressive," Simon Phillips, the Regional Vice President, began. "Please, have a seat," he motioned to the only empty chair in the office.

Jack sat. He crossed his legs, then thought better of it and placed both feet flat on the floor. He began to lean forward but felt awkward, so he leaned back a bit, with a slight slouch. His hands curled along the arm of the chair and he felt like a delinquent child sent to the principal's office for a scolding.

"Tell me Jack," Phillips continued, "are you related to anyone employed at the Advanta Healthcare Group?"

The possibility had never even occurred to Jack. Was he? He didn't think so. Was there some distant cousin he hadn't spoken to since he was eight years old, cleaning bedpans in an Advanta hospital in northern Kentucky? He gave his most truthful answer, "No." Then the obvious question, "Why? Is something wrong with my commission?"

"Well, that's why we called you in here today son," Phillips answered.

Jack straightened in his chair. "I am not your son."

His father had busted his ass to put Jack and his siblings through school and to keep a roof over their head and food on the table. No other man had earned the right to call him 'son'. Jack folded his arms and leaned back, comfortable in his chair now. He looked Phillips dead in the eye. The tension grew tight.

"Okay Jack. There is no need for this meeting to be adversarial, we're all on the same team here, I assure you," Melanie Richardson, the Human Resources Rep, responded. She reminded Jack of a junior high guidance counselor, condescending and toothy. They all sat in awkward silence for a moment or two. The air in the office felt thin. Phillips cleared his throat and continued.

"The reason you're here Jack is that you've had quite a year here haven't you?" The statement was more accusatory than congratulatory.

"Yes sir, I have. The Advanta Group sale was a big one. A huge coup. I brought a lot of business to General Systems that had formerly been with our competitors. Thirteen hospitals having made payment so far on brand new MRI machines for each and CAT scanners in addition at ten of them, with four more due to pay the first week of December if all goes well. I'd say that that's one hell of a year sir - for GS. I haven't seen a dime."

"I'd like to add," Jack said, "that the group has thirty-six hospitals in the Midwest and I secured a Preferred Sales Agreement with them for the region, so we're only just over one third of the way through the sales to this group. There'll be plenty more coming in next year and the year after that."

Phillips leaned forward, "Well. How did you happen to do that Jack? I mean, you've been here fifteen years and you've never produced numbers like this before. What's changed? Have you been holding back on us all these years?"

Jack leaned in too, matching Phillips body language and meeting him eye-to-eye. "I went after this sale and I got it. I've been working on getting Advanta for years. That's all there is to it. Sometimes you win and sometimes you don't. Maybe I'm becoming a better salesman, I don't know. Perhaps it's been your leadership sir." The sarcasm was thick.

"Mm-hmm," Phillips said sitting back in his chair and ignoring Jack's jab, "In any event, this is Mr. Fitzsimmons and Mr. Sheldon from New York." The two men looked up briefly from their Blackberries and nodded at Jack, then went right back to thumbing the keys of their smartphones. "They have a few questions to ask you about the Advanta deal Jack. Nothing major, just crossing the t's and dotting the i's and whatnot, you understand." Phillips seemed pleased to be washing his hands of the matter. "Afterwards, if you have any questions, please feel free to discuss them with Ms. Richardson, or Mr. Buchanan your district manager. I guess that's all for now. Go on back to your desk and Mr. Fitzsimmons will call for you when he's ready. Thank you."

The 'thank you' was a dismissal.

Jack felt that if he simply walked from the room upon dismissal, he would be relinquishing a certain level of dignity. He also wanted to remind them that he was not a stranger, but a long-time employee with a history at the company. He stopped halfway to the door and addressed Fitzsimmons. "Mr. Fitzsimmons, do you still lunch at the Fifth Avenue Deli?"

Fitzsimmons looked up from his Blackberry, annoyed by the interruption. "Hmm?"

"The Fifth Avenue Deli. My wife and I ran into you there on our last trip to New York. Still eat there often?"

Fitzsimmons put on a fake smile. "Oh yes. Yes I do, everyday in fact. I take my lunch there everyday; have for years, best soup in New York. Good to see you again Jack. This is just a formality. It won't take very long. I have a few e-mails to catch up on and we'll be with you very shortly. It's great to see you again. Don't worry about a thing." The smile disappeared and his attention was back to the Blackberry, his thumbs franticly dancing across the keypad.

It was then that Jack first saw the thick dark cloud come rolling in around his silver lining.

CHAPTER SEVEN

MONDAY JUNE 7, 2010

Jack sipped at his coffee struggling to shake the cobwebs. The voices of his children ripped through his head like firecrackers. He fought to hold his temper as they talked too loudly, chewed their cereal too loudly, sneezed too loudly, breathed too loudly.

"Seany, gimmee the Froot Loops, I want more," Timmy demanded.

"Timmy, say please," Amy scolded.

"Pleeeaaassseee Seany, gimmee the Froot Loops I'm soooo hungry!"

"Hang on," Sean responded to his little brother barely acknowledging him, "I'm reading the box."

"But Seany... I'm starving!"

"Sean, give your brother the cereal, then finish up and go upstairs and brush your teeth and get dressed."

"But Ma, I'm not done yet and I'm reading the box. You can get a free Yoda cereal bowl if you save up enough UPC symbols and go on-line..."

"Cool! Let me see!" Timmy grabbed at the box. A tug-of-war began over the box of cereal as the brothers yelled back and forth at each other. Jack could feel the back of his neck tighten. His teeth clenched and he could feel the muscle in his jaw push outward from his cheek at every little squeal and holler the boys let out. Their tinny little voices echoed in his head, gnawing away at his brain. The world around him seemed to move faster. His eyes couldn't keep up. He was caught in a whirlwind of annoyance, pain, and anger. He took in a deep breath to try to regain control but he couldn't breathe in deep enough. Then Timmy let out a blood-curdling scream.

"ENOUGH!" Jack's voice boomed through the kitchen and the boys froze in place. Jack had always been firm with them, but he rarely yelled. Sean and Timmy set the box of Froot Loops on the table together and went back to eating their cereal in silence. They wasted no time and were upstairs brushing their teeth in a matter of minutes.

Amy approached him from behind and, as he sat there staring out the window, she began to rub the muscles of his neck and shoulders.

"Whatcha thinkin' about?" she spoke in a soft voice.

"Same thing I'm always thinking about these days," he replied without changing his stare. Jack took a deep breath and let out a long sustained exhale. "This was their idea, their deal. Now they don't want to stand by it. Amy, it's just not right. It's a lot of money for us; for them, it's a drop in the bucket. I've seen the lunch tabs some of these executives rack up. I've been there as they fawned over seventy-five dollar bottles of wine that they put on their corporate card, and yet, these same people are fighting tooth and nail to keep from me money I legitimately earned. I want justice Amy. I need justice. That's what I'm thinkin' about."

Amy wrapped her arms around his chest and kissed the top of his head. "It's going to be fine Babe. It will all work out, okay. Hey, we have three great boys who are smart and healthy and well-behaved, except when they're fighting over Froot Loops that is. Although, it is a pretty epic Yoda cereal bowl."

"It is actually. Maybe I'll send away for it myself," said Jack, his mood taming.

"Uh-uh. That's mine." She grabbed for the box, but Jack was closer and beat her to it. They playfully tugged at it and Jack was smiling again. He pulled Amy onto his lap and they kissed.

Office life had actually gotten easier. No one at the branch wanted to go anywhere near Jack or his situation. They knew Jack and his problem were unstable powder kegs, ready to take out anyone who got too close or meddled too much. As a result, everyone from management on down steered clear of Jack.

It was Monday and Seth should be back from vacation. Jack was trying not to call Seth. If he were to call and get bad news about the negotiations, getting through the rest of the workday would be impossible. He was intent to wait at least until late afternoon. So he distracted himself with busy work. He got caught up on his paperwork, and did some cold calling. When he looked at the clock, it was only 10:30; he'd been at it for only an hour and a half. He decided it was time for a smoke. He grabbed a stack of envelopes and told Erin he was heading down to the mailroom.

The cigarette burned up a total of four and a half minutes and that included the elevator rides down and then back up. If Jack didn't get out of that office he was going to crack. He forwarded his office phone to his cell, packed his briefcase and informed reception he would be out calling on clients the rest of the day.

He'd barely gotten outside when he grabbed his phone and called the law offices of Seth Levine. Jack sat on hold for a good three full minutes before Seth picked up on the other end.

"Jack, how are you? I've been meaning to call; it's just been insane around here this morning. That's the problem with vacations, you fall so far behind while you're gone, by the time you catch up, you wonder if taking any time off was ever actually worth it. What's up my friend?"

"Seth, I waited for the mail Saturday. Nothing came. I was expecting a package from either you or them with the settlement proposal in it. I got nothing. Was there some kind of delay? Do we have a tracking number?"

"Yes, Jack, so sorry. It really has been crazy here. It seems there's been a delay. I was a little worried when they refused to put an offer forth through e-mail, that's how this is usually done. My copy never showed Friday either, but I didn't realize it until I got back in the office this morning. I was out of town, but that's no excuse. Look, I sent out an e-mail inquiring as to the whereabouts of said package. They responded this morning that they are putting the offer on hold..."

"On hold? What the hell does that mean?" Jack interrupted.

"It means, for the time being at least, we're in a holding pattern until I find out what the delay is. I have a call out to Rhonda Royce out there to see if she can give me some sort of explanation. If she doesn't get back to me before, oh, let's say three o'clock our time, I'll try again. Try not to worry Jack..."

"Try not to worry? Seth, this is my life here. I just don't understand how they can... I... It was a written contract! They have teams of lawyers on salary, when I signed the contract I had nobody on my side. And now they're trying to say I somehow... what? What are they trying to say Seth? How are they trying to get out of paying me?"

"Jack, that's what I'm trying to find out. That's why I have a call out to Rhonda Royce in New York. Let's see what they have to say and we'll take it from there. Look, if this thing goes to trial, you've got a great case against them, but let's see if we can avoid all of that and get you paid much sooner. I know it's hard, but just try to relax. Try to put it out of your mind. Can you do that Jack?"

"Absolutely not Seth. I haven't been able to put this out of my mind for the past eight fuckin' months! I'm sorry, I don't mean to take my frustration out on you, but fuck Seth, I mean really. Fuck! It's been a hell of a fuckin' ride that's all. It's starting to wear me down."

"I know Jack. These things are difficult. They take time. But listen to me, you are in the right here, okay? They took advantage of you and we're going to get your money. It will take time and it won't necessarily be a walk in the park, but trust me, they don't want this to go to court. Do what you can to unwind and I'll be in touch one way or the other this evening before I leave the office, okay?"

Jack put his phone in his pocket, started his car and drove north with no particular destination in mind. Seething, he just drove north.

CHAPTER EIGHT

Mrs. Kelly awoke from an afternoon nap to footsteps above her head. She leapt from her rocker where she'd fallen asleep reading the newspaper, and, in her housecoat and slippers, hustled outside to see what the noise was. There were four men with tools hammering away at her roof.

"You up there," Mrs. Kelly called out, "what are you doing? I thought you weren't supposed to start until Thursday."

"Que?" the man replied. "No habla engles."

"Where... is ... your ... boss?" she called up as slowly as she could expecting the man to suddenly be able to understand English perfectly now that she'd slowed it down. His reply was the same, "Que?"

Mrs. Kelly huffed in aggravation and walked along the side of the house looking up to find the man she'd spoken to on her front porch, but he wasn't there.

The men on her roof spoke in hurried Spanish as they pulled and dropped clay shingles from the roof to the ground below. Shards and chunks of green clay covered the sidewalk through the gangway, the lawn in the back yard, between the houses on the other side, and the front yard as well. The men moved quickly and were done and gone by noon. In place of the once beautiful green clay, they left behind the big blue tarp the man had put up when he first arrived at Mrs. Kelly's door.

Mrs. Kelly looked at the broken chunks of clay littering the ground around her home and thought she might cry. It had been such a beautiful home.

And the shame of it all. To just toss ninety-one year old clay tiles to the ground to shatter seemed unnecessarily wasteful and just plain stupid. Those had to be worth money simply for their historic value if nothing else.

She tried to phone the number on the card the man had given her, but she got his voicemail. She left a message asking him to call her immediately.

She went outside with a bucket and a broom and swept what she could off of her neighbor's property. She was no stranger to hard work, but it didn't take long before she began to tire out. "The rest can wait until morning when the men come back," she thought. In the meantime, she'd fix herself some dinner and draw a bath to soak her aching muscles. She'd shoveled up at least four large garbage bags of heavy clay shingles from her neighbors' properties and still her own looked like a construction site. At one point, she stepped on a roofing nail and it stuck deep into her shoe, just barely missing her foot.

She decided after her bath, she would call Jack and ask him what his thoughts were on these workmen showing up out of nowhere three days early and then leaving without cleaning up. When she called though, Jack wasn't home. There seemed to be worry in Amy's voice, which Mrs. Kelly thought odd. She knew from sitting on her porch on those sleepless nights after Harold died that Jack had worked later than this many times.

That night Mrs. Kelly lay in bed listening to the sound of the plastic tarp that was now her roof, flapping in the wind. She worried that she'd misread the nice roofer who'd come to her door and that he'd swindled her. She worried about Amy. She worried about her good friend Jack, whom she'd noticed still wasn't home at one o'clock when she finally turned out the lights and went to bed. He'd never come home that late before.

Amy looked up at the clock again. It was closing in on 7:30 and still no word from Jack. It wasn't too unusual for him to end up working late, but he usually gave her a heads up. She had actually expected to hear from him sometime this afternoon with some news from Seth about the settlement proposal. The fact that he hadn't called at all was what was worrying her now. She feared he'd gotten some bad news from Seth and the way he'd been acting lately, well, she was worried.

She resisted the urge to call him. If he had gotten bad news from Seth, then he probably needed his space to sort things out.

She wrapped up a plate from dinner and put it in the fridge for him. She nearly jumped out of her skin when the phone rang. She ran to it and nearly dropped it as she flung the receiver off of the wall.

"Hello?"

"Amy? Is that you?" the voice was familiar but Amy was too frazzled and disappointed to place it at first.

"Amy? You sound like something's wrong dear, are you okay?" Amy let out a deep sigh as she finally put a face to the voice.

"Yes Mrs. Kelly, everything is fine. I was just doing some cleaning. I must be out of breath, I'm sorry. What can I do for you?"

"Well, I was hoping to speak to Jack, is he home?"

"To be honest Mrs. Kelly, I haven't heard from Jack yet today. I was hoping this was him calling. He must have had a late meeting with a client or something. Is there anything I can help you with?"

"I just had a question for him about my roof. I'm having some work done on it and well... it's too much to explain right now. No emergency, just when he has a chance if he could either give me a call or stop by, I'd appreciate it. Just need some manly advice you might say."

Amy recalled seeing some workmen over at Mrs. Kelly's earlier in the day. "I'm sure he'd be happy to Mrs. Kelly. I'll tell him as soon as he comes home. If you don't hear from him tonight, I'm sure he'll be in touch in the morning."

"Oh, don't have him call tonight, it's late enough. He's worked a long day, let him enjoy his dinner and what's left of the evening and I'll speak to him tomorrow. Okay?"

Amy smiled. The old lady across the street could be a pain once in a while, but she really was a sweet and considerate woman. Amy often wondered how much of a pain she would be at that age without Jack to share the load of the waning years. "Okay Mrs. Kelly. Thank you. I'll have him call you tomorrow. Take care."

"Goodnight dear, and don't worry, I'm sure he's probably on his way home now. He's a good one you've got, if he's late, there's a good reason for it. Good-bye now."

"Good-bye Mrs. Kelly." As Amy hung up she wondered, as she occasionally did, whether Mrs. Kelly would be competition for Jack if she were thirty years younger. "Fierce competition," Amy concluded. She finished cleaning up the dishes from dinner and put the boys in the tub and got them to bed.

"Where's Daddy?" Timmy asked.

"He's working, duh," said Sean.

"Shut up Seany," Timmy countered.

"Boys, that's enough," their mother's tone told them she had no patience for misbehavior tonight.

"Sean is right though honey, Daddy is working late, but he'll be home tonight, okay?" She gave her little boy a kiss on the forehead and a reassuring smile.

Trevor had long ago locked himself in his room so as to avoid the younger ones.

With the boys tucked in, Amy went downstairs and made herself a cup of tea. She was never one to keep tabs on her husband. She didn't want to be one of those wives who'd use the cell phone as an electronic leash. "Where are you? Why are you late? When are you coming home? What are you doing?" Ugh, she hated the thought of it. But this was unlike Jack. He'd never been *this* late without calling before. She was legitimately worried now. She reluctantly dialed his cell and immediately got his voicemail. Her concern grew. She left him a short message, trying to make her voice sound as calm as she could.

She took her cup of tea into the front room and curled up on the couch with the most recent Stephanie Plum novel and waited beside the phone for it to ring. When it finally did ring, just after 2 a.m., it jolted her from a sound sleep.

"Hello?" her voice groggy but anticipatory.

"Amy," Jack mumbled, "I'm sorry." The line went dead.

CHAPTER NINE

Jack had driven north. He didn't have a destination in mind; he just drove north. When he reached Lake Geneva, Wisconsin, he stopped. The air carried the scent of coconut sunscreen, lake-breeze, and beer.

Lake Geneva is a small, quaint tourist town on the shore of Geneva Lake. The town was where the Chicago elite vacationed in the 1800's. Many of them built summer homes there that would wind up serving as their main residence while Chicago was being rebuilt after the Great Fire of 1876. Nowadays, middle-class tourists in search of summer fun have replaced the elite who, with the advent of air travel, can vacation in the other Geneva, the one in Switzerland.

There were a few things that drew Jack here. He'd come here as a kid with his parents and his grandmother. The ladies would shop, Grandma would buy him candy and an Indian tom-tom and tomahawk at the Ben Franklin.

Just over the Wisconsin border, Lake Geneva was only a two-hour drive from Chicago at most. The lake was clean and clear and blue. Once he was old enough to come here on his own, Jack did so often. He'd fish there, he'd swim there, he'd walk along the lakeshore trail. He brought dates there.

The water brought him peace. He was able to think. Watching the boats rock beside their buoys, listening to the waves lap up against the shore, feeling the cool lake wind against his skin. He'd watch as the sun set over the lake splashing a spectrum of warm colors against the water and across the sky until the day faded into night and wavy stars reflected back at him.

And then there were the bars, small, but lively. Some weekends they were just too damn crowded full of kids, but during the week, they were the perfect blend of party and sanity.

Jack stopped at a corner store and bought a six-pack of Old Style beer and a small Styrofoam cooler that he filled with ice. He took his cooler down to the lakeshore and sat on a grassy hill in the afternoon sun. From the not-too-distant beach, he could hear the sounds of children playing and splashing in the water, the voices of mothers calling out orders of 'be careful, don't hit your sister, you have to come in and eat something', and the sounds filled his mind with echoes from the past. For a moment, he was ten years old again, playing on that same beach, splashing in that same water, trudging through the sand to fill a hole with a bucket of water. Life was so simple then, so easy. Do your homework, eat your green beans, don't fight with your sister, look both ways before crossing the street, and be home when the streetlights came on. If you followed those simple rules, everything was okay.

His was a happy childhood. Jack came to the sudden realization that he hadn't thought much about his childhood days lately. He'd lost touch with that part of his life. There were moments after Trevor was born, that he'd think back to his own glory days of youth and hoped that he could provide as good an experience for his son as he'd had. Lately though, he felt old. Somewhere along the way, he'd lost that little-boy-Jack who used to swing on the monkey bars pretending he was Indiana Jones on an adventure through the jungle, who would take a whiffle ball and bat to the empty parking lot of a banquet hall near his house and imagine himself standing in the batter's box at Wrigley Field ready to hit the game winning home run that would finally bring a World Championship to his beloved Cubs, the little boy who would protectively hold the hand of his little sister at every alley and street crossing on the way to school and who would step in to knock the daylights out of any bully that teased her. What had happened to that Jack? The one with all the dreams and hopes and smiles? Was he dead? Did life itself snuff him out? Was he a victim of the inevitable loss of innocence that takes with it the hopeful world of imagination and dreams of a good day tomorrow? Was it simply the responsibilities all adults must face that extinguished that happy little boy, or was it this damn betrayal he was in the midst of fighting? The money was one thing, but if he allowed them to also rob him of that part of him that found great joy in life, that part of him that smiled brightly just because, that optimistic-happy-ready-to-play-Jack he'd been his whole life, then that would be as much his fault as it was theirs, and that would be the true crime of it all.

His phone rang. It was Erin at the office. Jack sent the call to voicemail and shut the damn phone off. He slammed down another beer and sank deeper into himself. His thoughts whirled in his head and switched back and forth from Amy and the boys to his own childhood to those bastards at General Systems and back again. After a while, his cooler held only empty beer cans and melted ice. Jack took the cooler to a garbage can and threw the whole mess away, cooler, cans and all.

He stopped in Potbelly's for a quick sandwich, and then walked the stores along Highway 50. At one point he thought he wanted an ice cream cone, but after two licks, he decided he didn't want it and threw it away.

The sun was beginning to set and the sky and the lake were ablaze in hues of orange and pink and purple. The beach emptied and the barrooms were just waking up. Jack went to one of his favorite haunts in Geneva and bellied up to the bar. He watched his reflection in the mirror behind the bottles and cash register as he sipped from a bottle of Miller High Life.

A revolving beer sign caught his attention and he stared at it as little colored points of light turned round and round seeming to bounce up and down as they turned. He sat mesmerized by the sign. Watching the lights but not really seeing them. He reverted into his mind, deeper and deeper into thoughts of the past few months. The meetings with his lawyer, the money he'd spent to chase the money he was owed, just to end up here, right where he had begun. No closer to any sort of resolution. No closer to taking possession of what was owed to him. Round and round the lights would go. Bouncing up and down. But the lights were just a mirage. It was simply a cone of different colors with black spaces blocking the light at intervals making them appear to bounce and dance, but in reality, it was just a spinning cone, a trick, an illusion. So much of life was an illusion. Once Jack became aware of what the sign was really doing, it lost its luster. He couldn't watch it anymore and turned back to watching his own reflection in the mirror.

What he saw was a good man. A husband. A father. An honest and hard working employee. A good neighbor. A man who, though he didn't go to church often, believed in God, believed in the tenants of his Catholic faith. Believed that honesty, and loyalty were to be valued. Believed that it is best to treat others as you would like to be treated. Believed that God truly helps those who help themselves, but also there are those who need a helping hand now and then. Believed that society has its rules and most of them are there for good reason. That the ten commandments really are compass points for life, regardless of religion, the main ideas put forth there are true, and righteous, and lead one to happiness and fulfillment. That man he saw in the mirror believed that. But the longer he stared, just as with the bouncing lights of the beer sign, the more he saw the truth in his own reflection. Was he really this man? This righteous, good-natured, God-fearing, friendly neighbor, loyal husband and devoted father? Or was that all an illusion as well? Was there more beneath what he showed the world? Was there more than what he revealed even to himself?

Jack felt a tap on his shoulder and jumped back to consciousness. He looked to his right. Sitting on the barstool beside him, looking curious and concerned, sat a beautiful woman. Her hair was dirty blonde, her eyes a soft, clean green. She had the softest, faintest trace of freckles across her nose. She appeared to be about Jack's age, the lines at the corners of her eyes were more pronounced when she smiled, but worked in her favor. Her lips were thin and painted pale pink. She wore a black dress that dipped low, but tastefully, revealing the slightest hint of cleavage. The hem rose high on the thigh of her crossed legs. She smiled and her green eyes lit and twinkled in the darkened barroom.

"Hello?" She sang smiling at Jack and waving her hand in front of his face as if to see if anyone were home inside that handsome skull.

It took him a second to realize she was talking to him and he answered her coolly. Trying not to seem as if he had drifted as far into himself as he had.

"Hi," Jack answered.

"Are you alright? The woman asked, with genuine concern.

"Yes, I'm fine. Why do you ask?"

"Well, you seemed far away. Are you sure everything's okay?"

"Everything okay? No. Everything is not 'okay'. But, I'm fine," Jack smiled at her, "Thank you for asking."

The woman extended a slender hand. "I'm Molly."

Jack took her hand in his. It began as a handshake but her hand seemed to melt into his. She was soft and warm and inviting.

"Jack Hanlon. Nice to meet you Molly."

"Nice to meet you too Jack. So, on vacation with the family?" Her eyes moved to acknowledge the wedding ring on Jack's left hand.

"Um, no. Just came up here to, I don't know, do some thinking I guess. How about you?" Jack looked but saw no ring on the woman's ring finger.

"Recently divorced. My family has a house on the lake. I came up here to get away and do a little thinking myself. What brings you to the Burley Boar on a school night Jack?"

"Rough day. Had to get away and decompress I guess. I just had to get out of the city. Thought some time away in a new location might give me some answers. A new perspective I guess."

"And how is that going?"

"Oh," Jack answered, "not very well."

"Well, answers like the ones it sounds like you're looking for are hard to come by on a barstool," she said.

"Yes they are. I don't drink much, at least not very often anymore. Like I said though, I had to think and somehow I wound up here."

"No need to explain Jack. I've been there several times myself. I have found though, that sometimes, the best

46

route to elusive answers is a little bit of distraction, if you don't mind the company. Also, talking it out with a neutral party sometimes opens channels to new perspectives and ideas you hadn't had before. But, if you want to be alone, I will turn my stool around and shut my mouth." She smiled a friendly, glimmering smile.

Jack was as mesmerized by her eyes and her smile and the dimples in her cheeks as he had been by the bouncing, dancing lights of the beer sign. He smiled back at her. "No, I would love the company. A pleasant diversion is exactly what I need, but no talking about my problems. Problems are boring."

"Okay Jack," Molly said, "what should we talk about?" Molly turned her stool to face Jack more directly. Jack matched her pose. They now were face-to-face. Arms resting on the bar - his left arm, her right arm - centimeters from touching. She reached for her wine and her arm brushed up against his. Wisps of barely visible blonde hair tickled his skin. The entire moment was over in a flash and Jack didn't know if it was purposeful or accidental. It was slight and it was quick, but he felt it in his spine.

Jack smiled at her and shook his head as he let out an exasperated breath. "'What should we talk about', ah, that's something I haven't heard in a long time. What should we talk about? In my house lately, hell in my entire life lately, there is just one topic of conversation and do you know what, I honestly believe it is close to driving me mad. I mean it, not 'man, this shit is driving me crazy' mad, I mean, 'Doctor, he was fine the last time we spoke, I don't know how he ended up shaved hairless wandering the park naked talking to the statues', lock him up and throw away the key' mad."

"Well, looks like I got here at just the right time. I'd hate to have met you hairless and naked in the park, I doubt we'd have struck up such a fast friendship if I had. There was a time in my life when that would have been alluring, but these days, not so much. Now that I already know you though, I would of course not hold such a scene against you. I'm much more forgiving of friends' insane antics in public than I am those of perfect strangers."

This made him smile. He raised his beer for a toast. "To new friendships." She lifted her glass to his and answered, "to keeping your hair, your clothes and your sanity." They clinked drinks and took generous swallows.

"Tell me about you," he said meeting her eyes again.

"Tell you about me?"

"Yeah, tell me your story."

She blushed a little, but never lost eye contact. In fact, she seemed to lean in a little closer to him. "My story? What is it you'd like to know Jack? Like I told you before, I'm divorced, recently. I'm staying at the family lake house."

"Tell me about you. Who is... um..."

"Molly," she reminded him.

"Yes, Molly. I'm sorry. I'm usually very good with names. I'm a salesman. It's a necessary job skill. Must be the beer I guess. Molly, tell me about you. What do you like, what do you want, how did you get here and where are you going? Talk to me Molly. I've been so damn wrapped up in myself I'm bored to tears. I want to know about you, about your life. We're friends now remember. I have to know about you."

"Okay, Jack, okay. Let me think where to begin. I was born in Naperville, Illinois, back when Naperville was still a small, growing suburb. I was a cheerleader in high school, went to business school at DePaul, graduated summa cum laude. Got a job at an investment firm. Met my soon-to-be-husband-soon-to-be-ex-husband at work. Got married, moved to Lake Forest, got pregnant, lost the baby, went into a deep depression, got pregnant again, had a beautiful baby boy named Joshua. Left the firm to be a mom. Got pregnant a third time and lost that baby too. After that the doctors told me no more babies. More depression. Gained some weight, husband started working longer hours, weekends. He seemed to be finding any excuse he could to not come home. I joined a running club with some of the other moms in the neighborhood and already belonged to the health club, but I started going to exercise rather than just for facials. Really liked running. I lost all of the extra weight and then some and even ran a marathon. I thought that would spark something between my husband and me that we had lost. It didn't. I knew he was cheating; it was just a matter of confronting the issue. But at the same time, he was a good dad to Joshua and I didn't want to break up the home, so I ignored it. Pretended it didn't bother me. It bothered me. I went out for revenge and slept with some random guy I never would have even given the time of day to just to feel better about myself and to throw it in my husband's face. It backfired. Revenge of that type usually does I suppose. I hated myself for sinking to that level, and he, well, he didn't even care, so a lot of good *that* did me. Finally, about six months ago I decided enough is enough. He'd stopped even trying to hide the affair. He was more hers than mine by then, and Joshua at seven years old could tell something was wrong. Kids aren't stupid you know. They know exactly what is happening, they may not understand it all, but they know. Anyhow, I saw how it was affecting my son and I saw how it was affecting me, so I decided it was time to call it quits. The divorce was relatively easy. We went our separate ways, but the starting new part, not so easy. Single mom, not so easy either. That's why I'm here. My mom and dad took Joshua for the week and I came here to think. To think about my life, where I'm going, what I'm doing, oh the whole goddamned thing. But, how long can you sit in an empty house and do that? So I decided I needed a glass of wine and I needed to feel pretty, so I put on my favorite little black dress and hightailed it down here to sip wine and think about my life. And that's when I saw you. Kind of like you said, I was tired of thinking about my situation. I wanted a distraction and there you were. And here I am talking forever about myself. Boring, I know. But you asked, so that's my story. Now it's your turn Jack, what's your story? How does a handsome gentleman such as yourself end up in a Lake Geneva dive on a Monday night?"

Jack waved down the bartender and ordered himself another beer and another glass of Rosé for Molly.

"My story. My story is short. Born and raised on the Northwest side of Chicago. Went to a state school where I met my beautiful wife. Got married. Had three great sons. Got a job in sales, job kinda went to shit, things at home have been better. Thought I'd be in a better place than this by this point in my life. Tired of being the fire hydrant in a world full of dogs. Got some bad news today, needed to think. Met you and I'm smiling for the first time in months. That pretty much sums it up."

"Sounds like a familiar story. That happens to a lot of people Jack, you'll bounce back," Molly was sincere.

"I neglected to mention the icing on the cake. When I found out about these big checks I was supposed to be getting, I started looking into college plans, put money away now, use it later for the cost of education and avoid taxes on the capital gains. It's a state thing. Years from now when my boys go to school, I'll have saved a small fortune and in the meantime, I would be able to sleep well knowing that no matter what else happened, if I were to die tomorrow, they would at least have a college degree and hopefully no debt."

"Why do I feel there's a 'but' in there?"

"Because, Molly, there's an enormous 'but' in there. BUT, I didn't get the checks, BUT I thought the money was on its way, SO I bought into a 529 plan for my three boys anyhow."

"Uh-oh, with what money, Jack?"

"With every penny Amy and I had in the bank. Figured I'd just replace it and then some once the big money started rolling in. That was last summer. In the meantime my company has tried every trick in the book to either not pay me at all, or pay me significantly less than they are contractually obligated to do. We were supposed to have come to a settlement, the papers were to be delivered to my house and my lawyer's office over the weekend, but today I found out they've put the offer on hold. I won't be getting any money anytime soon and it's getting harder and harder to lie to my wife about the savings account, harder and harder to make ends meet. Harder and harder to go into the office with a smile on my face and pour myself into the work to make money for a company that is stealing from my family. I'm tired of waiting and tired of fighting and tired of games.

Most of all, I'm tired of worrying. So let's talk about something else, anything else."

The bartender delivered the drinks and Jack motioned for him to take the money from the pile of bills he had in front of him. This time Molly raised her glass. "To friendly distractions," she said. "To friendly distractions," Jack agreed and they touched their drinks together. With that, Molly placed her hand on top of Jack's. She gave his hand a soft squeeze and their fingers intertwined. They sat like that for the next three hours, talking about everything from music, to television, to books, to sports. They shared stories about family vacations to Lake Geneva as kids. They'd both spent so much time over the years in the small vacation town that they figured they had probably run into each other at some point in childhood at the beach, or at the Ben Franklin, or at the Lake Aire restaurant for breakfast, without knowing it.

After a few hours and many drinks, Molly turned to Jack and said, "Look at us, it's a beautiful summer night and we're sitting here in this dank, stinky barroom. What do you say we go for a walk down by the lake, get some fresh air?"

"Sounds like a great idea Molly," Jack said, "I'm gonna hit the men's room real quick before we go, though."

"Good idea Jack. I'll hit the ladies' room and meet you back here in a minute," she said.

Jack's head was swimming. He stood at the urinal with his eyes closed. 'She's a pretty girl, but it's just a walk. We're talking. Nothing wrong with that. Just talking. Just going for a walk. It's okay.' He zipped up, bumped into the doorjamb, then found his way back out to the bar where Molly was waiting.

Music drifted through the night from the lakeshore Riviera ballroom. The local teen club was holding a dance in the upstairs hall. DJ lights flashed and flickered and spun through the open windows sending shots of blue and red and purple into the night sky. Holding hands, Jack and Molly walked to the end of the dock beneath the ballroom and looked out at the water. The lights from the dance hall above bounced and bobbed in the small breeze-blown ripples and lazy waves as they lapped against the pilings.

"It's so beautiful here," Molly folded her arms, chilled by the night air.

"It is. This is one of my favorite places on Earth," Jack responded.

Molly shivered a little. "Ooo, it's getting chilly out here."

Jack put his arm around her shoulders. His body warmed her. She felt safe and calm for the first time in a long time.

Then from the ballroom above, they heard the echo of the DJ's voice announce to the teens that it was time for the last dance. "Grab that special someone," he said, "it's the last song of the night. And we're going retro for this one." Then the song began. It was an old 80's tune. Jack and Molly recognized it immediately.

Molly's eyes widened. "The Bangles, Eternal Flame. God I used to love this song. Can we dance to it Jack?"

Jack grasped her hand in his and wrapped his other arm around her waist. Molly placed her free hand on Jack's shoulder, pressed her body against his, and they danced.

It's funny how a song can transport you in time and Jack was suddenly reminded of his first girlfriend, Missy McCarthy, and the high school dances at St. Vincent's. In a moment's time, he felt young again. He connected with that Jack he'd, just this afternoon, thought was dead.

The moonlight illuminated the end of the pier. Molly turned her face to Jack, meeting his gaze. He held her there for a moment. Now both his hands were wrapped around her hips, her arms wrapped around his neck. The night air seemed to make her green eyes glow. She looked younger and smaller here in the night, somehow more helpless and soft, but radiant. She pulled ever so slightly on the back of Jack's neck, pulling him to her, and soon their lips were just a whisper apart.

CHAPTER TEN

"Okay, for whom are we waiting?" Jacob Riis was in his late twenties and on top of the world. He'd been working at General Systems Inc. at their Manhattan headquarters for two years now and already had a corporate credit card. He could only use the card for office supplies and in an emergency when his boss, Rhonda, left her purse in the office, but still he felt as if he were on the fast track.

"Rhonda is the only one I think. Everyone else here?" Carrie Miller the newly appointed Vice President of Contractual Discourse announced. Carrie had one of those voices that made it appear as if she was perpetually annoyed. It was a survival instinct for an insecure person in a position way over her head.

Rhonda was always late. She did this on purpose.

On the call were the two men who'd met with Jack in the Chicago office when this whole thing started, Gerald Fitzsimmons the Executive Vice President of Legal Affairs, and Lloyd Sheldon the Associate Vice President of Legal Affairs, Ross Riggleman the Vice President of Project Management, a new guy from H.R. named Bruce Chung, Jacob and Carrie. The conference call was set to begin at 3:45 Eastern.

At precisely 3:52 Eastern, Rhonda Royce joined the call from the speakerphone of her office fifty yards away from Fitzsimmons and twenty feet away from Jacob Riis. "So sorry folks. Is everyone here? I assume so. Let's get started. What's our plan here?"

"Gerald here. Hi Rhonda."

"Hi Gerald."

"How are things?"

"Just dandy. If we could put all this Hanlon business behind us, it would be grand."

"I concur," said Gerald Fitzsimmons.

"We put the offer on hold," Sheldon spoke up from his west coast office in Los Angeles, "we think we can rescind it."

"On what grounds?" Ross asked.

"Well, in combing through the paperwork, we noticed the GSI-25 form was missing."

"That's just a simple clerical error, and I swore all the paperwork was in order when we received it, though that was almost a year ago, I could be mistaken. Do you think that gives us legal grounds to withhold payment?" Ross sounded unconvinced.

"What it does is it buys us time," declared Sheldon.

"This has been dragging on for a long time now. Are we really going find something new if given another week or so? His lawyer is going to laugh at this one."

"Let him laugh, it buys us time to find something we may have overlooked."

"Refresh my memory," interrupted Rhonda, "it's been a while. What exactly are the numbers?

"Well," Ross answered, "according to Mr. Hanlon and his lawyer, we owe him a total of $325,000.00 for the Advanta deal, a good deal of that the result of having hit the incentives and benchmarks put in place under the new contract."

"And the offer we had in place, until you put it on hold was... let me see if I have it here..."

"... two hundred thousand," Lloyd answered, "it's just a bit more than he'd have earned under the previous contract."

"That's still a lot of money, what does this guy want?" Rhonda piped in.

"I think he wants what his contract states," Jacob said.

"Well, he isn't going to get that," Fitzsimmons declared.

Rhonda glared at Jacob through her office window. He lowered his head like a scolded puppy.

"To be fair, he agreed to that settlement amount. I was to draw up the papers and FedEx them to his attorney for review," Lloyd stated, "but..."

"But why would we do that?" Fitzsimmons piped in, "if we don't have to, I mean."

"Why wouldn't we?" Riggleman retorted, "If you ask me, we're getting off easy. He legitimately earned the three and a quarter, we're saving ourselves over a hundred thousand dollars."

"Because, that's not how it's going to look from above," Fitzsimmons volume grew as he spoke, "My directive was to lower commission rates and retain talent at the same time when devising the new contract. That's why we put the unattainable incentives in there. Those incentives are what convinced these sales associates to agree to the lower commission and stay. They couldn't refuse the gamble. But no one was supposed to reach them. If we pay out a commission based even on last year's rates, heads are going to roll and I refuse to put myself on the chopping block because some son-of-a-bitch in Chicago had a lucky day."

"As of right now," Riggleman countered, "this thing has flown under the radar, but how long do you expect that to last? Eventually, Wade is going to get wind of this and heads are going to roll anyhow. Isn't it better to get it settled and move on and hope the rest of the figures for the year with the lower commission, make up for this one massive deal?"

"I'm not willing to take that chance, Ross. Look, this will get settled, and settled soon. Hanlon has a wife and three children, a mortgage and bills. Do you really think he's going to turn down say, a twenty thousand dollar offer and the chance to keep his job?"

"If he listens to his lawyer he will. Don't forget, the attorney only makes his big bucks on the final settlement figure."

"We hold the man's job in our hands, his livelihood. Do you read the papers? Have you seen the layoffs you yourself have made here in just the past few months? He's not going to push back very hard for very long. He needs his job plain and simple. We can probably get away with giving him a pat on the back and a gift certificate to Hooters and he'd be happy. Even better if we can find a legitimate reason to terminate his employment and pay him nothing."

"And if he doesn't fold. If he doesn't give us just cause to fire him? Then what?"

"It will never come to that," Fitzsimmons said with confidence.

"Now, if they do insist on taking it to court," Lloyd Sheldon hesitantly spoke, trying to get the conversation back on track. "If we're going to beat this in court, we're going to have to find either a loophole in the current contract, or some unscrupulous behavior on the part of Mr. Hanlon that either lead to this sale, or that we can hold over his head to encourage him to take a settlement of our liking."

"Blackmail, I like it. Anyone got any dirt on Jack Hanlon?" asked Rhonda. This was the kind of thing that got her excited about her job.

There was silence.

Eventually Bruce spoke up. "There's nothing in his file, but, wasn't his supervisor, the District Manager, who no longer works for the company I might add, the one who gave him the lead to Ken Hornsby at Advanta. We can claim that this supervisor told him to call Hornsby and that he was simply acting under orders. That the sale wasn't really his, it was his superior's."

"Wouldn't we owe the supervisor the commission then? I mean, it was a sale, someone makes commission right?" Rhonda asked.

"Well, not necessarily. We wouldn't owe the supervisor because, a) he doesn't work for the company anymore, and b) he was not a salesman and so he is not covered under the salesmen contract," Gerald answered.

"Sorry to interrupt here guys, but if I may be devil's advocate for just a moment," Ross chimed in, "don't our salesmen work off of leads from others all the time? Don't they get full commission anyhow?"

"These salesmen make me sick," Carrie said, finally adding something to the conversation, "they expect this outrageous pay for what? Doing their jobs? I mean, come on, just do your job and be happy you have one."

"It is what it is. Give them an inch and they'll take a mile," Fitzsimmons added, "there is no way he made this sale through legitimate means, at least that's my take on it. We constructed that contract to ensure nobody could ever reach those incentive levels. If he did, he did it illegally."

"Not on my watch," Rhonda stated.

"He'll have to take his medicine and like it. He will not win this," Gerald Fitzsimmons reassured everyone.

"I've been dodging calls and e-mails from his attorney, Levine, all day. What should I say to him?" Rhonda asked.

"Tell him we will be in touch tomorrow. Set up a time to get on the phone with him tomorrow afternoon. By then, we'll know what we're going to say to him. With any luck, we'll have figured a way out of this by then too. Either way though, we have tell him something tomorrow. Let's reconvene on this in the morning."

After the conference call ended, Gerald Fitzsimmons packed his briefcase, logged off his computer, and took a cab to the Plaza Hotel where he met his Executive Assistant, a leggy blonde in her early thirties who had taken a separate cab from the same office, for a few cocktails in the lobby bar and the night in the Presidential Suite.

Back home in Connecticut, Mrs. Fitzsimmons put her husband's dinner in the fridge for the third night in a row.

CHAPTER ELEVEN

TUESDAY, JUNE 8, 2010

Mrs. Kelly awoke at 5:30, early even for her. She lay in bed staring at the plaster-nipple cap of the old gas lines in the center of her bedroom ceiling wishing for sleep, but it was no use. She had a feeling of dread like she hadn't felt since those first weeks without Harold. She had always been a tough, independent woman. She didn't scare easily, but lying in her bed on this clear summer day, that damn blue tarp flapping from her roof, she had to admit to herself, she was scared.

At 6:00, she gave up on sleep and shuffled to the kitchen and put a pot of coffee on the stove. While she waited for the coffee to percolate, she brushed her teeth, got dressed, and brushed her hair. Mrs. Kelly stared at herself in her bedroom mirror.

"You are not a stupid woman," she said aloud, "how could you let this happen?" She fought tears, but cleared her throat and held her head high. "That'll get you no where. You're being silly. They'll be back. Soon the roof will be finished and all of this will be over. It was half a day. No big deal right? Right. So then why do I have this nagging feeling that I've been swindled? Because you're an old fool, that's why." She was silent for a moment. "No," she thought, "that's not it. You're a smart woman. You have good instincts. If he screws you over, fight back. Right now, I'll just have to have some coffee and be ready for the day. If they're not here by nine o'clock, I'll call him." She put her brush down, took a deep breath and returned to the kitchen to have her coffee, read the paper, and wait for the workmen to return - or not.

Good Morning America was blaring from the TV in Jack's hotel room when he began to come to. His head foggy and his mouth dry, he was lying on the cold sheets in his underwear with no pillow under his head. His neck hurt. He reeked of beer. At first, he didn't know where he was, and frankly didn't care. Slowly the events of the night returned to him and he felt a sick feeling of guilt grow in his gut.

He remembered going to the bar and staring into the mirror. He had been by the lake. There had been music. And a girl. Oh shit. The night pieced together like a word jumble, a little piece here, a little piece there, until the picture started to become clear. Smokey green eyes, an alluring scent of perfume, a little black dress, a hint of cleavage, an inviting smile, breasts against his chest - and trouble.

What had he done? Slender fingers. Had they held hands? Shit, he thought maybe they had. They drank, they laughed, they flirted hard, that he knew for sure. The details were fuzzy, but the feeling was there, it was residual inside him. What was her name? That perfume was amazing. Sexy. He remembered her smile vividly, the only vivid detail he held. Molly! That was her name, Molly. They'd talked for a long time. She was recently divorced and staying in a lake house. The lake. Little twinkling white lights like you see at Christmastime stretching from the boathouse roof to the trees dancing in the breeze and blurring like stars in an intoxicating dance. Dance. They had gone for a walk down to the boathouse. There was music. A wedding? No, a dance. The smell of the lake on the wind and that perfume. And then. That's where the 'oh shit' feeling came from. A kiss?

The night before -

She pulled ever so slightly on the back of Jack's neck, pulling him to her, and soon their lips were just a whisper apart. The woman was lovely. Jack felt a chill run up his spine. She smelled of lilacs. Her hair was soft and flowing and her lips beckoned him, hungry for his. Her breath smelled of cinnamon gum and wine. She was right there for the taking. Only the space of their breath between them, and from there, he knew he could have her, would have her, except - he couldn't. He pulled back from her and raised his chin to the sky. He sucked in the lake air, closed his eyes, and exhaled slowly.

"I can't," he said, slurring his words. "I wanna but I can't. You're a beautiful woman an' so generous to listen ta my troubles, but, I love my wife. She's waitin' at home, probly wondrin' where in the hell I am. I can't. I wanna, but I can't."

She put a chilled slender hand on his cheek, "She'd never know Jack."

He stared into those eyes, considering for a moment. "Nope, but I would. I can't do it. Sorry." Jack took a step back and held her fingers in his hands but there was space between them now, 'enough room for the Holy Spirit' as the nuns used to say at the grammar school dances. "She means too much to me. I hope you understand. And I'm sorry if I gave you the wrong impression. It was so nice to have someone to talk to and to take my mind off... ah... I'm an asshole. But this is where it ends. It has to."

Molly smiled a defeated smile. "I understand. There should be more men like you Jack. Anyhow, I had a wonderful night. Thank you."

"I did too Molly. Thank you. Um, I should be goin' though. Oh, wait, I should walk you to your car. It's late."

"I'll be fine Jack, but thank you. I'm parked right over there. Plenty of streetlights. Cops are out watching the drunks. I'll be fine. Take care and good luck."

"Thanks. You too." Jack turned and staggered up the street toward the hotel district. He was in no shape to drive all the way back home, so he got himself a room, crawled between the stark white sheets of the hotel bed, and flipped the television to an old black and white movie.

Just before passing out, Jack fumbled his cell phone from his pants' pocket, turned it on and checked his voicemail. There were several work messages from Erin, which he skipped through without listening, and one from Amy.

He dialed his home number, his head swimming and his tongue thick from too much beer. When she answered, he was barely coherent. "I'm sorry," was all he was able to get out. He ended the call and was out cold before Amy could say a word.

That sick feeling stopped growing, but it didn't dissipate. He'd come close to making a horrible mistake. What if someone he or Amy knew had seen him. He was sitting at a bar holding hands with another woman, walking along the lake with her, keeping her warm, and then almost…

…almost, but not. At least he had that. He hadn't been very well behaved, but he'd stopped and come to his senses before he'd done anything really wrong.

He got up, slipped out of his boxers, and took a hot shower. Steam rose around him and the heat penetrated his toxic pores. He needed coffee and he needed to get home. He'd be going home to a tired, angry, worried wife. He was not looking forward to that. He let the water pour over him, cleansing him.

CHAPTER TWELVE

Amy had phoned her mother before the boys were up for the day. She'd gotten zero sleep and needed desperately to be relieved of her motherly duties long enough to have an overdue discussion with her husband, and then hopefully get an hour or two nap.

Rosemary Shea arrived at the Hanlon home in the nick of time. It was only 9:30 and already the boys had spilled a box of cereal, had a sword fight with their Whiffle bats, and argued over a video game. Rosemary could see her daughter was on the verge of tears, but decided not to ask any questions. Amy wasn't much of a crier. Whatever was bothering her was important, and to have her break down in front of her boys was no good for anyone. Amy would come around to telling Mother her troubles when the time was right. Like a drill sergeant in a floral print dress, Rosemary rounded up the boys and marched them to her car.

Silence invaded the house. Amy stood in the center of the front room, arms crossed, staring out the bay window at nothing. Alone in the silence, her anger and worry morphed to genuine fear. She cursed the day Jack met that man in the parking lot of that Denny's. She cursed that day he'd made the biggest sale of his life. She wished none of it had ever happened.

Already, they'd lost too much from this battle. She wished her husband could let it go. But he couldn't, and she feared he never would. Now, for the first time in their married life, he'd spent the night away from home with no advanced warning, no explanation, not even a phone call other than the cryptic late night call to apologize, for what, she didn't know. This was not the man she'd married.

A chill ran through the quiet house and Amy shivered. She retreated to her bedroom, crawled under the covers and attempted to sleep.

Amy was still awake when she heard Jack come home. She didn't get out of bed. She'd rehearsed all night what she'd say to him when he returned, but now that the time had come, her mind was blank.

Jack put his keys down on the table beside the door and was taken aback by the tangible silence around him. Typically, the house would be teaming with activity. Amy would be vacuuming, the boys would be running around making a racket, the TV would be blaring SpongeBob with no one actually sitting and watching it. At those times he'd wished for some peace, but the silence now was cold and empty.

He took a deep breath and headed toward the stairs to the bedroom he shared with Amy. They rarely fought. He hated when she was angry with him, hated the feeling of having upset or disappointed her.

He wanted to get everything out on the table (well, almost everything, leaving out the part about the attractive woman he'd almost kissed). Apologize and hope she forgave him, take the licking he deserved and slowly return to normal, that was the plan. In time, she would forgive him. But he dreaded having to go through it all. He felt the same as he did as a child when he'd gotten in trouble and heard his father come home. He knew the belt was coming and he wanted it over, but he dreaded the moment that approached between now and then.

Jack climbed the steps slowly and entered the bedroom.

They sat in silence for a moment.

"I'm sorry. I should have called you earlier while I was still sober. I shouldn't have just…"

Amy pulled the blanket to her chest and curled the top of it in her arms, her expression never changing. She kept her back to her husband and stared at the closet doors in front of her.

"Anyhow, I talked to Levine finally. The company put the settlement offer on hold. I don't know why. He claims he doesn't know why. I had to get away. I had to go somewhere to think; shit, I had to go somewhere to breathe. I just got in the car and started driving. I didn't want to come home and face you. I didn't want to come home and lash out at the boys because of something some asshole in New York did. I just – drove. I wound up in Lake Geneva. I walked by the lake. I walked the main street by the stores. Then I went to the Burley Boar for a drink and wound up staying till it closed."

Jack paused for a moment. No response from Amy. Just cold silence.

"By that point, I was in no shape to drive home. I got a hotel room, passed out, woke up this morning and came right home. I know I worried you. I'm sorry."

Amy didn't respond right away. She lay in her bed soaking up all she'd heard. Still facing the closet doors, her back to Jack, she finally said, "Next time, call."

Then silence. He'd rather she get up and start yelling and screaming at him, start throwing shoes at him or something. But she didn't do any of that. Instead, she quietly burrowed deeper in her covers and waited patiently for sleep, summarily and silently dismissing him.

Jack got up from the bed and went downstairs to the kitchen to boil water for tea. He microwaved some canned soup, and sat at the kitchen table smoking a cigarette and flipping through the Sun-Times, occasionally taking a sip of either the soup or the tea, but neither was empty before it was cold.

He finally fell asleep in front of the TV watching the afternoon Cubs game.

When he awoke a couple hours later, the Cubs were beating the Mets 4-2 and Amy was gone.

The buzz of the doorbell startled him. He peered out the curtain. It was Mrs. Kelly, and she was crying.

CHAPTER THIRTEEN

"Allow me to ask a question," Fitzsimmons declared to the reconvened group of executives, "have we contacted the customer about this yet?"

Fitzsimmons had come to the office straight from the Plaza Hotel feeling renewed. A clandestine romp with a young woman in a luxury hotel will do that. Like drinking from the fountain of youth.

"Well, we decided it was premature to do that last year. We agreed we didn't want to do anything that might compromise the sale or the renewal of the contract when the time came," Sheldon answered.

"When was the original contract signed? I'm in my car and don't have the paperwork in front of me," Ross Riggleman said.

"The sale was signed and authorized by Ken Hornsby on August 8, 2008," replied Jacob.

"Then a courtesy call to the customer is in order considering the approach of the two-year anniversary of the deal is approaching," said Fitzsimmons. "Ross, why don't you reach out to Mr. Hornsby and make sure everything has been satisfactory for him, and, while you're at it, feel him out for his impression of our Mr. Hanlon. Find out exactly how this middle-of-the-road salesman blasted through all of our incentive offerings in one agreement."

"I'll give him a call as soon as I get back to the office," Riggleman replied.

With that, the conference call ended. Ross Riggleman hit 'end' on the screen of his cell phone, placed it on the nightstand, then leaned over on his elbow to face the beautiful young actress he'd been pursuing for two months, as she lie naked next to him, smoking a cigarette and checking her Facebook page on her iPhone. He was looking for a quickie before he had to check out and get back to the office, but alas Facebook held more interest for the girl than did he.

Ken Hornsby was in a sour mood. He answered the last of his e-mails before shutting down his computer and packing it in for the day. It had been a hell of a day. One of those days when he wondered why in the hell he hadn't retired yet. The work was fine, a little tougher in this bad economy, but he'd been through rough economies before. It was the people he couldn't stand anymore. When did everyone become so phony? When did they begin to care less about getting the job done and more about getting credit for work they hadn't done to move up that corporate ladder where they mistakenly thought the work got easier? Had it always been this way? He thought it probably had. He could remember several names from the past thirty-some-odd years of people who'd tried to take the easy way, people who'd backstabbed and jockeyed themselves into positions they weren't equipped to handle. They had been the exceptions though. Now, it seemed that kind of behavior was the norm, and that now it was the honest hard-working fellas and gals who were the exception.

Maybe he had just stayed too long at the party. Maybe he was just getting old and tired. But what waited on the other side for him? Sleeping in and having late breakfasts with Martha? Tending to the lawn? Afternoons stuck in front of the idiot-box watching Supermarket Sweep on the Game Show Network? He'd rather drop dead in his office than endure that. He had devoted his life to his work and his family. Now the kids were grown and gone. His wife, God bless her, would want to kill him after a few weeks of him diddling around the house. And the work, well that was always supposed to be a means to an end, but to what end? A sedentary life of non-import, waiting in a recliner for the grim reaper to come? Each day exactly like the day before? Sure he could travel, but where? And really, how long could you do that? Live out of a suitcase in hotel after hotel? The novelty of that would wear off quick. What he needed for his retirement was a plan. He didn't have one. So he stayed. And he hated every second of it.

As he packed his briefcase and was about to turn out his light, the phone rang.

"Mr. Hornsby, there's a Mr. Riggleman from General Systems on the phone for you. Would you like me to send him to voicemail?"

He had no idea who Riggleman was, but General Systems was a big supplier, so he took a deep breath and decided he should take the call. "No, Sara. I'll take the call. Thank you. Feel free to go home whenever you'd like. After this call, I'm done for the day."

He wondered why it wasn't Hanlon calling. In the nearly two years of the deal, Jack had been his only contact over at G.S. to this point.

"Thank you Mr. Hornsby. I'll see you tomorrow. Have a good night."

"Thank you Sara. You too."

With a click, Sara was gone and Ross Riggleman was on the line.

"Mr. Riggleman, Ken Hornsby here. What can I do for you?"

"Ken, how are you? Is it late there in Chicago?"

'Fucking L.A. people think there is only one time zone, Pacific', Ken thought, 'if the man has a clock and half a fucking brain he should be able to figure out what time it is in Chicago on his own.'

"To be honest Mr. Riggleman, I was just packing up for the day. Is this a pressing matter?"

"No, I just wanted to check in with you and make sure you're happy with our products and services."

"I am. Is that all?"

"I should tell you sir, that I am the Vice President of Project Management for General Systems. I am calling you today because you are one of our largest and most valued customers and I felt that your account was worthy of a personal phone call from the corporate offices to thank you for your business and to ensure your satisfaction with our company."

"V.P. of Project Management? Is there something wrong with the account? I assure you that Advanta Health is usually very timely with its payments to our vendors. If something has been overlooked I'd be happy to..."

"No, Ken, everything is just fine with the account. Your payments have been prompt and are up to date. We couldn't be happier on this end. I just wanted to make sure you were happy with our people on your end."

"Yeah. Things are great. Thanks for checking in." Ken Hornsby was ready to go home to his dinner. He had no patience for bullshit at this hour.

66

"Great. I see that the two year anniversary of our contract is coming up and I was wondering if there was anything you might need in addition to what you've already ordered, or if there was anything I could do for you?"

"What happened to Hanlon? He's the salesman I signed the deal with. Has he left your company? Usually, it would be his job to make this kind of call, not the VP of Finance. What's going on here?"

"Mr. Hanlon is still in our employ. I just wanted to..."

"Wanted to what? Undercut him on an additional sale?" Ken genuinely liked Jack, which was a rarity with most people these days. His conversations with Jack were short and to the point, with no hard sell and no bullshit.

"No sir, it's not that. It's just that, well," Riggleman went into the lie he'd planned for this call in case he needed it, "we've gotten some complaints from other customers about Mr. Hanlon's performance and I just wanted to make sure that you felt that you were receiving the quality of service you expect from General Systems."

"I'll be honest with your Mr. Riggleman," Ken Hornsby was getting more agitated by the second. It was bad enough he had to deal with the politicking in his own workplace, let alone having to deal with someone else's bullshit. "I have not received the level of service I expected from General Systems."

"I'm sorry to hear that Ken. I assure you that Mr. Hanlon will be dealt with in..."

"Let me finish Mr. Riggleman," Hornsby interrupted, "what I expected from General Systems was a complete and utter lack of service at all. I expected that if I were to sign a contract with a salesman from GS that that would be last goddamn day I would hear from him until the contract was up for renewal. I expected that any problems we had with your machines would be forwarded from said salesman to some clown in India whose name is Krishna Mohamed Patel or some shit, but calls himself Larry and has never seen a GS machine in his life. I expected your machinery to be substandard and expensive. In short, and excuse my French sir, I expected that if I ever signed a deal with General Systems that I would get royally fucked in the goddamn ass!"

"I'm sorry to hear that Ken..."

Again Hornsby interrupted, "I'm not finished. I fended off that Mr. Hanlon of yours for several years. Phone call after phone call, I would lie and tell him I was too busy, or had just made purchases from a competitor, whatever it would take to get him off the phone. He kept on me. He was polite on the phone, and didn't give me the usual salesman bullshit. He wore me down. So finally, I agreed to meet with him with every intention of listening to his pitch and telling him no and sending him on his way in hopes of never hearing from him again. Then I had the pleasure of meeting him. Not here. Not where he knew who I was and had his game face on. Not where he knew the right ass to kiss, but in a parking lot of a fucking Denny's. Without knowing who I was, he changed my flat tire and wished me good luck. When he told me his name, I knew who he was, but he still didn't know who I was. I tested him to make sure this wasn't some bullshit game. He passed. I figured if General Systems was smart enough to hire an honest and polite young man as Jack Hanlon, maybe I had been wrong about the company. I was impressed by his presentation. He put to rest my fears of being lost in the shuffle of such a large corporation, and he convinced me of the quality of your products. That is not at all what I expected. Any questions or concerns my company has had about your machines, Jack has personally looked into and gotten the correct answers for us. I have never been directed from him to an automated operator nor to India. I have never gotten lost in the shuffle. He has tended to this account better than anyone I have ever dealt with from any company. If you tell me others have complained, then I have to doubt either their sincerity or yours. Now, it's time for me to go home to my wife and my dinner. I urge you Mr. Riggleman, that if you want to keep this account, and you want any future sales from the Advanta Group, that you have Jack Hanlon call me himself. Not you. Not anyone else. Jack. That's all. Is there anything else you wanted to ask me?"

"No, that's all, Ken."

"Have we met Mr. Riggleman?"

"No Ken, I don't think we have."

"Neither do I. So stop calling me Ken like we grew up on the same fucking block together. It's Mr. Hornsby to you. My friends call me Ken. You, Mr. Riggleman, are not one of my friends."

With that, Ken Hornsby hung up the phone, snapped his briefcase shut and stormed from his office. He couldn't wait to get out of the cesspool of business and into his recliner. 'Maybe', he thought, 'retirement wouldn't be such a bad thing after all.'

Ross Riggleman held the receiver of his office phone in his hand, stunned by the exchange that had just taken place. After a couple of seconds, he got a new dial tone and placed a call to Gerald Fitzsimmons.

It was late in New York and Fitzsimmons was on his way back to his home in Connecticut, debating on making a stop at the club for a martini and a sandwich when his cell phone rang. The caller ID told him it was from the L.A. office.

"Fitzsimmons," he said.

"Gerald, Ross here. How are you?"

"Heading home."

"Great. Good for you. Listen. I just had an interesting phone conversation with Ken Hornsby from Advanta."

"Get anything good? Do they hate Hanlon as much as we do?"

"No, not exactly. But I wanted to relay our conversation to you before I forget the details. I don't think there's anything you can use, but I thought, hell you're the lawyer, maybe there's something I'm missing. Anyhow. He had a glowing review of Jack. Loves him. That's why I didn't want to put this in an e-mail."

"I understand," Fitzsimmons said, "What did the man have to say?"

Riggleman relayed, almost word for word what Hornsby had said about Jack Hanlon. He ended with the threat that if Jack Hanlon wasn't the salesman, GS could expect no more business from Advanta.

Gerald Fitzsimmons soaked in what he'd heard. He didn't say anything for a long time. So long in fact that Riggleman thought that the call had been dropped.

"You still there Gerald?"

"Yes, yes I am. Listen, let's not worry about not getting any additional business from Advanta. Business is business and if the price is right and the merchandise is good, they'll order from us no matter whom the salesman is. Hornsby has a board to answer to after all. Plus, they've already invested plenty in our products; it would cost them a lot to re-train their personnel on different equipment. That's an empty threat. But from what you've told me, I think we have grounds not only to deny payment to Mr. Hanlon, but to fire him as well."

"Really," Riggleman couldn't understand what part of what he'd told Fitzsimmons was the key to getting rid of Hanlon.

"I honestly don't think Jack Hanlon is going to be a problem for us any longer," Fitzsimmons said, "It's time to put this thing to bed. My next call will be to his attorney. I'll fill you in on the details in the morning. Good job Ross. This nightmare is over. We got him!"

CHAPTER FOURTEEN

"Mrs. Kelly, you're crying. What's wrong?" Jack grabbed her hand to help her over the threshold and shut the door behind her. He'd seen the old woman upset before, but he couldn't recall ever seeing her cry other than at her husband's funeral. Even at the wake she was stoic. She was talkative and lonely, but she was a tough old broad. To see her in tears was alarming.

"Jack, I think I made a big mistake," she said between sobs.

70

"Come into the kitchen and have a seat. I'll make us some tea. Tell me about it, I'm sure we can fix whatever the problem is," Jack said.

He followed the old woman into the kitchen and put fresh water in the kettle and lit the stove. He sat down next to her and gently took her hand.

"What mistake have you made, Mrs. Kelly?" he asked.

"Well," she swallowed a sob and, with a quivering voice, told Jack the story. "Remember the storm we had last weekend and I asked you to remove that big branch from my yard?"

"Yes."

"Well, a man came to my door, a roofer, he said he was doing some work in the neighborhood and noticed some damage to my roof and asked if he could take a look and I told him okay and then he said the roof was in desperate need of repair and the insurance company would drop my coverage if I called them and he could fix it quick for twenty thousand dollars if I paid twelve thousand up front and said he could start next week but then yesterday morning a bunch of men were tearing my roof off and left it that way and they didn't come back today and I'm worried that I'm an old fool who's been swindled out of twelve thousand dollars and Jack, that's a lot of money. I don't have that kind of money to lose."

Jack had been so wrapped up in his own problems, he hadn't even noticed that the century-old, green clay roof had been removed from the old woman's house across the street.

Jack patted her hand and told her to slow down a bit. Mrs. Kelly stopped talking and took a deep breath and tried to stop her hands from shaking.

"Let me get this straight, the man told you *not* to call the insurance company?"

Mrs. Kelly nodded.

"And you paid him twelve thousand dollars."

Mrs. Kelly nodded again.

"That kind of roof you have shouldn't need to be replaced, Mrs. Kelly. What he quoted you sounds like a repair job, those roofs are expensive, but they last forever. You're telling me they just tore all of the clay shingles off the house?"

"Yes," she said.

Jack took it all in for a moment. It was obvious the old lady had been the victim of a crime. "Did he give you a business card or anything?"

Mrs. Kelly reached into the pocket of her housecoat and produced the business card the man had slipped through the chained door. She gave it to Jack.

"Okay. I'm going to give the man a call. I'll tell him I'm your son or something, I don't know. I'll ask him when he plans to return. I don't want you to worry too much, Mrs. Kelly. Okay?"

The shaking subsided and Mrs. Kelly took in a deep breath and exhaled. The teakettle whistled and Jack rose to turn off the stove and pour the tea. Before he could get to the stove, the phone rang. He shut off the fire under the kettle and rushed to the ringing phone.

"Hello?"

"Jack, it's Seth," Levine's voice was somber.

"Seth. What's wrong?"

Seth exhaled before speaking. "I just received a call from Gerald Fitzsimmons at GS."

"Yeah?"

"Jack, I don't know what happened exactly, but he informed me that GS would no longer be negotiating with us. That you had broken company policy and that had resulted in your acquisition of the sale to Advanta. He said that it was a clear case of malfeasance and that he would be forwarding to me your termination papers."

"Termination papers? How did this go from a commission dispute to termination? On what grounds?"

"On the grounds that you knowingly and willfully broke company policy. Beyond that, I don't have the details. Like I said, he told me he'd get me the official paperwork tomorrow."

"Seth. You have to do something. I didn't do anything wrong. How could they do this?" Jack's hands began to shake.

"I don't know Jack. Trust me, whatever it is, we'll fight it. But I can't know what we're up against until I get the official complaint. I just thought I owed you a heads up. Jack, I don't know what they have up their sleeve, but he sounded very confident. This is looking like it's going to be a long battle after all."

"Yeah.

"Can you think of any inappropriate behavior you may have engaged in during your employment with GS?"

"Seth, I go to work, I do my job, I come home to my wife and family. I don't scam, I don't cheat, I don't even bring home pens or post-it notes from the office. I don't harass the women, I don't go over on my entertainment budget. I tow the line." Jack was starting to shout. "What kind of fucking bullshit are they pulling Seth? What the fuck is this? This should have been simple!" Jack was short of breath and reached in his pocket for his Marlboros but they weren't there. His head began to pound and he became dizzy.

Mrs. Kelly went to the teakettle, found the cups and the Lipton and poured two cups of tea.

"Seth - Seth - you have to fix this. You have to help me. I can't lose my job. I can't. I can't lose my job and I can't lose the money they owe me. How am I gonna survive?"

"Jack, we'll fight this. We'll win this. Tomorrow I'll know exactly what we're up against, okay. Until then, try not to worry..."

"Try not to worry? I have a wife and three kids who depend on me to feed them, to keep a roof over their heads, how the FUCK can I not worry, Seth?"

Jack slammed the receiver down hard enough to knock the phone off the wall.

His face was contorted and red and dripping with sweat. His fists clenched tight, his knuckles flushed red then white. Jack laid his head against the kitchen wall next to where the phone had once hung. Then, with a sudden and violent explosion, he put his fist through the drywall with such force he punched a hole clear through to the adjacent room. Had he struck a stud, his hand would have shattered.

When he turned to face Mrs. Kelly, his eyes were red as blood; his hair was a matted, sweaty mess. She saw in his eyes, behind the blood and tears, an anger and emptiness that startled her. She was afraid to speak. She slowly carried the teacups to the kitchen table and set them down with care. She avoided eye contact with Jack and sipped her tea.

Jack's head was spinning. He wiped his eyes of their wetness and rubbed drywall dust from his throbbing knuckles.

He staggered to the kitchen table and dropped into a chair.

Mrs. Kelly laid a wary hand on his arm.

The two sat there in silence as they sipped their tea and meandered through the dark and twisting corridors of the betrayal-stunned mind. Each searching for answers. Each seeking a justifiable resolution. Each scared to death that there was no way out.

CHAPTER FIFTEEN

Gerald Fitzsimmons sent out a late-night e-mail summonsing the group to a mandatory conference call to take place at nine eastern, Wednesday morning. He instructed them all to have a copy of the Official General Systems Employee Code of Ethics Handbook with them. Jacob Riis was the only one in the group who had one readily available; the others had to download it from the corporate intranet.

The usual suspects were on the line: Rhonda Royce, Lloyd Sheldon, Carrie Miller, Bruce Chung, Jacob Riis, Ross Riggleman and, of course, Fitzsimmons.

"Okay everyone," Fitzsimmons began, "I'd like you to open your Employee Handbooks to page 115 under the section entitled Gifts, Favors, Conflicts of Interest. I trust you're all familiar with your Employee Handbook." This got a collective laugh from the group.

"I'd first like to draw your attention to Directive 206 which states: 'Employees shall not give gifts or favors greater than the limitations spelled out in Directive 204-B to any business contact unless the gifts or favors are part of an Official General Systems Company approved promotion. Employees should avoid any situation or circumstance that may give even the appearance of impropriety.' The limitations spelled out in 204-B by the way," Fitzsimmons continued, "is $50.00 U.S."

"Okay," Carrie Miller wasn't sure where Gerald was going with this. She wondered how he'd discovered her quiet agreement with several company vendors.

"Bear with me Carrie. This will all come into focus in just a moment." Gerald Fitzsimmons' smile could be seen through the phone lines.

"Now I'd like to draw your attention to the bottom of that same page to the section sub-titled Commercial Bribery stating 'Federal and State Laws prohibit an agreement in which an employee engages in behavior in which a benefit is offered or accepted, without the consent or knowledge of the employer, and the gift is offered or accepted with the understanding that the person receiving the gift will use his/her influence to benefit the person giving the gift.'"

"Gerald, I mean this as a complement," Rhonda Royce said, "You are one clever son-of-a-bitch. That is brilliant."

"I'm sorry, I'm still lost," Carrie said.

"I have to admit, Gerald, I'm a bit confused too," said Riggleman, "I assume this has something to do with the Hanlon problem, but I don't see how this helps us, unless you found he had a deal under the table with Hornsby."

"I knew it!" Carrie shouted, relieved that it wasn't she they were after. "There's no way that moron could have brought in a sale that large without cheating."

"Well," cautioned Fitzsimmons, "it's not that clear cut. But I'm certain it will work. It will at least hold up in court long enough for us to wear him out and deplete his financial ability to continue fighting. It also gave us legitimate grounds to terminate him, which I did last night."

"You fired him last night?" Riggleman was shocked and angry.

"Bruce and I contacted his attorney last night and informed him of his client's termination. Bruce, Lloyd, and I will be drafting an official written notice this afternoon for immediate delivery to Mr. Levine."

"Oh my god, what did he do? You're killing me Gerald. Tell me. I have to know," Carrie was giddy.

"Well, Carrie, it seems our Mr. Hanlon ran into the buyer for Advanta in a parking lot before their meeting where he proceeded to change the man's flat tire."

"What? He fixed the guy's tire? I don't get it."

"Lloyd, I asked you to get some information for me this morning, do you have that handy?"

"I do Gerald."

"Good, please tell the group here how much it would cost to have a tow truck come out and change a flat tire in Schaumburg, Illinois."

"The cost ranges from $65 to $150 provided he didn't need a tow and provided he wasn't a member of AAA or some other auto-club."

"And if he were in an auto-club, what is the average response time for a tow truck to come out and fix a flat tire at say 8:30-9:00 in the morning in the summer in Schaumburg, Illinois?"

"Well, that all depends of course on how busy the towing companies are and traffic variances from day to day, but on average I found it takes about an hour to an hour and a half from the time the call is made until the spare is on the car and the car is ready to be driven again. Most of that time of course is spent waiting for the truck to arrive on the scene."

"And approximately how much does Mr. Hornsby earn per hour if you were to break his salary down?"

"He is of course, a salaried employee, but his salary divided into a straight forty hour week comes out to about $100.00 an hour. But of course a man in Mr. Hornsby's position, well his time is more valuable to both he and his company than just his salary. He makes million dollar decisions on a daily basis, an hour of his time is extremely valuable."

"Time is money, is it not folks? The way I see it, one way or the other, Mr. Hanlon's little 'favor' saved Mr. Hornsby well over $50.00. I further argue that it was that favor that influenced Mr. Hornsby to give Jack Hanlon the contract, he as much as said that to Ross last night on the phone. That my friends is a direct violation not only of the Corporate policies of General Systems Inc., but also, if we can convince a judge, which I admit will take some convincing, is in violation of the Federal Commercial Bribery laws."

"Do you really think that will stand up in court?" Rhonda was skeptical.

"It will stand up enough to get us to court. It will stand up enough to give us leverage we didn't have before. If we can't use it to leverage Jack into dropping this nonsense, then maybe the threat of legal action for a man facing retirement soon will convince Mr. Hornsby to go along with the program so to speak. And there's always the threat that we will take the matters to the Feds for criminal action that we can dangle over both of them. Eventually, one of the other will decide it isn't worth the fight and the hassle and the matter will be dropped."

"I'm just trying to learn here, but what happens if it doesn't get dropped? Will it work in court?" Jacob Riis was taking diligent notes.

"It can work," Lloyd added, "if we can connect the dots and present our argument convincingly. It's going to take a lot of leg work and long hours for us in legal affairs, but it can work."

"And if it doesn't," Riggleman noted, "then we just set him up for a very lucrative wrongful termination suit."

"Not by the letter of the law Ross. By the letter of the law, he broke company policy, that's all we have to prove."

"You don't have to prove he knowingly broke corporate policy?"

"What I need to do is convince a judge he knowingly broke corporate policy; there is a difference. It'll work, you'll see. If you'll excuse us now," Fitzsimmons added with an air of haughtiness, "Bruce, Lloyd, and I have a document to draft for Mr. Hanlon's attorney."

CHAPTER SIXTEEN

Jack and Mrs. Kelly had sat at his kitchen table for an hour, sipping their tea and staring unfocused at the wall in silence. When the front door opened and the boys rushed in, Mrs. Kelly stood up, and without a word, nodded at the kids and walked out the front door passing Amy on the way.

"What's with her?" Amy asked Jack, then saw the broken phone on the floor and the hole in the drywall and knew Mrs. Kelly wasn't the one to worry about. "What is it? What's happened?"

"I don't know. I have to walk. Please don't wait up. We'll talk about this all tomorrow. I just can't do it tonight." With that, Jack walked out the back door and roamed the neighborhood until well after midnight.

His first phone call after a sleepless night was to Levine.

"I'd never met the man before. I saw an old guy with a flat tire and offered to change it for him; I had no idea who he was."

"That may be true Jack but..."

"It is true Seth. We have to fight this. This should be a slam-dunk in court. Just let me tell my story and..."

"Jack... Jack... nothing is a slam-dunk in court. Even if they were to admit you didn't know who Mr. Hornsby was when you changed his tire, they will still argue that your doing so led to your getting the sale."

"They made a lot of money off that sale! If my changing the old man's tire got me the sale, they should be happy about that."

"Yes, of course they should, but we're in a situation where if they can win this thing in court, they still get to keep the proceeds from the sale, and not have to pay you anything. What they're doing is morally wrong, but they may have the law on their side, as fucked up as that may sound."

"That sounds very fucked up. So you think I should take the $200,000.00 offer and just forget the whole thing happened. Fine. I just want this over. Tell them they have a deal."

"I wish I could Jack, but they rescinded that offer, remember?"

"So what are they offering now?"

"Three months severance and compensation for any unused vacation days. You're looking at about fifteen grand before taxes, then there's my fee of course, so all in all you'll walk away with a few grand in your pocket and no job."

"I have no job," Jack had yet to say it aloud. He heard his own words and let them sink in for a moment.

"Jack, they've fired you on the grounds that you violated corporate policy. You have no job."

"We have no choice then Seth. We have to fight it in court. It's the only chance I have. Even if I don't win the full amount, maybe I'll at least get what my regular commission would have been under the old contract and get to keep my job at least long enough to find a new one."

"And if you don't win, you walk away with nothing."

"I'm right and they're wrong, and I have no other option. Tell them we'll see them in court."

"Okay Jack, you're the boss. I'm sorry. I hope you're ready for this. These kinds of lawsuits tend to drag on. I would suggest you start your job hunt now because, even if you win, and that's a big if, it could be years before you see a dime from them. You'll have to live somehow between now and then. I wish I had better news for you Jack. Again, I'm sorry."

Jack was sweating when he hung up the phone. His entire adult life, ever since he became a husband and a father, every financial move he made, every penny he spent, every decision he made was based on making sure the essentials were taken care of first. He had done the math and figured out how much they would need in savings to get them through six months of no income and still be able to make ends meet. That money was untouchable unless absolutely necessary, unless he found himself out of work, or, God forbid, they had some kind of medical emergency that exceeded what insurance would cover and he needed the money to care for either Amy or one of the kids. But, he had spent it. Not on a motorcycle or a boat, not on a vacation or a car, not on dinners and movies and toys, but on his sons, on their college tuition, and on that only because he was expecting to be able to replace it and then some within a few weeks time. But then the shit storm came. Everything went to hell. If he were to withdraw the money from the Brilliant Beginnings 529 fund, a good portion of the money would simply evaporate due to penalties and taxes.

Jack dropped into his beat-up old recliner, lit a cigarette, and rubbed his temples. It was good that Amy and the boys were gone for the day; he needed time to think.

Jack spent the rest of his day calling and e-mailing former co-workers and any contacts he'd made over the years, hoping one of them could lead him to a job opening. They all promised they'd get back to him if they heard of anything, but as it stood, no one had an opening.

By now, the Great Recession was in full swing. Companies were laying off workers on a monthly basis. To add insult to injury, the Affordable Care Act had passed through Congress and had been signed by the President. Republicans vowed to repeal it, Democrats vowed to implement it, but the new law was a mystery so far, and how it would ultimately affect business was anybody's guess. The in-fighting in Washington between the two parties raised questions as to whether there ultimately would be a law or would not be a law, even though it had been passed and signed. In business, uncertainty is the enemy, and at this point, uncertainty seemed to be the rule of the day. All of these factors created fear on Wall Street and in the boardrooms. As a result, hospitals stopped buying new equipment and hence, manufacturers of that equipment had halted hiring and began cutting the workforce. There were no jobs in medical sales, at least until everyone had figured out if there would, in fact, be new rules, if so, what the new rules would be and what those new rules meant for the bottom line.

But a good salesman can sell anything, so Jack expanded his search outside of medical sales to industrial sales of any kind he could think of, hotel and leisure sales, and prescription drug sales. The downturn in the economy had hit every corner of the economic engine hard. People were losing their jobs left and right, and those who had been fortunate enough to not get laid-off were hanging on to their jobs with both fists. No one was leaving one company for another; no one was vacating a position for a higher one. Everyone who was lucky enough to have a job was digging in and staying put.

However, there was one market that opened up because of the bad economy. Jack hated the thought of it, but he had to put food on the table. He had to earn a living. He grabbed his car keys and went in search of a job in the one place he thought he could find one.

CHAPTER SEVENTEEN

Mrs. Kelly returned home well after darkness had fallen across the city. She locked the deadbolt, dropped her keys on the table by the door, and switched on the hall light. The quiet empty enveloped her and, though the house was hot and muggy from being closed up all day, she shivered. She went from room to room turning on lights and opening windows hoping to find some relief from the choking, chilling silence.

She put the kettle on for tea and turned the kitchen radio to the Cubs game. While she waited for the kettle to whistle, she went to her bedroom, shed her day clothes and put on a loose fitting housecoat and a pair of slippers. It felt good to be free of the sticky nylon blouse and stockings. The stockings left behind an awful itch she couldn't scratch enough to relieve.

Upon returning to the kitchen, she shut the stove off under the kettle and decided instead to have a cold beer.

There was one left in the fridge from the six-pack she'd bought for the annual block party a few weeks before. She let the screen door spring shut on its own with a swift snap, took a seat on the cushion she kept on the top step of the back porch, looked off into the distance and sipped at the beer trying to wash down the day.

She'd gotten up at 11:00 am, much later than usual. The first two hours of the day, she spent tottering around the house trying to think of what she should do about the roofer. The number on the card he'd given her had apparently been a cell phone that had since been shut off. She dressed and went out to survey the roof from the street. It was a horrid sight. The blue tarp had loosened in one corner and billowed in the wind exposing the nakedness beneath it. Another couple of days, and it surely would sail from her roof off into some neighbor's yard or worse, onto the windshield of some passing car on Montrose Avenue.

Mrs. Kelly couldn't bare the sight of it any longer and went into her house and called her insurance company. The woman on the phone, very curtly told her that she would send a man out but that because it was not an act of nature, it most likely would not be covered by her policy.

The next hour was spent flipping through the Yellow Pages for a reputable roofer who could come undo the damage left by the thief who'd stolen her money and left her home in shambles. Appointments were set up with four companies for later in the week to survey the job and place bids.

It was nearly three o'clock when Mrs. Kelly left the house, bus pass in hand, to go to the police station to file an official complaint against the roofer. The afternoon sun beat down and the breeze that had been blowing the blue tarp earlier had died leaving behind a stale humidity that made it difficult for her to take in a full breath.

The visit to the police station was as fruitless as the call to the insurance company. A tall, gaunt young man in a police uniform shuffled papers and half-listened while Mrs. Kelly went through in painstaking detail what had transpired.

When Mrs. Kelly finally finished her story, the man slapped a form on the counter in front of her and told Mrs. Kelly to fill it out and they'd look into it. There was a tone of disinterest and dismissal in his voice. After slapping a pen on the counter, he turned his attention to his smartphone.

Mrs. Kelly wasn't about to be brushed off that easily.

"Listen here," she began too softly to be noticed, so she repeated herself more forcefully, "Listen here I said!" The desk-officer looked up from his phone. Mrs. Kelly continued, "I've been robbed. A good portion of my life savings has been stolen from me and I'm not gonna just fill out a goddamn form and be dismissed. Now I have paid taxes here my entire life. There was a time in Chicago that when you needed a police officer, you actually got to speak to a police officer, not some scrawny little asshole who spends his days sitting on the flat bone where his ass should be, playing bullshit kid games on his telephone like a fourteen year old girl. You should be ashamed of yourself sitting behind a desk, an able bodied man like you. Either be a policeman and help me, or grow a pair of tits and be a girl Friday, but do *not* dismiss me like I don't matter. Now if you can't help me Ichabod, point me in the direction of someone who can."

A stifled laugh came out as a snort from a detective who'd stopped on the staircase to watch the show. He wasn't alone; Mrs. Kelly now had the attention not only of the officers behind the front desk, but also of the entire first floor of the crowded police station. The cops all snickered, not at her, but in support of her. "Hey, Ichabod want me to water your horse on my way out," one thick-necked mustached officer chided as he went out the front doors. "Hey lady," a female officer called to Mrs. Kelly, "Ichabod's a new one. Most of the gals just call him pinky." She waggled her little pinky finger at the desk-officer and the place erupted in laughter. The scrawny desk-officer turned beat-red and bit his lip for lack of anything to say.

"Maybe I can help," a kind, but masculine voice declared from behind Mrs. Kelly. She turned to see a young black man in his mid-thirties dressed in a short sleeve dress shirt and a Sears tie. His hair was short and dark. He smiled at her and a dimple formed on his left cheek.

Mrs. Kelly softened. "I hope so," she said.

"I'm Detective Alan Rayson of the Robbery Division. If you'd like to follow me, we can go up to my desk and you can make a formal complaint and give me the pertinent details."

Mrs. Kelly followed the Detective up the flight of stairs past other policemen and some straggly looking characters. Detective Rayson lead her to an old beat up metal desk and offered her a seat. The chair was steel with a green vinyl cushion. The vinyl was cracked in several places revealing the yellowed foam underneath. Detective Rayson took his seat on the opposite side of the desk and pulled out a notebook and pen.

"I want to apologize Mrs. ..."

"... Kelly."

"I want to apologize Mrs. Kelly for what happened downstairs. Used to be the desk was a job for old-timers and officers who were injured in the line of duty. Now it seems like the preferred destination for the lazy ones who like wearing the badge but don't like doing the work. It's too bad. Now why don't you tell me what happened, Mrs. Kelly."

As Mrs. Kelly told Detective Rayson about the storm and the roofer who'd come to her door and the check she had written him and the Mexicans who had torn the roof off and how she hadn't seen neither hide nor hair of any of them since and how the phone number he'd given her was now disconnected, the detective took notes. When she was finished, he looked up from his notebook and gave her a sympathetic smile.

"This happens a lot Mrs. Kelly. Don't beat yourself up too much about it."

"I feel so stupid." She was fighting back tears.

"Don't. These guys who do this, are pros. They take in a lot of people with this scam, smart people. They go to great lengths to look legit. It's hard to tell the real workmen from the con artists."

"Can you catch them?"

The detective took a deep breath. "I'm not going to lie to you Mrs. Kelly. We'll do everything we can to catch him. But I can't promise you anything. The Mayor has manpower pretty thin around here. Citywide actually. I'd love to say that we could devote a team to just look into this kind of scam because I'm sure it's happening all over the city, but that's just not realistic. If we could, we'd catch the bum within a week or two, but the way things are, it's just not doable. But, I will make sure that while my team is out, that they keep an eye out for the vehicle you described to us and for roofers and workmen who seem out of place or not quite right. If we have anything, I will call you. I'm sorry I can't offer you more than that."

"I am too. You've been very kind to an old lady and I appreciate that, but I think this warrants a call to the Mayor's office to demand he hire more police officers."

"I wish you luck on that. Our union has been asking for that for years now. Seems Mayor Daley thinks there's more need for potted plants in the middle of Milwaukee Avenue than there is for more police officers. Of course, you didn't hear that from me."

"Of course not. Thank you for listening to me. Kick that little twerp downstairs in the shin for me if you get the chance. If I do it, I'll probably go to jail."

Detective Rayson laughed at that and said his farewells to Mrs. Kelly. On the bus ride home, she stared out at the passing apartment buildings and bungalows and wondered what in God's name had happened to her city.

PART TWO

DUSK IS MERELY THE SLOW, IMPENDING DEATH OF THE DAY

Revenge... is like a rolling stone, which, when a man hath forced up a hill, will return upon him with a greater violence, and break those bones whose sinews gave it motion.
— Albert Schweitzer

CHAPTER EIGHTEEN

THURSDAY, NOVEMBER 18, 2010

The light of day dimmed behind the blanket of a gunmetal sky. The biting rain slashed at Jack's face. The cheap vinyl dress shoes and thin socks he wore were not intended for Chicago Novembers. The vinyl tops hardened in the cold and with each step, the shoes would hammer the tiny bones at the top of Jack's feet. The wet and the cold soaked through the thin rubber soles and into his heels causing them to throb and ache. His toes numb, he stood waiting in the used car lot as a young man went back and forth between a '95 Chevy Monte Carlo and a '96 Jeep Cherokee, inspecting each one, reading the sticker, then going back to the other and doing the same. This had been going on now for twenty minutes. Jack had been working at the car lot now for four months and he'd hated every second of it.

Traffic along Milwaukee Avenue slushed by in a stream of salt crystals, dirty-melted ice, and rubber on wet asphalt. Jack envied those people in their cars. As he saw them they were *'comfortable people encased in the warmth of their own vehicle, the heater blowing hot air at them while soothing music calmed and erased the trials of the day. Content people heading toward home-cooked meals and loved ones, some silly TV show, a good book, and then bed. Even the passengers on the city bus were to be envied; though they'd surely spent long minutes waiting on the corner in the harsh weather, they were now encased in the soft light and warmth of the bus taking them to the cozy shelter of home.'*

'All of those warm, happy people passing by. People with no problems. People with careers. People with jobs they liked and a way to pay the mortgage. People who hadn't had the misfortune of having been employed by those thieving bastards at GS. Lucky people.'

As the day grew dimmer, the spotlights above the car lot came to life, bathing the small square space, packed with cars and gravel and a trailer-office, in cold, white, artificial light. It was a day of perpetual dusk, the sun having never made an appearance. Then true darkness approached just before 4:00pm and the temperature dropped ten degrees in half an hour. That's when the freezing rain hit.

It was the kind of day that made Jack long for his mother's homemade stew or his grandmother's chicken soup. He watched the rain slash diagonally through the white lights above the lot and felt the sting as the ice bit his skin. He longed for home. But, of course, that home didn't exist anymore.

Things had been strained between Amy and him lately. The boys kept their distance too. Home no longer felt like home and Jack no longer felt like Jack.

Something deep within him had changed. Something important was missing.

"Excuse me, excuse me," the young man's voice snapped Jack back to the freezing lot.

"Yes."

"Have either of these cars been in an accident?" the young man inquired.

"No sir, they have not. Either one of them." That was the answer Jack had been instructed to give to that question, though the owner of the lot, Frank Bugiardo, never bothered to look into the history of any of the cars they sold.

The young man looked back and forth at his options again, then shoved his hands into his pockets and said, "I'll be back tomorrow. I want to do some homework on the computer." And with that, he walked away.

Jack knew the man was not coming back. Anytime someone said they'd be back tomorrow, it meant they wouldn't be back at all. Jack climbed the steps into the trailer where Bugiardo was waiting.

"Well, what happened out there?"

Frank Bugiardo was a round, burley man. His face was always exertion-red, even while sitting. His dark, oily hair, slicked back along the dome of his head, was thin enough to expose the top of his scalp. The top button of his shirt always hung undone so as not to strangle him. He smelled strongly of sweat and Drakkar Noir.

"Said he'd be back tomorrow. I guess he couldn't decide between the Chevy or the Jeep," Jack replied.

"Well, did you help him along with his decision?"

"I told him about each of them. I told him all the perks of both cars. I thought he was gonna make a purchase. They're both good cars, I figured..."

"You figured. You figured wrong. You know I've been trying to unload that Chevy for four months now; why did you let him walk away? He would have driven out of here in that Chevy if you would have done your job." Bugiardo shook his head and let out a throaty humorless chuckle, "You are one of the shittiest salesman I've ever seen. And that's sayin' a lot, 'cause I have seen the shittiest of the shittiest, and you're shittier than any of them."

Jack took a deep breath. He stifled the urge to grab the fat man by the shirt collar, pull him to his feet, and throw him through the aluminum wall of the trailer. Instead, he lit a cigarette and took a deep pull. "I told you, take that shit outside. What're ya tryin' to give me cancer?" Bugiardo grumbled reaching for his cigar.

Jack took his cigarette back out into the cold.

The job market was not showing any signs of recovering anytime soon. His contacts and friends had nothing for him. In September, Amy got a part-time job at the local Big-Box Bullseye as a checker. Jack did his time on the lot. Amy got home most days around 4:30, in time to cook dinner for the boys. This left Trevor in charge of his brothers for an hour between getting home from their new public school and Amy arriving home from work. At first he resented the added responsibility that coincided with the elimination of his allowance, just as he had resented having to leave all of his friends behind and change schools. But he was a good kid and soon settled in to the new routine. He made sure the door was closed and locked behind them, and took good care of the boys and the house until his mother got home.

At nine o'clock Jack said goodbye to Bugiardo, was waved off by the fat man with a grunt, and descended the steps of the trailer. The bright floods above the lot shut off and Jack was left in near darkness until his eyes adjusted to the change. The freezing rain was beginning to accumulate on the ground in the form of slush and icy puddles. Jack stepped through the lot trying his best to avoid getting his frigid feet even wetter. The only thing worse than cold, was cold and wet, and it was a long way home.

Jack trudged along Milwaukee Avenue, passing beneath the orange glow of the street lights' sodium vapor. He looked over his shoulder, but there was no sign of a bus coming, so he lowered his head to shield his face from the frozen rain and trudged on.

The wind and the rain ripped the last remaining leaves from the trees and sent them whirling through the air, then the leaves, soaked heavy, would fall to the ground, wet, tattered, and dead, to decay. The tree, unrecognizable as the lush sturdiness of breath and life it had been, was now stripped of its once awesome glory, to stand naked and dark in the cold. During summer, the tree was limber, swaying in the soft breezes and the summer storms. Now though, its branches creaked and croaked and one thought the beast might crumble and topple to come crashing to the earth. What had once been strength and shelter, was now a danger, something of which to be frightened. A thing of ghost stories and children's nightmares. Jack, his feet numb, his ears burning red, his eyes watering and his nose running, shivered as he stepped among the naked trees, his shoe heels cracking against the sidewalk with each step. He caught his reflection in a shop window, and he barely recognized himself. Jack lowered his head and continued his journey. He had miles to go, and it was only November. Jack feared what winter would bring.

At last his home was in view. Like everything else in the world, the house looked cold. The porch light was unlit. From inside, the icy light from the television flashed through the window sending differing shades of blue through the pane to reflect off the rain-drenched pillars of the front porch.

The boys would be in bed by now, and Amy close to sleep herself. Jack longed for the warmth of his home, but dreaded the loneliness that would greet him when he finally did arrive. That's what his life had been the past few months, long dreary days, followed by dark, lonely nights. He ascended the steps of his house. The key no longer slid easily in the lock and he had to wiggle it and jerk it to get it in. The lock was difficult to turn and the door, swollen from the weather, stuck to the jamb and had to be shouldered open.

Once inside, Jack pushed the swollen door shut, making more noise than he had intended. Amy lay on the front room couch and acknowledged Jack's arrival home with a half-hearted wave, her eyes never leaving the television screen, her lips pursed shut.

Things had been this way for a while now, the two drifting apart. Little conversation, no small talk, none of the little private jokes they used to share. There was no laughing, no smiling, no touching. No little warm embraces and no kisses hello and good-bye as there had been just a few months before. Now there were only cool pleasantries, long hours apart, and diverging ideals.

Amy for her part had tried to make things work. She'd tried very hard to keep the family together as it had been. She'd caress Jack's hand, only to have him pull it away. She'd rub his shoulders after he returned from a long day at the car lot, though she herself had spent endless hours on her feet at work, and then again at home caring for the children. She got no response from him. He was fixated. His body, worn and tired was home, but his mind was someplace else.

At night, after the boys had gone to bed, she would try to seduce him. She'd brush her hair in the manner he liked, dressed herself in the thin, short, satin teddy he'd bought her one anniversary and sidled up to him. Her breasts firm and alert, her legs soft and inviting, her lips poised to pleasure him, her goal to relieve him, to take him away, if only for a few passionate moments, from the theft, the money, the ego-blow of having been fired, the law suit, but there was no diverting Jack from those things and so, she was rebuked.

She bought him new clothes and sturdier winter shoes, he returned them stating they couldn't afford them. She baked cookies, cooked his favorite meals, all for naught.

Amy spoke softly, but directly to him, stating firmly that she wanted no part of the money, that he should let the whole thing go, but he dismissed her attempts at solace as charity. He would lament that he'd let her down, that he'd disappointed her and the boys and that he would continue to fight for what was rightfully theirs.

Months of trying. Months of insisting. Months of giving all she'd had to the marriage with seemingly no reciprocity wore on Amy. She was at a loss. She had run out of ideas and had grown weary of trying. Eventually, she closed herself off. She was unsure and afraid of what Jack was becoming. He was no longer the man she'd fallen in love with and that realization sent shivers through her core. Worse, she was becoming more and more certain that her Jack was gone for good, that regardless of the results of his fight, that he would never return to being the man she married. He had become cold and hard and cynical, and she began to hate him for it.

Jack walked straight to the kitchen without saying a word. The refrigerator door illuminated the otherwise dark room. He found a cold plate of chicken, green beans, and noodles covered in foil. He ate the chicken cold, leaning against the counter-top in the dark while the green beans and noodles revolved in the microwave.

He took his plate of reheated food to the kitchen table and sat in the dark staring out the window at the freezing rain pelting the back porch railing. Jack hated what he'd become. He hated lying to people about the cars they wanted. He hated gouging them for more than their purchase car was worth, while simultaneously screwing them on the other end for their trade-in. The customers at the used car lot were not wealthy people. They were people just like him, hard-working people just trying to find a mode of transportation to get them to and from work while they raised a family, fed the kids, clothed the kids, raced them to and from little league practice or basketball practice and dance recitals and paid their taxes. People clipping coupons and buying cheap shoes so they could keep a roof over their heads and still have some kind of a decent life. These weren't people looking to impress the neighbors with the fancy hood ornament or the status-symbol make and model of the latest hot number. They just needed a car. And Jack would've gladly sold them what they needed and with enough of a mark-up that both he and the lot made a fair profit, but that's not how it worked. No, that's not how it worked at all. Not at Frank Bugiardo's lot. He couldn't scrub the scum off of himself, no matter how often or how lengthy he showered. The grime was inside him. It had stained his soul. Until he was free of that stain, that grime, that scum, he could not like himself.

He felt Amy slipping away from him too. 'And why wouldn't she,' he thought. She had trusted him, had put all her faith in him to provide for her and the boys so she could stay home and raise them. They had agreed early on, before there were any kids, before there was even a hint at any kids, that children should have a mother at home to raise them if that were at all financially possible. Amy was a college-educated woman. She had ambitions of her own. She was not afraid of hard work. But, if they were going to decide to bring children into the world, and she did so want children, then it was going to be she who raised them. That was her decision. It was a job she took very seriously, and one she enjoyed.

But she'd had to go out and get a job well below her abilities because she'd been out of the workforce for so long. The boys, they've had to adjust to life on their own, without mother or father around when they got home from school, a new school, a school they weren't accustomed to. They had to drop all of their extra-curricular activities because, for one thing, the family couldn't afford the fees, and for another, there was no one to get them to and from.

That beautiful girl who could have had any man she wanted, had chosen Jack, and now, as a result, she was forced to pinch every penny, to take on a minimum wage job, to work twice as hard as she already had been. She wasn't a high-maintenance woman, and here she was having to give up the simple dreams and desires she *did* have because he had failed her. That was the key word right there: 'fail'. At the heart of it all, Jack felt like a complete and utter FAILURE. He had failed his children, he had failed himself, but worst of all, he had failed Amy.

When you fail the one you love, it's difficult enough just to face her everyday knowing you're a failure, let alone sleep with her. He saw her advances and attempts at seduction as charity. Give the boy a little pick-me-up with some good old-fashioned sex. Make him feel like a man again. And that only made things worse. That intensified the dark thoughts, the self-loathing, and he couldn't do it. He couldn't take her knowing she deserved so much better, knowing he was not a man as a man should be.

Jack heard the television in the living room turn off. He heard Amy's footsteps on the stairs. She was off to bed with an early start to work in the morning. A sliver of light from the pole in the alley washed across the otherwise unlit kitchen. Jack sat in silence, nibbling at cold chicken and thinking dark thoughts.

CHAPTER NINETEEN

Mrs. Kelly lay under a green and yellow afghan knitted for her by a friend years ago. Even beneath the afghan, a nightgown, and a sweater, Mrs. Kelly could not get warm. Money was tight and she was delaying turning the furnace on until she absolutely had to, and even then she knew, she'd have to keep the thermostat set low. She felt the November chill in her bones, the freezing rain made her ache and shiver. It was as if there was a block of ice inside her belly, chilling her from the inside out.

Besides the money she'd given to the con artist, she had to pay out nearly forty thousand dollars to a legitimate roofer to replace the clay tile roof the con artist and his men had unnecessarily destroyed. "He tore off a clay roof?" the real roofer had asked. "There was no need to do that. Even if there were damage, which from what I see now there doesn't appear to have been any, it would have been a matter of minor repairs." He'd gone on to tell her that installing a new clay roof was the only route and a very costly one. "The downside to owning an historic Chicago bungalow," he'd told her.

Her savings were depleted to a frightening degree.

To save on the electric bill, she had but one lamp lit. The radio she used only in the mornings, and the television almost never.

The lamp cast a soft yellow glow across the room forming dark shadows in the corners. Occasionally, the headlights of a passing car would sweep through the room bringing the shadows to life, enlarging them and moving them across the room, then just as quickly they'd sink back into their corners leaving only the distant sound of rubber on cold, wet pavement and she was alone again.

To pass the time, Mrs. Kelly would look back through old photo albums of happier times when her husband was with her and her children were young. Those were the good times.

The pictures and boxes and mementoes from the past had been tucked away on the top shelf of her bedroom closet collecting dust for years. She was not one to look backwards. She'd gone through them all just after Harold died, but had soon felt it prolonged the grief so she'd shelved them and moved forward with strength and conviction, determined to not let her husband's passing, though she'd loved him so, mean the end of her life as well.

Lately though, she found herself drawn to them again, searching for some part of herself she felt she had lost. Searching for that strength again that she had found all those years before when her whole world had been taken from her, suddenly and devastatingly.

She recalled that afternoon when she came in from the yard where she'd been doing her gardening. As she ascended the wooden steps of the creaking, wooden back porch, she called out to Harold who had gone inside for a drink of water after having turned over the dirt along the side of the house between the brick and the gangway, complaining of the heat and not feeling so well. She'd been after him for weeks to turn the dirt so she could plant some hostas.

She pulled open the wooden screen door, it's spring squeaking as it stretched open, and she could see Harold's feet jutting out from behind the chrome legs of the kitchen table. He lay face down on the linoleum, his face bloated and blue. She rushed to him and knelt beside him. He was gone. The cause of death would be determined a sudden and massive heart attack. He'd retired from the elevator union six months earlier. Decades of work and overtime, bills and kids and a mortgage all behind them, this was supposed to be the beginning of the golden years. This was the time to reap the benefits of a life spent toiling and sacrificing. It was to be the time to finally be together living life on their terms, doing what they wanted, when they wanted, or doing nothing at all if that's what their moods demanded. Time to enjoy what was left. But that time was so much shorter than either imagined. They hadn't gone anywhere. They hadn't done anything. They had talked about what they were going to do. They had a list of places to go and things to do and friends to visit. They'd done none of it. Harold retired in January and they spent the winter months and the spring at home, doing what they always had, taking care of the house, the car, the laundry, the groceries, all the little things that eat up time. Then, on that June day, time had run out. Harold was gone. The list left meaningless and undone. And Irene Kelly left alone, a widow, with some money in the bank, a house that was paid for, a car that ran, and some freshly turned dirt between the bricks and the gangway, ready for hostas.

She was sad and she was angry. Angry with herself, angry with Harold, and angry with God. For the first time in her life, Irene Kelly, always the good Catholic, started skipping Sunday Mass. Months went by after Harold's funeral without her stepping foot inside a church. She'd pass by on occasion, sneer at it, and keep on walking. Her friends tried to lure her out, but to no avail. She dropped out of the weekly Bridge game. She stopped meeting for coffee at her friend Eleanore's apartment. She stopped meeting the ladies at Super Cup for Sunday breakfast. She stopped walking three houses down to share a quart of beer with Mrs. Berger on late Friday afternoons. Instead, she sat in the house staring at those pictures of the good old days.

Then one early September morning, while she was sipping her coffee on the front porch, the Hanlon's came out of their house. It was the first day of school and little Trevor was dressed in his Catholic School uniform, a pale blue collared shirt and navy blue slacks, ready and anxious to start the first grade. Mrs. Kelly watched, unnoticed, from her porch across the street. Jack was dressed in a crisp shirt and tie; Amy wore a yellow summery dress, the weather still quite warm. Little Seany in shorts and Cubs t-shirt picked dandelions, and the baby Timmy was bundled up under the shade of his stroller.

Mrs. Kelly watched as Jack took out a disposable camera and snapped pictures of Trevor looking so proud and smart in his new school clothes. Then the family walked down the street toward St. Christopher's School. Jack pushed the buggy and Amy took hold of Seany's hand, and off they went. Before they were out of sight, Mrs. Kelly spotted Jack's hand grasp Amy's and give it a good squeeze. Then the family was gone, disappeared behind the giant oaks that lined Mobile Street. Mrs. Kelly wept. There was something so beautiful and so touching about the sight of that family celebrating one of the precious milestones of life. Two people in love escorting their first born off to his first day of school, the little ones in tow. She'd lived those days too. She wept for the happiness such moments brought, and for the sorrow that would one day befall them as it had befallen her. That one-day when the kids were grown and the 'firsts' are over. That day when you think life is going to get easier. That one day when you think you and life-long partner can be sweethearts again. That one day when it all comes crashing down. That day that begins like every other day with coffee and breakfast together, the 'what shall we do today dear' discussion at the kitchen table followed by a trip to the bathroom, brushing of teeth, the mundane ritual of getting dressed, and then -- disaster. The end. The end of forty-eight years together. The end of everything you've known.

Mrs. Kelly was still on the front porch, eyes wet but no longer weeping, when the Hanlons returned, minus one child. Jack and Amy stopped at the foot of their steps and hugged. Mrs. Kelly could tell Amy had been crying. It's difficult to see your baby off to school, she remembered. The first one is always the hardest. Jack held his wife close and kissed her forehead. He whispered something in her ear and it made Amy smile. Then, the embrace was interrupted by Seany who had decided he needed to pee and proceeded to 'water' the bushes in front of the Hanlon house, with navy shorts and fire-truck drawers dropped down to his ankles and his bright, skinny, white ass out for all the neighborhood to see. Mrs. Kelly was overcome by a laughter that sprung from somewhere deep within. It flowed through her, enveloping her, soothing and healing her broken heart and her weary spirit.

Amy shrieked in horror and lurched at the boy, but Jack grabbed her arm and Mrs. Kelly heard him say, "It's too late now, just let him finish." Then the two of them broke out in laughter. Amy covered her mouth and buried her head in Jack's chest, suppressing the embarrassment and the laughter for fear it would encourage her son to make a habit of this.

When Seany had finished his business, he awkwardly pulled up his pants and turned to his parents and smiled, proud of himself for having taken care of business so efficiently. Amy shook her head and, still suppressing a smile, took the boy's hand and led him into the house. Jack carried the stroller up the stairs, and unstrapped the baby. As he lifted Timmy from the stroller, he spotted Mrs. Kelly across the street and smiled and waved at her, shrugged his shoulders as if to say, "kids, what're ya gonna do?" then followed his wife inside.

"Life goes on," she thought, and she realized that there was still joy out there somewhere, brought to life by the sight of a little boy's pale bare bottom as he peed in the

98

bushes. There is still a life to be lived. She went inside, collected her photo albums, and stored them on the top shelf of her closet, close enough to get to if she needed them, but out of sight and out of mind. It was time to start living again. She hadn't taken them down again until this past October.

Months had passed with no word from the police. For the first two months after her visit to the police station, Mrs. Kelly would call Detective Rayson to ask about the progress of the investigation. Though he was always cordial, she knew her case was not at the top of his priorities. There'd been no sightings of the man and no other reports of similar scams being perpetrated. He assured her he would keep on it, but until the man struck again, there wasn't much to go on. Eventually Mrs. Kelly gave up and stopped calling.

She saw the man in her nightmares and in her daydreams and she imagined what she would say to him, what she would do to him, if ever given the chance. These were dark thoughts and she tried to free her mind from them, but she couldn't. She'd be doing the dishes and his face would appear and in her mind she'd punch him. She'd be folding the laundry and catch herself thinking about him being beaten in a jail cell by the guards or other inmates. She'd be showering and her mind would drift to thoughts of him being water-boarded like a terrorist until he confessed to his crimes.

Mrs. Kelly closed the photo album on her lap and placed it on the floor beside her chair. Then she picked up a box she hadn't opened since even before Harold's death. Inside the box, she found Harold's army uniform, folded neatly. She laid the uniform across her lap and dug deeper into the box. Next she found a stack of letters bound by a blue string of yarn. Beneath that was an American flag that Harold had kept from his youth, only forty-eight stars on it. At the bottom of the box, lay a revolver. She had always been against Harold keeping a gun in the house, but he carried it with him for safety after he'd been robbed twice while working in the public housing projects. They'd compromised. He could keep the gun, but he had to keep it out of sight and out of reach of the children. Harold buried the gun at the bottom of the box and put the box high on the shelf in the closet. He kept it there until it was needed.

Now in the lamp lit gloom of her living room, her lap covered by a worn afghan knitted years ago by a friend, Mrs. Kelly held her husband's old revolver in her hand. It was heavy and cold. She raised it up, aiming at the wall in front of her and she felt the power it contained. She squeezed hard on the heavy trigger, pulling the hammer slowly back and back and back until at last it slammed down fast and hard on an empty chamber. 'Bang', she said, imagining the scam artist roofer was in her sights. And she smiled.

CHAPTER TWENTY

CHRISTMAS 2010

As the world rejoiced at the birth of the Savior, Jack and Amy Hanlon mourned the death of their once vibrant love. Despite the festive decorations, the tree, the lights, the manger, the garland, the musical snow-globes, the robotic Santa building a toy, emptiness hung in the Hanlon house.

Tensions between Jack and Amy had only intensified, and the added financial pressures of the holidays strained the relationship even more. The boys noticed, of course, how could they not. The house was perpetually quiet while an undercurrent of anger and resentment electrified the home, waiting to zap any one of them at any time. The reactor of the nuclear family was in meltdown and it seemed as if there were no way to reverse the impending implosion. The alarms rang loud on Christmas Eve, and by Christmas Night the little bungalow on Mobile Street, where once there lived a happy little family, was now simply ground zero of its destruction. Lights still lit, tree still adorned with ornaments and garland, Santa still working away on that wooden toy, but all that had made the house a loving home snuffed out like a Christmas candle leaving only a smoky twirling trace of what had once been a bright flame.

Jack awoke Christmas Eve morning at six a.m., still tired from a restless night's sleep. Amy lay next to him, her dark hair a tumbled mess beneath her head. Errant strands spilled across her face as she slumbered. Lost in the respite of sleep, she looked ten years younger. Jack sat up and watched her for a long moment. She was beautiful. She was his dream girl. She was all he'd ever wanted. That he was to share a bed with so lovely a woman was still, after over a decade of marriage, almost incomprehensible to Jack. He recalled how optimistic they were when they married so long ago. Just two kids fresh out of college, ready to take on the world together as a team, armed only with their love for one another and the belief that love was enough; that with hard work and a little sacrifice, it would all work out just fine. It had been so good for so long, how did he let it all slip away from them? They'd both expected so much more happiness than he was able to provide.

He got out of bed and headed for the shower, then a cigarette and coffee, a quick breakfast, and off to work. To have a used car dealership open on Christmas Eve was simply asinine Jack thought, but the reality was that it *was* open and Jack was expected to begin his ten-hour workday at eight a.m..

Christmas Eve had for a long time been Jack's favorite holiday, even more so than Christmas Day itself. Christmas Eve held all of the anticipation while at the same time maintaining a serenity lacking amidst the craziness of the following day. It was the calm before the storm.

His usual Christmas Eve routine was to get up early, before Amy and the kids awoke, and head down to Dinkel's Bakery, where his Grandmother had taken him when he was a child, to buy coffee cakes and sugar cookies and Pfeffernüsse. From there he'd grab a cup of coffee and watch the people bustle past on Lincoln Avenue and get lost in the shimmering sway of the candy cane decorations swinging above the sidewalk from the streetlights. Then it was off to the Paulina Market where he'd buy the veal cutlets for the traditional Hanlon Christmas Eve dinner of veal-parmesan and spaghetti, a tradition that began the first

Christmas Jack and Amy spent as a married couple. It was one of Amy's favorite dishes and, Jack remembered, the one she'd ordered on their fourth date.

Jack enjoyed shopping on Christmas Eve. It wasn't a matter of procrastination, but simply a preference. Though Amy took care of most of the boys' presents between Halloween and Thanksgiving, Jack waited until that final day. He would head to the little boutiques or to the mall to get that special gift, the one he thought Amy would adore. Then he'd pick up a small present for each of the boys. It didn't seem right for them to not get at least one gift that was chosen and purchased by their Dad specifically for them. He chose all of these gifts for Amy and each of the boys carefully. His choices always reflected a keen observation of want and need that made his gifts precious tokens of his love and a much-anticipated part of Christmas for them all.

Upon arriving at home, usually just past noon or one, Jack would take the veal to the kitchen and open a bottle of red wine. Then he'd take his packages down to the basement where, once everyone was asleep, he'd wrap them. The house would smell of potpourri and Amy's cookies baking in the oven. That's when the open house would begin. Everyone in the Hanlon's circle knew that their home was an open house on Christmas Eve and throughout the day old friends, neighbors, and family would drop in for a short visit, knowing there would be snacks and wine and beer and coffee and cookies awaiting them. The Richters, the O'Malleys, the McEnerys, the Cross's, the Zajacs, the Alaimos, the Pufpafs, Juliana Downes and her boys, all descended on Jack and Amy's home bearing gifts and receiving gifts in turn. It was a stopover on the way from home to family parties, for a little talk and a few laughs and the acknowledgment of fine friendships on a day in which one tends to reflect on his blessings.

Mrs. Kelly would arrive around six with candy and presents for each of the boys. Then Jack's in-laws would come over and the house would erupt with the joyous screams of little boys tearing open Grandma and Grandpa's gifts. The scene would repeat itself about a half hour later when Jack's parents arrived.

After dinner and dessert and a reading of the Polar Express, Amy would whoosh the boys off to bed with warnings that Santa wouldn't come if they were awake. The guests would say their good-byes and head out into the night. Jack and Amy would clean up the dinner dishes, then cuddle under a blanket in front of the TV to watch an old movie, usually either It's a Wonderful Life or Going My Way, their favorites. Inevitably, Amy would fall asleep on Jack's shoulder before the movie was halfway through. He'd hold her close, then, when the movie was over, he'd wake her with a kiss and she'd go off to bed leaving instructions as to where each of the boys' presents were and who got what.

It was like being a child again as he lay the presents out beneath the tree and assembled those toys that needed assembling. He made each pile look bigger than it actually was by placing the colorfully wrapped gifts just so. Jack remembered the feeling of coming down the stairs Christmas morning to a pile of presents, and wanted to provide his sons with that 'wow' feeling he had when he was a boy.

When the toy-land beneath the tree was complete, he'd check the locks on the doors, shut off the TV and climb in bed with his beautiful wife, happier than he'd expected he could, or would, ever be. It was, for Jack, the best day of the year.

This year however, things would be drastically different. There'd be no trip to the bakery. No trip to the meat market. No shopping for Amy's gift on Christmas Eve, nor any special gifts from Dad to the boys this year. There'd be no visiting with old friends, no time spent catching up with cousins. No dinner with his parents, his in-laws, or Mrs. Kelly.

It wasn't so much that he had to work on Christmas Eve that bothered Jack, hell, that's life. He was far from the only one spending the day somewhere other than where he wanted to be. It was that this year, not only would Jack's Christmas Eve be spent in a used car lot waiting for customers who would never show, to sell cars that, on this day at least, would never sell, working for a miserable man who despised him for reasons unknown, but also because, when he did finally make it back home, the day wouldn't be getting much better.

Jack showered and dressed and left the house for work. The only other task he had on his agenda was to stop by the bike shop and pick up the bike Amy had ordered for Trevor, who had out-grown his old bike. It was the only thing the boy had asked for this Christmas, and though expensive, Amy and Jack had saved up enough to buy the bike, a reward for four straight quarters of straight A's and a perfect attendance record. In fact, they had just gotten enough to buy the bike with Amy's last check, the one that arrived just two days ago.

The shop was a five-minute drive from the car lot, and open until three o'clock. Jack planned on using his lunch break to get to the shop to pick up the bike. But sometimes, the best-laid plans fail.

Mrs. Kelly awoke Christmas Eve morning to WGN radio on her alarm clock. She shuffled to the kitchen and made a pot of coffee. Sitting alone at the kitchen table, she remembered Christmas Eves past. She could recall the children bouncing off the walls almost as soon as they got out of bed waiting for night to come so they could go back to bed and get up for Christmas morning. She remembered Harold getting up, grumbling his way through the morning's first two cups of coffee and first three or four cigarettes. Then he'd announce to the kids that it was time to get dressed. The kids would immediately rush upstairs to their bedrooms and change out of their pajamas and into the day's clothing.

Once dressed and back downstairs they would tug at Harold's arm begging to head out to the stores for the day. It was their annual tradition. Harold thought it important to include the children in the shopping for their mother's Christmas presents since it was they who benefitted most from her hard work and sacrifice.

He'd finish off his coffee and take a last drag from his cigarette then he'd head off to the bedroom to get dressed in his cleanest white t-shirt and a pair of brown polyester pants for a day at the department stores. He'd take the kids to Sears and they would shop for dresses and slacks and scarfs for their mother. Mrs. Kelly didn't know it, but Harold saved a few bucks a week all year long for her Christmas present. Whereas Jack shopped on Christmas Eve because he liked the fun of the spontaneity of it, Harold Kelly shopped on Christmas Eve because that was when he finally had saved enough money to give his wife a proper Christmas. Along with his yearlong savings, each child contributed a little from his/her allowance. Money that, upon their father's orders, they were supposed to have been saving for their mother's Christmas since August.

From there, they would take the bus to the Ideal Pastry bakery where they would buy their mother her favorite cookies and donuts, plus a cookie for each kid. After that, he'd take them to the Irish Imports Shop, where they would usually purchase a record of Irish songs like the ones Mrs. Kelly's parents would sing when she was a child.

Her folks had both been born in Ireland and met here in the States. While little Irene was growing up, her parents would play songs from the homeland and dance around the front room of their one-bedroom apartment with their little girl. Mrs. Kelly didn't know what happened to those records after her parents died, but every Christmas Harold would surprise her with a record album of the songs of her youth.

Harold was a stickler for tradition, and so, there was never an artificial tree in the Kelly residence, and there was no tree in the Kelly residence until Christmas Eve. So after the Irish Imports shop, it was straight to the C-Davis Truck Rental lot, where the trucks had been temporarily replaced by Christmas Trees, to choose the perfect tree for the Kelly family Christmas. Mrs. Kelly often wondered if it was truly tradition motivating her husband to shop for trees on Christmas Eve or if it was the fact that he could haggle the salesman down so easily at such a late date. The pickings were scarcer, but you couldn't beat the price and he always managed to bring home a tree that, once decorated at least, would be brilliant.

She smiled a bitter-sweet smile as she conjured up the vision of her husband dragging a six foot tall Christmas tree onto a city bus with children in tow dragging shopping bags from Sears and the Irish Imports, bumping into other riders, needles flying and falling off the tree throughout the bus, bags and packages bumping against knees and seats. It was no wonder she never got a porcelain tea set or Waterford crystal for Christmas, it never would've survived the journey.

Once home, the children would run the shopping bags up to their rooms where they'd wrap them while Harold took the tree and a hacksaw to the yard and sawed off the bottom few inches. She could see him in her mind's eye out there in the dark snowy yard in his work boots, polyester pants and plaid winter coat sawing off those few inches of tree trunk so that the fresh cut could soak up enough water to make the tree last until the Feast of the Epiphany when it would finally be taken down and the Christmas Season would officially end.

Next came the annual hour of Harold lighting the tree, mumbling words not appropriate for such a sacred Holiday, as he fought with tangles and burned out bulbs and flashing strands that had never flashed before.

Then, with the tree firmly placed in its stand and fully lit, Harold sipping from a fresh brewed cup of coffee (with a three count splash of Jameson), and enjoying a well-earned cigarette after a long day of children, store-clerks, crowds, tree salesmen, and those goddamn Christmas lights. Then Mother was presented with one record from the Irish Imports (the others to be saved for the morning). The sounds of the Emerald Isle would play on the phonograph as the children decorated the tree with the family ornaments Mrs. Kelly had brought up from the basement while they were out shopping.

With the kids in bed, the stockings stuffed, and the presents beneath the tree, Harold and Irene Kelly would slip off to bed where it was time for another Christmas Eve tradition. Both of them bursting with love - love for their family, love for their blessings, love for their Savior, and love for each other - they would nestle in beneath the covers, legs rubbing the other's to produce some warmth, arms wrapped around the other, bodies pressed together, they would embrace and envelope each other in a physical love that only years of marriage can invoke. That well practiced tradition complete, they would both settle in to drift off into a solid slumber.

Mrs. Kelly recalled the Christmas Eve back before the Union years when Harold was a mechanic down at Weekly's Auto Shop, when, as they lay there in the peaceful aftermath of marital relations, the room dark and warm, Harold broke the silence.

"Are you happy?"

"Were you not paying attention? I'm not that good an actress."

"No. I don't mean that. After so many years, I can tell when I've gotten the job done and when I haven't. I mean, in general, with our life here. With your life, are you happy?"

"What kind of question is that? Of course I'm happy. I'm very happy."

"Oh, we struggle though. It gets tough for you I know. Garrity up the block just bought a second car for his wife to do the shopping with while he's at work. Shotz just bought braces for his boy's teeth. I can't do that. I'm lucky to pay the insurance man his weekly premiums."

"Will you stop. I don't want a car to do the shopping. That Shotz kid needed braces because what he inherited from his father was such a mangled mess of a mouth that people were beginning to mistake the kid for a horse. Our children inherited your good looks."

"Hardly. They got their good looks from you, and their brains too. Those kids are gonna be somethin' one day, every one of 'um. They got the stuff. They won't have ta live hand to mout da way we do."

"First of all, we don't live hand to mouth Harold. We have enough to pay the bills and put food on the table. We own a house for Pete's sake. No one in my family ever lived in a house before you and I moved in here. My sister was jealous for years. We are able to give our kids a wonderful Christmas every year. The reason it seems like we live hand to mouth is 'cause we don't spend it all. We don't live on credit. We have money in the bank and not everyone can say that. Granted, it's not much, but it's there. You worked hard for that money and I'll be damned if I'm going to let it go to some shopkeeper somewhere, or a credit company, or worse, let some car salesman skim it away from us. That money is ours. It's there for us, for our old age if some emergency doesn't come along in the meantime. I sacrifice around here because you sacrifice so much out there. You come right home instead of stopping off at a tavern. You don't gamble or play the horses. Not a lot of wives can say that about their husbands. So why should I be sauntering around town in some fancy dress? You sacrifice, I sacrifice, and together we make one hell of a team."

"I'll tell ya one thing, I hit da jackpot when I married you sweetheart."

"That's right you did, and don't you forget it Harold Kelly. But, truth be told, so did I."

There was a long pause before Harold spoke again. "Promise me one ting dear."

"What's that?"

"If somethin' ever happens to me, I mean when the kids are grown, if somethin' ever happens to me and yer still young enough to enjoy yerself, use dat money we're savin' to get somethin' outta life. Don't save it to pass on ta da kids, or to leave for the goddamn Government ta take, use it, spend it. Do all the tings we plan to do..."

"Stop it. Nothing is going to happen to you. If you cut down on the cigarettes and the bacon you'll be around for a long, long time and we will grow old and decrepit together."

"But if..."

"Enough Harold. It's Christmas Eve, I don't want to talk about this."

"Just promise me you'll take good care of yourself."

"Okay, I promise. Can we drop it now?"

"Yes."

"Harold, you are a good father and a wonderful husband and a fantastic lover. I couldn't be happier, so you make me a promise too."

"What?"

"Stick around so that I won't have to keep my promise."

"You got a deal."

They kissed then rested their heads, each silently counting their blessings. There's something about when things are so right that can give rise to a feeling of impending doom. The feeling that it's all too good to last, that something catastrophic is coming around the bend to take it all away. Harold fought that feeling until he fell asleep. Irene Kelly knew what he was feeling and she loved him for it, she just wished she could ease his worry. Eventually, she fell asleep too. Their bed warmed by their bodies and their love. At the foot of the bed lay a green and yellow afghan, an early Christmas gift from a childhood friend.

Mrs. Kelly got up from the kitchen table, her vision blurred by the welling tears of nostalgia and loneliness and anger, and poured another cup of coffee. She wondered if the kids would call today.

CHAPTER TWENTY-ONE

Everyday at precisely noon, Gerald Fitzsimmons, the Executive Vice President of Legal Affairs for General Systems, would emerge from the revolving doors of GS Tower in Manhattan to the bustling sidewalk of 5th Avenue and walk two blocks to the Fifth Avenue Deli. There he would order half a turkey sandwich and a bowl of soup. The woman behind the counter would hand him a small plastic card with a large black number on it. The soup changed daily, but the sandwich was always turkey. He would visit the men's room to wash his hands. That task completed, he'd find a table as far to the back of the place as he could and sit facing the wall. He'd turn off his phone and wait patiently for his number to be called. When his food was ready, a loud and hurried man would bark out the number and Fitzsimmons would collect his food. He would eat alone. This he did everyday; it had been his ritual since he first began working for GS in Manhattan seventeen years before. He enjoyed the solitude of it. That's the great thing about New York, you can be surrounded by people and still be completely alone. You get lost in the crowd. There's anonymity among the throngs.

The fact that it was Christmas Eve, didn't change this routine. A man in his position within the corporation certainly could have taken Christmas Eve off, most of the rest of the office had, including his receptionist Sheila. But Gerald Fitzsimmons took the ride in from his Connecticut home to his Manhattan office as if it were any other day. He'd have done the same on Christmas Day if he thought he could get away with it. It wasn't that he was that dedicated to 'the company store', it was that his work gave him pleasure whereas staying at home made him miserable.

The city sidewalks were teaming with last-minute shoppers. Gerald wound his way through them the best he could. The traffic flow was different than on a usual day. Unlike the regular crowd, holiday shoppers kept a different pace, moved in a different manner, and had a different agenda. It made the movements of the crowd unpredictable and he had to stagger his step a couple of times to avoid crashing into a shopper who'd suddenly stopped to peer in a window, and he'd been bumped more times than he could count by procrastinators rushing to hit all the stores before time ran out on them.

When Gerald returned to his office, his phone was ringing. With Sheila having taken Christmas Eve off, he had to answer his own phone which pissed him off to no end, but she had vacation time and he had to let her take it.

He picked up the phone on the fourth ring.

"Answering your own phone these days?"

"Sheila's off."

"What a bitch."

"Tell me about it. What can I do for you Rhonda?"

"Well, first I wanted to wish you a Happy Holiday."

"Happy Holidays to you too Rhonda. Going anywhere special?"

"Ugh, Eric wants to spend Christmas with his children. My mother told me to find a nice Jewish boy and get married, I picked a gentile schmuck who never goes to church, doesn't believe in God, but wants to spend Christmas with his awful kids whose bitch of a mother will make life a living hell I'm sure. I want to go away somewhere nice. We'll see. How about you?"

"Home. Christmas in Connecticut."

"Gerald, how cliché. Sounds like a Hallmark special on Lifetime. Poor you."

"Yeah, well, we'll see. Maybe I'll make a trek out to California. I don't know."

"Well good luck with that. The other reason I'm calling is because I heard a trial date has been set for the Hanlon bullshit. I wanted to know if you needed any assistance from my office in regards to that issue..."

"I appreciate your offer Rhonda, and I'm sure I will be in touch eventually in regards to that, but right now, we're finalizing our research and forming our argument. I've given your number and e-mail to Randal and Susan and I'm sure if they have any questions, they'll be in touch."

"Two months isn't a lot of time. I'm sure you'll be putting in a lot of overtime, please don't hesitate to call me if you need anything."

"I don't know how much overtime *I'll* be putting in, hopefully not much, but my staff will be. I just want this goddamn thing over."

"Gerald, you and me both. The shit seems to be moving up the ladder. There are big shake-ups in the works, and I don't want this thing hanging around our necks when they start looking to swing the axes upwards."

"Yes. It can be looked at from several perspectives depending on what one's motivation is. You could say we're saving the company a lot of money, or you could say we opened up a Pandora's box that never should have existed in the first place. Honestly though, who would have thought any of those salesmen could ever reach those bonus levels? Certainly not me or I would've told Riggleman to make them higher. His point is they had to at least seem attainable or the sales force would see what we were trying to do and balk. We'd had enough talent flee to our competition as it was at the time, so I went along with him. The difference is, he figured if we end up having to pay one or two guys that would incentivize the others, they'd work harder and increase their numbers and still not reach the big money bonuses but die trying. He had the numbers all figured out. My thought was, why put them anywhere within reach and have to pay *any* of them that type of money? If we could increase it ever so slightly and ensure nobody would get there, that would increase sales without ever paying out a penny over the reduced commissions. People are gamblers by nature, Rhonda. There is a one in a million chance to win the lottery, but everyone plays expecting they'll hit the jackpot. That's how Vegas makes all their money, the silly dreams of unrealistic people. Those sales associates would've stayed regardless, and not one of them would have even come close to where I wanted the incentive levels to be, including Hanlon and his Advanta deal. But you know Ross, he has this silly idea that the world needs to be fair."

"So Riggleman wants to pay Hanlon?"

"He did at first. He told me, 'why create a problem', but solving those problems is what I do. I never thought Hanlon would take it this far, Christ, the guy has three kids and a mortgage, why risk everything and pay lawyer's fees and court costs and risk his career? I thought we could back him into a corner and he'd cave, but the man's an idiot and he didn't do it. He keeps trying to fight us. And he'll go broke doing so before he ever sees a dime. He'll never be able to sustain the costs long enough to see it through. He'll destroy himself. Oh well. Sometimes you have to know your place and just be happy with what you've got. Jack Hanlon will learn that lesson the hard way I guess. He's just like one of those guys in Vegas chasing his losses by losing the rest of his bank."

"Like you said, he'll learn, if he hasn't already. Well, I'll let you go. Remember, shoot me an e-mail if you need anything, and you have my cell if it's something you don't want to discuss in an e-mail. There is no way in hell some salesman who got lucky is going to end up making more than I do if I have anything to do about it."

Fitzsimmons laughed, "Same here Rhonda. I have your cell and I'll use it if I have to. Take care. Bye."

Jack stood on the steps of the modular office trailer of the E-Z Credit Used Car Lot, smoking a cigarette and counting the minutes. The hours he'd been there had dragged by with not one potential customer in sight. He checked his watch again and saw that it was 11:35, only twenty-five minutes until his lunch break.

He and Amy had been saving for months to buy Trevor the new bike he wanted. Amy would drive by the shop twice a week to see if the bicycle was still in the window. That particular model was on back-order from the factory. They had the one display in the store and that was it. When she was sure they would have enough to buy it in time for Christmas, she went inside and made a down payment towards the bike. The man at the shop told her he could hold it for her for two weeks, but beyond that, if someone came in for the bike, he'd have to sell the one they had and she'd have to wait for another one to come in sometime after Christmas.

As of last evening, they had the money and the bike was still in the window.

Jack looked forward to his trip to the bike shop. Not only would the bike make his son happy, but the purchase would remind him of why he dredged through his days at this god-awful job. A bright spot in an otherwise dreary Christmas Eve.

Jack burned time by restlessly wandering up and down the aisles of used and abused automobiles shined up to look like jewels. The minutes to noon ticked by on Jack's watch. At 11:55 Jack headed toward the office to tell Bugiardo he was taking his lunch, when a man dressed in a wool overcoat and decent shoes ventured onto the lot. Jack hoped he had no intention of buying a car or speaking to a salesman. He prayed it was just a guy with some time to kill who'd been passing by and decided to take a look around. Jack checked his watch again.

He couldn't ignore him, and he couldn't go to the bike shop until the man left.

"Hi, sir. Happy Holidays. Did you have any questions about this car?" Jack asked half-heartedly. The man was short and bald, his eyes narrow-set and dark. His face was soft and puffy sitting on a small frame. Jack thought he looked like a bag full of pink gravy.

"Actually, yes I do."

Any other day, this would be great news, motivated buyers were easy sales, but today it just meant no lunch for at least an hour, and that's if the asshole were to choose a car quickly. If he waffled, then wanted a test drive, damn, it could be after two o'clock before Jack could get to the bike shop.

"I'm looking for a vehicle for my daughter. She turned sixteen about a month ago and I thought it would be a great Christmas present to hand her the keys to her very own car. I'm going to end up buying her one eventually anyhow, so why not kill two birds with one stone. Gets me out of having to shop for clothes she's just going to return. Plus it will piss off my ex-wife to no end. What I'm looking for is something reliable and safe."

"I understand, I'm a father myself Mr..."

"Ward. Felix Ward."

"Pleasure to meet you Mr. Ward. I'm Jack Hanlon. Were you thinking of this Pontiac here?"

"Well, I don't know. It's a nice looking car. I could see her driving around in it. I'm a little hesitant buying American."

"American cars get a bad rap unfairly. This is a solid car. It's very popular among young girls and young women. It's safe. This one has only 52,000 miles on it, which is low for a used car. It's an excellent choice."

"Ummm, I don't know. I think I'd like to look around some more. What else have you got?"

Jack decided to go for broke. He took Ward to the most expensive car on the lot, figuring one of two things would happen, he'd either buy the expensive car and Jack would get a wonderful Christmas commission, or the price would drive him back to the Pontiac and the sale would be quickly completed.

"Let me show you this. This is the perfect car for your needs. First of all, it's a BMW, German engineering so it's reliable, high resale value, and it's small. Why is that a good thing? Well, the major causes of accidents among teen drivers are cell phones, this car has hands free blue tooth built in, and the other is distraction from within the vehicle - passengers. With a small car like this, your daughter isn't going to get stuck being a bus driver for a pack of kids. Fewer passengers means fewer distractions. Plus, the BMW on the front will ensure she loves it and your ex-wife will hate it that much more."

"Well, you have a point there. It really is a nice car. It's a little more than I intended to spend. Like you said, the Pontiac is a nice car too, and small as well."

"It is."

"I'm going to have to think about this for a minute Jack."

"Of course, take your time, Mr. Ward."

Jack looked at his watch. Precious minutes were eaten into his lunch break already.

Ward strolled back to the Pontiac, stopping along the way to examine the price stickers on some of the cars he passed. He looked the Pontiac over for what seemed like an eternity, then strolled back to the BMW. Then back to the Pontiac again. Then back to the BMW. He sat in them both. He sat in the back seat of them both. He kicked the tires. Jack could only assume he did this because he'd heard that's what your supposed to do when you buy a used car. He stared at the sticker on one, then he stared at the sticker on the other. Finally, after half an hour, he decided to take the BMW for a test drive.

Jack got the keys from the office. The fat man was there, but he didn't say a word, his head buried in his laptop.

The test drive took about fifteen minutes. Along the way Ward grilled Jack on the safety specs and the options. Felt him out about the flexibility of the price. Began to complain about small, insignificant things he claimed he didn't like about the car. This was good news for Jack because it meant the man was going to buy the car and was working on getting a good deal on it.

The fat man was on the phone when Jack and Ward returned to the lot.

"So, what do you think?"

"It's okay I guess."

Jack had no time for games today. The temperature was dropping rapidly. It was Christmas Eve for Christ's sake and he had to get to the bike shop before 3:00 to get Trevor his present. It was the only task Amy had given him.

"What's holding you back from buying this car for your daughter Mr. Ward?"

"Honestly Jack, it's the price. It's quite a bit more than I intended to spend. She's a new driver, she's going to bang it up."

"Wouldn't you rather she bang up in a sturdy safe car like this one as opposed to a rickety, unreliable, unsafe car?"

"Of course, but..."

"The price."

"Yes."

Jack peered at his watch; it was just past 1:00.

"Well, Mr. Ward, it's Christmas. Why don't you tell me what you're willing to pay for this car and we'll take it from there."

Ward threw out a number that was ridiculously low.

"It may be Christmas Mr. Ward, but I'm not Santa Clause. I'd love to sell you the car at that price, but I just can't. Let's go inside and see if we can come up with a number we can both live with."

"Well Jack. I was just down the block at Gateway and they happen to have the same model BMW, same year, with less miles on it and they're willing to sell it to me for the price I gave you. So either you beat their deal, or I go buy my car over there."

The bastard! He was shopping for the Beemer the entire time. He knew exactly what he wanted. If he would've just come out and said that from the beginning, Jack could have saved precious time spent fucking around. He was livid. He fought to keep it from showing.

"Well, Mr. Ward, I'll have to talk to the owner first and see what we can work out. If you'll wait right here for a minute, I'll be right back." Jack turned toward the mobile office knowing full well that Bugiardo would never let that car go at that price. His only hope was that the year was ending and that maybe he'd rather have the cash than keep the inventory. He went inside. Bugiardo was on the phone.

"Excuse me for interrupting Mr. Bugiardo, but..."

Bugiardo waved him off. Jack waited. He checked his watch.

"Mr. Bugiardo," he said again, "a man wants to buy the Beemer."

Bugiardo gave him an aggravated look, but ended his phone call. "Why are you buggin' me if the guy wants to buy the fuckin' car Hanlon?"

Jack told him about the competing offer.

"Tell him to go fuck himself," Bugiardo replied. "If Gateway wants to give cars away, let 'em. If he can get that price from them, tell him to go there, it serves them right. They'll be out of business before summer givin' cars away like that." He picked up the receiver and dialed.

Jack went out to the lot where Ward was waiting. "I'm sorry Mr. Ward, we can't match their price. If you can buy the car there for that, you should take the deal."

Ward, who had been pleasant throughout the hour transformed into something entirely different. His eyes narrowed, his brow furrowed, his face reddened.

"Really? You go talk to your boss and send me on my way? You expect me to believe that bullshit? I know what this car is worth and I know it's fucking Christmas fucking Eve and I know your end of the year inventory will cost you if you don't unload it by next week, so fuck you. If

117

you think I'm going to fall for that crap, you're dumber than you look, you fucking cocksucker. What do you take me for, some kind of fucking moron who's never bought a car before? Go fuck yourself."

Well Merry Goddamn Christmas, huh? It was clear that the supposed competing deal from the other dealership was a lie; an attempt to get him to lower his price below what the car was worth. His blood pressure rose.

"Mr. Ward, I'm not trying to pull one over on you, you were the one trying to pull one over on me. There is no BMW down at Gateway, I called them," Jack lied, "they never heard of you and they told me they haven't had this model on their lot since September, so if anyone is lying here sir, it is you. Now, you have wasted too much of my time as it is. The sticker price is the sticker price, do you want the car or not?"

"Fuck you."

Jack wanted nothing more than to reach out and grab Ward by the throat and throttle him until he turned blue, but he didn't. He knew that would be the end of his job, he'd probably end up in jail, and the little shit would sue him for everything he had left, which wasn't much.

"Merry Christmas to you too, Mr. Ward." Jack turned and walked to the office. Bugiardo was on his way out.

"Keep an eye on things here Jack, I'll be back."

"Mr. Bugiardo, I haven't had my lunch yet. I need to get over to the..."

"Jack, I know it's Christmas Eve. I know you have a family to get home to. As soon as I get back, you can go home. I won't be gone long, and before you go, I have an envelope for you."

It would defy everything Jack had witnessed from the asshole for him to be giving out a Christmas bonus, but then again, Christmas can do strange things to people.

"Mr. Bugiardo, I appreciate the job and you letting me go home, but I really need to get to the bike shop by 3:00. That's when they close and I promised my eldest son a bike for Christmas. He's a good kid and I can't disappoint him."

"No worries Hanlon. I just have to make a quick run. I'll be back in fifteen, maybe twenty minutes and you can punch out for the day and have plenty of time to get where you need to go. I promise. Do you really think I want to be here on Christmas Eve? I have a family too ya know. And I intend to get back to them as soon as I can. I just have to make this quick run, so do me a favor and keep an eye on things for just a little bit and I'll be right back and then you can go home. Okay?"

Jack took in a deep breath. "Okay Mr. Bugiardo. I appreciate your understanding. But I really have to get to that bike shop by three. I'll come right back and work late if I have to, I just have to get there by three."

"No problem, Jack. I'll be back in half an hour." And with that the fat man left.

Jack sat down at the pressed-board desk and picked up the phone. He dialed information and asked for the number to the bike shop.

"North-branch Bikes."

"Hi, what time do you close today?"

"Three o'clock."

"That's what I thought. Listen, I'm at work right now and I know I will get there by three, but I might be cutting it close. I know exactly what I want, there's a blue Varsity Road Bike in your front window. My wife put a deposit down on it and I have cash for the rest. I'll be there before you close, but like I said, I may be cutting it close. Can you hold it for me?"

"It's Christmas Eve sir. As much as I'd like to say we'll hold it, we only have the one left and I can't promise you that if someone else comes in for that bike I won't sell it to them, especially if you aren't sure you can get here by three. My staff want to get home to their families too. I told your wife I could hold it for two weeks three weeks ago. You're lucky it's still here."

"I understand that, really I do. I will be there by three, I promise, before three. If you could just hold that bike for me, it's for my son. For his Christmas present."

"Okay, I'll hold it, but you have to get here before three, I'm not staying open a minute later. I have family coming over tonight."

"I understand. I'll be there as soon as I can. Just don't sell that bike."

Jack hung up the phone and watched the clock as time steadily ticked away. Fearing he might not make it in time, he called Amy to see if she could get to the bike shop. Her cell went to voicemail and she didn't answer at home.

CHAPTER TWENTY-TWO

At 2:45, with no sign of the fat man, Jack had resigned himself to the fact that he wouldn't get to the bike shop in time to get the bike for Trevor. At 3:20, there was still no sign of Bugiardo. Jack would have left, had thought long and hard about it, but he knew that if he were gone when Bugiardo got back, that would be the end of his job, and, as much as he hated it, his family needed him to keep this job.

He'd tried calling Amy to tell her what was going on and see if she could get to the bike shop in time, but she wasn't answering. He'd tried calling her mother, and his parents, but to no avail. He tried friends, other relatives, but it was Christmas Eve and the few who answered their phones were nowhere nearby.

Jack sat in Bugiardo's worn swivel chair, fuming. 'I'll be back in fifteen, twenty minutes,' he'd said. 'Half-an-hour tops.' It had been hours and there was still no sign of the fat man.

When the day had begun, the temperature was a balmy 32 degrees Fahrenheit, by four o'clock it had dipped into the teens. The weather forecasts were calling for a bitter cold Christmas.

At five-thirty, the fat man finally stumbled through the door. His tie was off, his shirt was buttoned wrong, and there was lipstick on his collar. He reeked of alcohol.

Jack jumped to his feet. "You said you'd be gone twenty minutes, it's been over three hours! Where the hell have you been?"

"What business of yours is it where I been? I been where I been, so mind your own fuckin' business."

"I told you I had to get to the bike shop by three for my son's present. You said you'd be back."

"I had business to attend to. Your kid'll get over it. You shouldn't spoil him like that anyhow. Trust me, I did ya a favor." The fat man plopped down into his chair. "You can go home now."

Jack fumed. He took in a deep breath to settle his temper. "You said you had something for me," he said through gritted teeth.

"Oh yeah," a smile appeared on the fat man's face and he reached for an envelope in the top drawer of his desk, nearly losing his tenuous balance as he did so. "Here you go Hanlon."

Jack took the envelope, opened it, and went pale as a ghost.

The manager at 'the Bullseye', as they called it, held a small Holiday party for the employees in the break room. When their shift ended, they all gathered for cupcakes and coffee. The young people each grabbed a cupcake and wolfed it down, forgoing the coffee, then bolted. After about fifteen minutes, there was only Amy and four or five older women in their fifties and sixties, two men also in their sixties, and the manager, Bill Tallman.

Tallman was thirty-five years old, with broad shoulders and curly black hair. His bright blue eyes always seemed to be smiling. By the way he treated her and looked at her, Amy suspected Bill Tallman had developed a little crush on her. Truth be told, he was a good-looking guy. Amy was quite flattered by the attention.

The older women and the two men were engaged in quiet conversation and Amy found herself standing alone beside the coffee carafe. Tallman approached under the guise of checking to see if the coffee needed refilling. It didn't. He turned to Amy as if just noticing her and smiled.

"Hello Amy. Merry Christm... I mean, Happy Holidays."

"Happy Holidays to you too Bill."

There was an uncomfortable silence for a moment. Amy looked at the wall clock.

"This was really nice of you," she said, "the cupcakes and coffee I mean. I know you didn't have to do this."

"People don't want to work on Christmas Eve. I thought it was the least I could do. A little gesture of appreciation. Recognition that they had given something up to be here today."

"Well, not every manager would do that, Bill. It was very nice of you."

"Thank you, Amy. That's nice of you to say."

Again there was a long uncomfortable moment when neither said anything.

"So," Tallman began, "do you and the family have big plans for tonight?"

"No," Amy said as matter-of-fact as she could, "usually we have friends and family over for kind of an open house, but not this year. Just a quiet night at home with the kids."

"Because you had to work here today?"

"No!" she responded too abruptly, "I mean, well yes, sort of, but actually my husband is working today too, so..." Amy had the sudden realization that this was the first time she'd mentioned her husband to Bill Tallman.

"What is it your husband does?"

Amy was surprised by the embarrassment she felt. She'd never felt that way about Jack before, certainly not with his last job, and not with this one either, until now.

"He sells cars," she said.

"Oh, a car salesman. I have a cousin who sells cars. I don't like him very much."

Amy couldn't help but notice the dig.

"What dealership does he work for? Maybe he can get me a deal."

"It's a little lot on Milwaukee."

"The easy credit place? I know where that is. I can't believe anyone buys their cars there. I suppose, if that's your only choice, but what a scam."

Another dig.

"I didn't mean that your husband isn't a good guy. That came out wrong."

Amy forced a small smile, avoiding eye contact.

"Is he a good guy Amy? What's he like?"

"Oh, you know, he's a regular guy. A good father. A nice husband. Yeah, he's a good guy."

"A nice husband. Boy, I hope my wife is more enthusiastic when someone asks her about me."

"What's that supposed to mean?"

"I mean, 'nice'. Not much passion in a word like 'nice'. You'll have to excuse me; I'm a bit of a snob when it comes to words and such. English major."

"I see that's worked out for you."

"Ouch. Yes, I didn't plan on working at Big-Box Bullseye my entire life. Had big dreams of being a writer and teaching at a University, but well, life gets in the way sometimes. Got married young and then children and then, well, here I am."

"Is your wife proud of you? Is she happy?"

"Oh, I doubt it. My wife and I don't see a lot of each other. She was raised with unrealistic expectations. I'm sure she's not happy. But life is what it is. I'm not really all that concerned about her happiness anymore."

Amy glanced at her watch without really noticing the time, then downed her coffee and extended her hand to Tallman.

"I need to be going Bill. Thanks again for the party."

"Amy, I hope I didn't insult you. I didn't mean to."

"It's fine. You didn't. He is a good guy. He's just going through something right now. For better or worse, right?"

"I suppose," he replied. She could feel the lust in his eyes; it was both exhilarating and disgusting to her and she made her exit. Bill Tallman never took his eyes off her until her firm rear-end was gone from the room and out of sight.

When Jack opened the envelope Bugiardo had given him, he found two slips of paper. One was a check for fifty dollars; the other was a pink slip.

"What is this?"

"It's your Christmas bonus. You're welcome."

"No, I mean this...." Jack stuffed the pink paper in the fat man's face, inches from his blood-shot eyes.

"It's the end of the year, I can't afford to keep ya around. You suck as a salesman and frankly, I don't like you. The fifty bucks is a gift because it's Christmas time and you got kids. Be thankful you got that much. I told ya I did ya a favor. You were about to go out and blow a wad on a new bike for your brat. I knew you couldn't afford it. Now get the hell outta here."

"You had this ready." Jack's face reddened. "You had this planned, and still you had me sit here to watch this shit-hole even though you knew I had to get to that bike shop, all the while knowing you were gonna fire me when you got back."

"Well, that's life in the big city asshole. You can't sell cars worth a shit, so get out." The fat man turned his back to Jack and opened his laptop.

Jack's knuckles turned white. His fists were clenched. His face was on fire. He grabbed Bugiardo by the back of his neck and spun him around in his chair to face him. Then he grabbed the fat man by his larynx and lifted him up from his chair by his throat.

The fat man reached for Jack, but Jack already had pulled his face so close they were nose-to-nose and there was nothing for the fat man to grab but Jack's ribs, and the fat man's strength, what little there was, drained from him as he fought for a breath.

"You son-of-a-bitch," was all Jack could muster. A rage built inside him that he'd not experienced in years.

Today's events along with the frustration of the past six months had reached its capacity and Jack simply erupted.

124

Bugiardo's face turned beat red, then purple. Jack had cut off the airway as he shoved the fat man against the wall causing the trailer to rock on its cinderblocks. Jack had one hand on Buiardo's forehead, pushing it into the faux paneling, the other clenched firmly around the fat man's windpipe.

Just as he was about to crush the fat man's throat, something inside told him to stop. He released, but then let loose with a barrage of punches and kicks and knees, forearms and elbows that brought the fat man to the floor dazed and bloody, gasping for breath and unable to defend himself.

Jack grabbed the fat man's thin greasy hair just above the ears and pounded his skull into the floor a half dozen times. Then he stood and kicked Bugiardo in the ribs and the groin and the head.

Jack flipped Budiardo onto his back straddled his chest. He thought of every guy he'd had to gouge the pocketbook of for a beat-up old car and he punched the fat man. Blood spilled from a cut beneath the left eye. He thought of every family he'd had to lie to about the integrity of a car, and he punched the fat man again and again and again. A rib cracked. He thought of every insult he'd had to absorb and ignore, and split the fat man's lip. The right eye began to discolor and swell. He thought of every useless second he'd spent beneath those awful floodlights waiting for customers who'd never show, and he pounded the fat skull into the floor. He thought about GS and the money they owed him, and he struck the man in the throat then busted his nose. Blood spewed after the cartilage cracked. He thought about Amy and the boys and what had become of his marriage and his family, and he drove his knee into the fat man's groin.

Bugiardo had given up what little fight he'd had in him by now, but Jack kept on beating him, slipping in the growing pool of blood as he delivered the punishment.

He lifted the fat man's leg by the ankle then lowered his foot on the knee, shattering it in pieces with a loud crack.

Bugiardo let out a horrid scream.

Then Jack did the same to each of his arms, grabbing the fat man by his bloated wrist then lowering a powerful kick to the rear of each elbow. One-by-one, the arms bent backwards then shattered.

With all his limbs broken, his nose bent sideways, his ribs fractured and his head swollen, Bugiardo passed out from the pain. Jack straddled the fat man's chest again and delivered a barrage of punches to his head, face, and neck until Jack's rage had been exercised from his soul.

He stood above the bloodied, bloated body of his now former employer knowing that this Christmas was not going to end the way he'd hoped it would when he'd gotten out of bed this morning.

Standing over the fat man's broken body, Jack rubbed the blood and pain from his knuckles and wiped the sweat from his forehead. He took a deep breath but, as he did in the new silence of the trailer, he had a strange feeling he was being watched. He looked toward the door, and there standing frightened and in shock, mouth agape, was Felix Ward, who'd come back to buy the Beemer.

CHAPTER TWENTY-THREE

With frozen hands, Amy put the keys in the door ready to put the world away for a bit and enjoy Christmas. 'Hopefully,' she thought, 'Jack will have dinner started and be in a good mood.' She turned the lock, braced herself for the rushing shout of children, and leaned in to the swollen door. As expected, the boys all came running.

"Mommy's home! Mommy's home! Mom, did you get us anything? Merry Christmas Mommy! What's in the bag? Is that for me?"

"No, it's not for you and never mind what's in the bag."

"Where's Daddy, Mommy? Is he home too? Can we have cookies? Trevor said no cookies until you got home."

"Wait, what do you mean, where's Daddy? He's not home yet?"

"No, he's not. Can we have cookies?"

"Fine. Fine. Have cookies. Dinner's going to be a while anyhow, I guess." Amy dropped her bag containing Jack's Christmas gift and went right to the phone. She tried his cell but it went straight to voicemail. "Damn it!" She slammed the phone down. "Trevor!"

"Yes Mom."

"Come here." Amy's head was splitting and the cold still burned on her cheeks. Despite all that had occurred in the past six months, she never dreamt for a second that Jack would do anything to spoil Christmas. Even with his moodiness, this wasn't like him. She worried something might have happened to him, something bad, an accident, a robbery, something awful to keep him from home on Christmas Eve.

Trevor bounded into the room.

"Have you heard from your father today?"

"No, Mom. Is everything okay?"

"Yes. Everything's fine. I just expected him to be home by now. Mr. Bugiardo probably made him work late, that's all. Go back to whatever it was you were doing. I'll get dinner started."

Trevor went back to his video game. Amy went to the kitchen and pulled some spaghetti from the cabinet along with a jar of Ragu, and started a pot of water. Far from veal-parmesan, but as long as they were together, it would feel like Christmas. The only missing ingredient now was Jack. Amy's worry grew.

The water in the pot came to a rapid boil just as the phone rang. Amy dumped the noodles into the water and rushed to the phone. Her heart was racing. She prayed it wasn't a hospital calling to tell her Jack had been in an accident. She grabbed the phone with bated breath.

"Hi," Jack's voice was soft and weak.

"Jack, what's wrong? Where are you?"

"I'm at the sixteenth district police station."

"Oh God, are you alright? Were you in an accident?"

"No. I wasn't in an accident. I've been arrested."

Amy's racing heart sank. She was shocked and too furious for words. Too disappointed. Too sad. Maybe on any other day, maybe she could deal with this, but not today. Not on Christmas Eve. Not with their boys counting on him. She took deep breaths, trying to keep her composure, contain her anger, and hold back the tears.

The silence was tangible.

"Amy? Amy, are you there?"

"I'm here."

"Amy, I'm sorry. I'm so, so sorry."

"Why were you arrested?"

"Aggravated battery."

Amy didn't have to say anything. Her silence said it all.

Can you call Seth and ask him to come down here. They're telling me I can't go before a judge until after Christmas, so..."

"You're going to spend Christmas in Cook County Jail." Her voice was level, monotone, simply stating a fact.

"I'm hoping Seth can work some magic. Can you call him?"

"Yeah, I'll call him."

"Thank you. I'm so sorry Amy. I'm so sorry," his voice cracked with each word then he broke into uncontrollable sobs.

Her thoughts went to her children. What would she tell the boys? Why is Daddy not home for Christmas? They would be confused and heartbroken.

"Yeah, you're sorry. You said that. I'll call Seth. Merry Christmas." She didn't wait for his reply before pulling the phone from her ear and hitting the 'end' button.

Seth was home and said he'd see what he could do.

Amy plated spaghetti for each of the boys and brought it to them in the family room where they sat in front of the television. They were hypnotized by a Will Ferrell movie and didn't ask a single question about their father.

Then Amy went up to her bedroom, called her mother and broke down in tears.

She knew she had lost her husband. Not to another woman, not to an untimely death, but to an obsession, an unfaltering hunt for some sort of justice. Some acknowledgement that he was right and they were wrong. It wasn't even about the money anymore, she wasn't sure it ever was. Jack had been wronged and couldn't deal with the fact that it may never be righted, and so he went on this crusade for recompense, and that is how she lost him. A casualty of a war of his own making.

That night, she tucked her three boys into bed, put their presents beneath the tree (minus one bicycle), climbed into her own bed, and mourned the death of her marriage.

CHAPTER TWENTY-FOUR

Jack stood in the holding cell of the sixteenth district police station, his head against the lead-paint chipped wall. His hands had begun to swell. The cell smelled of urine and booze. In the opposite corner, an old man sat on the floor, his arm folded over bent knees, his back against the wall. He rested his chin on his arms, his grey beard stained yellow, his eyes blood-red and half shut.

A gravel voice broke the silence. Jack opened his eyes and turned toward his cellmate.

"Do not give in to sadness, torment not yourself with brooding. Gladness of heart is the very life of man, cheerfulness prolongs his days. Distract yourself, renew your courage, drive resentment far away from you; for worry has brought death to many, nor is there aught to be gained from resentment. Envy and anger shorten one's life, worry brings on premature old age. One who is cheerful and gay while at the table benefits from his food."

The filthy bum looked, not at Jack, but straight ahead as if speaking to an invisible crowd. He was still sitting on the dirty floor, his back against the wall.

"Do not let your anger lead you into sin and do not stay angry all day. Don't give the Devil a chance. Get rid of all bitterness, passion, and anger. No more shouting or insults, no more hateful feelings of any sort. Instead, be kind and tender-hearted to one another, and forgive one another as God has forgiven you through Christ!"

The man continued sermonizing to the invisible crowd. 'Why is it,' Jack thought, 'that the crazies can all recite Bible verses word for word?' "The nuttier they are, the better they know the Bible," he mumbled under his breath.

The old man struggled to his feet, using the wall to help him keep his balance. Once he was standing, he placed his back against the wall and lifted both hands, arms outstretched toward the jail ceiling, and with his crusty voice rising in volume and intensity, he preached:

"You have heard that it was said, 'An eye for an eye and a tooth for a tooth.' But I say to you offer no resistance to one who is evil. When someone strikes you on your right cheek, turn the other one to him as well. If anyone wants to go to law with you over your tunic, hand him your cloak as well. Should anyone press you into service for one mile, go with him for two miles. Give to the one who asks of you, and do not turn your back on one who wants to borrow. You have heard that it was said, 'You should love your neighbor and hate your enemy.' But I say to you, love your enemies, and pray for those who persecute you that you may be children of your heavenly Father, for he makes his sun rise on the bad and the good, and causes rain to fall on the just and the unjust. For if you love those who love you, what recompense will you have? Do not the tax collectors do the same? And if you greet your brothers only, what is unusual about that? Do not the pagans do the same? So be perfect, just as your heavenly Father is perfect."

Jack could only stand and watch the show. When the old bearded man finished pontificating, he dropped he head and rested his hands on his knees as if he had just finished running several miles. He was quiet then.

Jack watched the old man. He'd seen bums before, but usually, he could just walk away from them; now he was forced to listen to the crazy ramblings. Then, from the cuffs of the old bum's filthy jeans ran a yellow-tinged pungent river flowing into a puddle on the floor and inching its way across the cell toward Jack. Then the bum raised his head and stared directly into the eyes of a bewildered Jack.

"Do not pay back evil with evil," he said.

Jack took two steps back to avoid the river of piss. The old man slid down the wall and returned to his original position, sitting now in a puddle of his own piss, slouched over bent knees, folded arms resting on the knees and chin resting on the arms.

Seth Levine had a lot of friends down at the State's Attorney's Office, but to get anything done on Christmas Eve was a long shot. In addition to that, Aggravated Battery is not one of those crimes they just let people slide on. He had two things on his side though. The first was that Jack, at his age, had never once had a run-in with the law. No record whatsoever. The second was a little bit of leverage he hoped would encourage Mr. Bugiardo to drop the charges.

Bugiardo had been taken to Our Lady of Victory Hospital where he was treated for four broken ribs, a broken nose, two broken arms, a broken leg, minor contusions and cuts, and a concussion.

Seth put a call out to a former law school classmate of his who now worked as an Assistant State's Attorney, left an urgent message asking her to call him immediately, then raced over to the OLV Emergency Room, hoping to catch Bugiardo before he was released.

He was in luck. When he arrived at the ER, Seth inquired about Bugiardo's condition under the auspices that he was the patient's brother. He was told that Bugiardo was admitted and would be spending the night for observation. Though official visiting hours were over, Seth was able to persuade the desk nurse to let him up to see his victimized 'brother'. Persuasion is what lawyers get paid for, after all, and Seth Levine was pretty damn good at it.

He knocked lightly on Bugiardo's door but didn't wait for permission to enter, rather he just slid in through the half-opened door and smiled at the man he found bound in plaster and traction.

"Hello Mr. Bugiardo, how are you?"

"How the fuck does it look like I am? Jesus Christ you hospital fucks are some stupid mother-fuckers," the fat man replied.

"Oh, I'm not from the hospital. My name is Levine. I'm an attorney. I represent Jack Hanlon."

"Get the fuck out of here you cocksucker!" He bellowed so loudly he could've awoken the morgue.

Seth closed the door behind him and approached the bloated, plastered man. Seth whispered in Bugiardo's ear. When the nurse came rushing in to see what was wrong, Bugiardo told her everything was okay. He was just having some fun with his brother but they would promise to keep it down.

Those skills of persuasion can work wonders when applied correctly. After the nurse left, Levine and Bugiardo had a long discussion about trials and lipstick and whereabouts and whatnot. All the things that would come out in a public trial if this matter were pursued. He added some names of top divorce lawyers he'd be happy to recommend to Mrs. Bugiardo.

It didn't take the fat man long to put two and two together and realize that pressing charges against Jack Hanlon could eventually prove quite costly in divorce court later. He agreed to drop the charges, of course admitting nothing, but rather in the Christian spirit of charity on this Holiest of nights.

Seth Levine dialed the sixteenth police district, told Bugiardo whom to ask for and what to say, and handed him the phone. By midnight, Jack would be sitting in Seth's car on the way home.

Mrs. Kelley sat in the third pew of St. Christopher's for Midnight Mass. Above the church, the bells rang out in celebration of the Savior's birth. A re-birth for humanity. A new beginning. Around her, joyful believers sat straight listening to the Parish Men's Choir sing Away In A Manger, half-drunken revelers whispered just a bit too loudly for church, and anxious, exhausted children fought off yawns and drooping eyes.

132

The church was filled. If this many people attended Mass on a regular basis, there'd be no need for the special collections or the fund-raisers to fix the aging boiler.

Above her, gold leaf and baby blue vaulted ceilings arched to an apex. Marble columns stretched high to the ceiling. A twenty-foot tall crucifix hung from above the marble altar displaying Christ in agonizing death, while, at the foot of the steps, lay a wooden infant Christ child sleeping in the crèche. To one side stood the golden tabernacle, home to the Eucharist, the living body of Christ, to the other side, marble statues of the Holy Family.

The church had been built in 1910, with grandeur and elegance. The building itself, when viewed from above, formed a cross, with a long aisle leading from the front door to the Altar, and a shorter horizontal cross-section for pews and confessionals and votive candles. It was Spanish-style complete with two bell-towers on either side of a gilded entrance. The building sat on a narrow one-way city side street with redbrick two-flats across the way.

Mrs. Kelly searched for comfort this Christmas Eve. She searched long and hard for that place in her heart where she could find forgiveness... forgiveness for the man who had robbed her of her savings, her security, and the promise she'd made to her deceased love. Robbed her of her dignity, her self-respect and her confidence. Robbed her of peace of mind and future happiness. She gazed up at the dying Christ, nailed to the cross for the sole purpose of forgiveness. Nailed to His death, a death He freely accepted, so that mankind could be forgiven of their sins and for the salvation of their souls. Her own soul among them. Her own sins forgiven. Through forgiveness, lies life eternal. Thus far, she hadn't found that place of forgiveness for her offender yet.

Long lay the world, in sin and error pining, till He appeared and the soul felt its worth...

'What has changed?' she thought, 'over two thousand years later, and what has changed? Thieves come right up to your doorstep, children starve, wars rage, devastation abounds, diseases cured in one part of the world still killing in other parts of the world, and greed rules. Selfishness taken to the Nth degree. And after over seventy years of living, you're left with a soul that feels no worth whatsoever. What has changed since He appeared, dammit?!'

Mass began in the name of the Father, the Son, and the Holy Spirit.

Mrs. Kelly bowed her head, closed her eyes, and listened to the priest, the congregation's responses, the choir singing, but was soon lost again. Lost in that dark place from which she had hoped coming to Mass would free her.

In that place she was eye-to-eye with that scoundrel. He would smile his wicked smile and flash her money at her, now converted into a bundle of hundred dollar bills that he'd fan out and wave at her, mocking her, smiling and laughing at her gullibility. But in that dark place, the smile wouldn't last. It would turn to a look of horror and regret, the look of a man pleading for his life, for forgiveness and mercy from his victim. For in this dark place she was no longer the helpless victim, no longer an old and feeble woman. Here she was in charge. Here she held all the cards. Here he was indeed at her mercy and she would have none. Here she would get her money back and here she would enact her revenge.

Lamb of God, you take away the sin of the world: have mercy on us...

Here in this dark place he would fall to his knees, begging and crying for a second chance. Here she would stand over him as judge and jury and executioner. Here she would dispense justice with one loud crack of pin hitting bullet. Here she would stare into his cold dead eyes and here it was her turn to smile.

... My peace I leave you, my peace I give to you. Look not on our sins but on the faith of your Church and grant us

the peace and unity of your Kingdom where you live forever and ever...

In that dark place, she saw a pathway to the light. From there she could regain all that had been taken from her, her money, her dignity, her security, her self.

The Peace of the Lord be with you always... And also with you... Let us offer each other a sign of Christ's peace...

A nudging elbow brought her back from that dark place to the here and now. She extended her hand to the woman next to her and commenced to exchanging handshakes with those around her. When she turned to exchange the sign of peace with a young family seated in the pew behind her, something caught her eye. She thought for a moment she was truly losing her mind. She had to look twice.

When she was sure of it, a rage built inside her like none she'd ever felt. There he was, about halfway back in the church and one aisle over. Sure as shit it was he, the one she'd just been daydreaming about killing. The man who'd stolen her life savings was shaking hands and smiling and wishing a Merry Christmas to her fellow congregants of St. Christopher's Catholic Church. He was half-turned so she couldn't see his face full on, but she knew it was 'him'. If she'd had a gun right there at that moment, there was no doubt in her mind that he wouldn't survive past the Breaking of the Bread.

But she didn't have a gun. She didn't have anything. So she did the one thing she could think of doing.

The officer assigned to lockup stepped up to the jail cell. "Hanlon, your lawyer's here, you're sprung," he said. The officer took a look at the cell floor. "Oh, Christ. Did he piss himself again? Goddammit!"

"Yeah," answered Jack, "the Holy Spirit took over him and he let it all out."

"Hey," the officer yelled to the old bum, "Pastor Pissalot, you mind lettin' me know when you feel a sermon comin' on? I'm tired of cleanin' up after you."

The bum shot a vacant glance at the officer, gave him the middle finger, and looked away again.

The officer unlocked the cell door and Jack stepped out. He led Jack through the basement of the ancient station house toward the stairs to freedom.

"Otis," he yelled as they walked, "grab the mop. The bum pissed all over the floor again."

The temperature had dropped into the single digits, with a wind chill factor below zero. As the bells tolled to signal the beginning of Christmas Day, Jack was at once happy to be out of jail, but dreading having to face Amy. He had a strange thought about bells and how they are used for both celebration and mourning.

Levine's car pulled up in front of the darkened little bungalow on Mobile Street at about 12:20 Christmas morning. Jack held a dozen cheap roses and a package of Skittles he'd picked up at a 7-11 on the way home.

"A dozen roses and some candy isn't going to fix shit on this one friend," Seth had told him. But Jack felt he had to do something, make some kind of gesture, and at this late hour, it was all he could think of.

Seth put the car in park.

"Thank you Seth, really. I owe you big for this."

"Oh, you'll get the bill, don't you worry about that."

Jack smiled a weak smile. "Seriously, thank you. Have a good night." Jack reached for the door handle but stopped when Seth grabbed his arm.

"Jack."

"Yeah?"

"I'm worried about you. This - this kind of thing - what you did tonight, it's not like you. I know I'm just your lawyer and you're my client, but in the past few months, hell, I've grown to like you. Trust me, I don't say that about many of my clients. But I like you and I like Amy, and you've got a good thing going here, okay? You got treated shitty, that's for sure. No doubt about it. But don't let that ruin everything. I'm going to try my damnedest to get back what you lost, but I can't promise I'll succeed. What I *can* guarantee you is this: if you keep acting the way you have been, and keep going down this road, you're going to lose what's really important. You're a lucky guy Jack, don't let them steal that from you too."

Jack soaked it in. He knew Levine was right.

"Thank you Seth. I appreciate that. And I appreciate all you've done for me. I've tried to let it go. I've tried to move on. It's not easy. What I'm doing, I'm doing for Amy and the boys."

"No, what you're doing is trying to save face. What you're doing in the process is losing Amy and the boys. Stop it now. You need a job. Get your mind straight and find one. I'll help you if I can. But as far as General Systems goes, forget it. Put it behind you. Stop fighting, stop thinking about it, stop fixating on it. Let me do that. That's what you pay me for. I'll fight that war, you get yourself together and rebuild what you've broken here."

Jack fumbled with the door handle but eventually got it open. When he stepped out of the warm car into the freezing cold, he slipped on a patch of ice, lost his balance and dropped the roses. They fell to the frozen earth, losing petals and scattering from their neat little bunch into a flay of stems and flowers and thorns. Jack tried to gather them up as neatly as possible, but the prettiness of them disappeared. The shock of the cold drew life from them and they seemed to wilt and whither before his eyes. Still, he hoped, the thought would be enough.

Jack snuck into the house, took off his shoes, and tiptoed past the Christmas tree with the boys' presents stacked beneath it, and up the stairs to his bedroom. He undressed and climbed into his bed.

"I see Seth was able to work some Christmas magic," Amy said without turning to face him, her head still on the pillow.

Jack snuggled in close beside her and put his arm around her. She shrugged it off, turned towards him and rested on one elbow.

"Listen, I don't want to hear it. The boys are going to be up at the crack of dawn and goddammit, we're gonna give them a good Christmas. Not one word, not one discussion about tonight, you understand? The day after, they're going to my mother's and you and me are having a long talk. That's the end of it. Now, I'm going to try to sleep because I'll be damned if you're going to ruin tomorrow the way you've ruined everything else. Now go downstairs and leave me the hell alone."

With that she turned her back to him and rested her head on the pillow. Jack got out of bed and sulked downstairs. He took a small throw off a recliner and plopped down on the couch. He grabbed the remote, turned on the TV, and tried to settle in.

It's A Wonderful Life was on. He tried to watch it, but couldn't. This year the uplifting movie simply added to his depression. He flipped through the channels three times before settling on an infomercial for a power juicer. Beside the couch, on an end table, sat a snow globe he'd bought for Amy the year Trevor was born. He took the fragile glass in his hands and shook it. Little white flakes swirled through the world inside almost hiding the family that lived there. A man, his wife, and a little boy in a sled barely visible through the whirling storm Jack created when he shook up their world.

He wound the key on the bottom of the globe and listened to the tiny plinkety-plinks play the melody of *My Favorite Things*. The tears poured down his face and he sobbed like a child. When the crying subsided, he fell asleep, cold and alone, face still wet with tears, nose running and throat sore, with only the flashing blue of the television to keep him company.

... He took the cup, again He gave you thanks and praise, gave the cup to His Disciples and said...

"Thief!" Mrs. Kelly's voice bounced off the marble and echoed through the church, startling everyone. Bowed heads jerked up and every eye glared at her as she stood amongst the kneeling crowd pointing at the man she'd identified as the roofer who'd stolen her money.

A mumble grew through the church. A young man sitting behind Mrs. Kelly stood and placed a gentle hand on her shoulder.

"Is everything alright ma'am?"

"That man! That man right there," she said still pointing a quivering finger, "stole my life savings from me!"

The congregation turned to see at whom she pointed.

"What man?"

"That one, right there." The young man's hand fell away as she moved through the pew, stepping over legs and purses. When she was out of her pew she marched down the aisle of the church. Her heels cracked against the marble floor like gunshots that rang out through the church and echoed back to her. Her steps were deliberate and steady as she closed in on her target, her finger still pointing.

She stopped when she came to the pew where the bewildered man knelt. Her accusing finger stopped an inch from his nose and stayed there. Her face contorted with anger and her eyes welled with tears, though none would fall. Her breathing was fast and forceful through her nose like a bull about to charge. With a confused smile he pointed his own finger at himself and meekly asked, "Me?"

"You know goddamn well I mean you, you son-of-a-bitch," Mrs. Kelly announced with no hesitation, her profanities echoing through the church as her shoe heels had.

"Honest ma'am, I don't know what you're talking about," the man said. He was embarrassed and confused.

"You don't know what I'm talking about my ass. You know what you did. You know exactly what you did to me. Admit it. Here in front of God and everybody, just admit it dammit!"

The man looked on in awe.

"ADMIT IT!" She screamed.

At that point two of the ushers sidled up beside her and gently, but firmly, took her by the arms and led her to the nearest exit. Mrs. Kelly went along, her eyes and her pointing finger never leaving the man in the pew. The tears let loose now and streamed down her reddened cheeks as she was led out of the church and into the cold.

CHAPTER TWENTY-FIVE

The rectory had a chill. Mrs. Kelly sat on a leather chair much too large for her small frame. Her feet dangled off the floor like those of a child. She'd been waiting there with one of the ushers, an older man, tall and thin, wearing a maroon sports coat and grey slacks, since she'd been ejected from Mass for causing a scene.

"Father Kuzinski would like to see you when he's finished with midnight Mass," the usher told her.

And so she sat like a schoolgirl outside the principal's office, waiting to be scolded for acting up in class.

"He's not going to sick the nuns on me is he?" she asked. She got no response.

At about 1:30, Father Kuzinski came into the rectory. He was tall and heavy, with white hair, a bulbous nose and a kind smile. He looked at Mrs. Kelly with empathy. He thanked the usher, wished him a Merry Christmas, excused him, and took a seat in a leather chair across from Mrs. Kelly. His Chicago accent was as thick as hers.

"So..." he began, "here we are."

"Father forgive me, isn't that what I'm supposed to say? Then you give me penance, some Hail Mary's, some Our Fathers, and we go on our way, right?"

"Well, that depends, is this a confession?"

"You tell me."

"Mrs. Kelly, you've been a parishioner here for a long, long time, and a good one at that. You volunteered often at the school when you had young children, you've donated time to the Lady's Sodality, you are a frequent attendee to Mass every Sunday, although I've recently noticed your absence the past few months. Tonight's outburst, well, I don't doubt that it was for good cause."

"Then you believe me?"

"No, I didn't say that. I believe you believe that the man you pointed out stole your money," he replied.

"Then you don't believe me. You think I'm nuts."

"I didn't say that either. Why don't you start at the beginning and tell me what happened."

Mrs. Kelly recounted what had happened. Her memory was good, her mind sharp. Though it had been nearly six months, she gave details and dates perfectly. When she finished, Father Kuzinski sat rubbing his chin, soaking it all in.

Finally he said, "Mrs. Kelly, I wish you'd have come to me sooner. That's what I'm here for. Not for just saying Mass and hearing confessions. I'm here to help in any way I can. If nothing else, I'm a great listener, but I also have friends over at the police station. I have a friend in our Alderman. And I have other parishioners who come to me with problems, some of them have come to me with the exact same problem you have. This guy has been all over the parish preying on our older residents. You aren't the only one, so stop feeling stupid; you aren't stupid. He has swindled several people and several very bright, streetwise, intelligent people at that. So it is nothing to be ashamed of. However, I can tell you that the man you accused in Mass tonight is not the man who stole from you."

"How are you so sure?"

"Because I know the man. He's been a parishioner here for about eight years. His children go to school here. He's a good man. Part of our Father's Club. He donates his time, and his money generously. And he's not a roofer, not even close. He's an accountant with a firm downtown. He has a large enough salary that he doesn't have to go about scamming old folks out of their life savings."

"I swear it was him Father. I know it..."

"I know you think you know it, but I'm sorry dear, you're wrong. It's not him. Think about this Mrs. Kelly, wouldn't a man doing what you described find a place far from his home to commit his crimes? Why would he do it in his own neighborhood where he could be seen and recognized at the Jewel grocery shopping, or standing at a bus stop, at the park with his kids, or attending Mass?"

"But he looks just like..."

"Mrs. Kelly. I've asked the man you pointed out in church to stay around and speak to us. Is that okay?"

"He's here?"

"He's waiting in the vestibule. He's a good man and he agreed to delay his Christmas in order to talk this over with us. Mind if I bring him in?"

"No. Go ahead. I have to be sure. I want to look into his eyes. I wanna hear his voice."

Father Kuzinski opened the door and welcomed the man inside. He was a stout man, black curly hair peeking out of his collar where his tie once tamed it. He smiled at Mrs. Kelly before taking the seat Father Kuzinski had occupied before. The good Father sat behind his desk.

"Mrs. Kelly, this is Mr. Dom Sicci. Like I said, He's a long-time parishioner here at St. Christopher's. Dom, this is Mrs. Kelly."

Dom stood to shake Mrs. Kelly's hand. She did so reluctantly.

"Pleasure to meet you Mrs. Kelly."

Mrs. Kelly stared into his eyes. They were deep brown just like the man on her porch that day. She looked at his chest and noticed a gold chain tucked into his shirt.

"A crucifix Mr. Sicci?" she said sliding a finger beneath the thin gold chain.

"This?" he pulled the chain from his shirt. "No ma'am, this is a horn charm. It's an Italian thing for good luck." He held out the gold charm in his hand. It looked more like a golden fang than a horn, but it was definitely not a crucifix. "Wards off the evil eye, they say. My mother gave me a crucifix for my confirmation but I'm sad to say I lost it when I was in high school. Careless kid I was. And please, call me Dom."

Dom took his seat again. He crossed his legs and rested both hands on his knee. Mrs. Kelly took a good look

142

at his left hand. There was no wedding ring as there had been on the con-man roofer.

"Not married Mr. Sicci?"

"Well, that's kind of a long story. No Mrs. Kelly, I'm not. I was married, years ago, to a beautiful woman. I made the mistake a lot of men make, I guess. I spent a good deal of my time at the office. In the meantime, she spent a good deal of time alone. She worked and she had the kids to look after, but I guess she needed more. She met a man, someone she worked with, and took off with him. That was about nine years ago. Just before I moved to St. Christopher's."

"I'm sorry to hear that. Do you still have your wedding ring?"

"No. I sold it. I simply couldn't look at it any longer. It was time for it to go."

Dom's manner of speaking was more articulate than that of the man on her porch so many months ago. He spoke so genuinely of his former wife, and his gold chain did not display a crucifix as the roofer man's had. Mrs. Kelly was overcome with a feeling of dread.

She glared at him for a moment in a new light. She stared at the receding hairline and the brown eyes. She studied his mannerisms and the curvature of his mouth. The resemblance faded. After a few moments, she burst into tears.

Mr. Sicci and Father Kuzinski glanced at each other then both went to the old woman to console her.

"I'm so sorry. Forgive me. Please forgive me. You... you looked just like him." She sobbed like a child. The men each placed a hand on her shoulders, but she was inconsolable. "Please go Mr. Sicci. Please go and forgive me. I'm embarrassed and ashamed. Please, go enjoy your Christmas and find a place in your heart to forgive me." She sobbed.

"Of course Mrs. Kelly. I forgive you. You've been through a lot and I understand. Please, don't think about it another minute. All is well. All is forgiven. Okay?" He smiled at her hoping for a smile in return. He didn't get one. "I'll leave now because you asked me to, but please don't

143

feel bad about this anymore. It's okay." With that, he slid his hand from her shoulder, shrugged at Father Kuzinski, and left.

Mrs. Kelly stood to leave.

"Please, sit."

"Time for the lecture, ay Father?" She said wiping the tears from her eyes, her voice hoarse and uneven.

"No. But I would like to talk with you. Can you tell me more about what happened?"

"What more is there to tell? I'm broke. A lifetime of working and scrimping and saving and Father, I have very little left. You see, not only did I pay him out the money he asked for, but then I had to pay more to a real roofer to fix the Godda... goshdarn mess. We never had a lot Father. I've been poor father, dirt poor. My parents came from Ireland with very little. I lived through the Depression. I don't want to be poor again. We worked so hard. I don't need much, but now I'm worried. I may have to go back to work. Imagine me, at my age. What would I do?"

"You mentioned your children, could they help you out?"

"Oh Father, they mustn't know. I am an independent woman. They'll think I lost my marbles. They'll stick me in one of those old folks homes to eat Jell-O and wait for the grim reaper."

"I'm sure they would be happy to help if they knew..."

"No."

"Sometimes we have to swallow our pride Mrs. Kelly. As difficult as that is, sometimes we have to do it."

"Absolutely not! The police are still looking for that bastard and when they find him, I'll get my money back."

"Mrs. Kelly, I'm not certain that's the case. Chances are, he's spent your money and all the other money he's swindled. You may get some satisfaction in seeing him go to jail, but I don't think you'll be getting your money back."

"I don't want to see him go to jail, Father. I want to see him dead."

144

"Now Mrs. Kelly, are you listening to yourself? Life is precious. It's God's greatest gift. You wouldn't want to see a man dead over money now, would you?"

"The Hell I wouldn't. Besides, it's not just the money, it's..."

"It's pride, Mrs. Kelly. You told me yourself, you feel like a fool. You're angry that he tricked you, that he got the better of you. That's understandable, but hating him and wishing him dead isn't going to get you peace. It's only going to lead to more misery. You have to let it go. As difficult as that will be, you have to let it go."

"Easy for you to say. It didn't happen to you."

"I know."

"You know? That's all you have to say is 'you know'? There is so much about this that you *don't* know Father it could fill up a Third Testament of the Bible."

"Mrs. Kelly, please..."

She stood from the too-large chair and planted her feet firmly in front of the sitting priest. She wiped the remaining tears from her eyes, threw her shoulders back, slung her big purse over her forearm, and cleared her throat. "Father Kuzinski, I'm leaving now. I appreciate your concern, but I can handle this on my own. Now if you'll excuse me, it's Christmas and I have things to do." With that, she stormed from the rectory office.

"Think of what happened tonight Mrs. Kelly," the priest called after her, "there is more misery like that waiting for you if you continue down this..." She was out of earshot before he could finish the sentence.

Jack was awakened by the sound of his boys bounding down the stairs. Typically, Amy would wake him up to get the video camera ready to capture the excited rush from the second floor to the downstairs tree and the goodies that waited beneath it. But this year, they were up and coming before he had even opened his eyes.

Amy poked her head in the family room. "The boys are up. Christmas is starting."

"I'll get the camera."

"No. No video this year. I'll take still pictures, but no video." She was adamant. Jack lifted himself from the couch and wandered yawning into the front room where his boys had already tore open a couple of presents each and strewn wrapping paper about in the process.

"Are you sure you don't want me to tape..."

"Jack, I said no," Amy tried to disguise her anger so as not to alert the boys, but Jack got the message.

"Okay." Jack sat in a wing chair and watched as his boys opened their presents. They were happy and excited and oblivious to the fact that their world was about to change forever. Then Jack watched his wife watch their boys.

He watched her in awe. In awe of her strength. In awe of her beauty. In awe of how well she was holding herself together despite her anger. In awe of her undying love for their sons.

He reached for her hand and grasped it in his. She gave his hand a squeeze then pulled away. He took the squeeze as a sign that, though she was very angry, she still loved him and he smiled at the thought that they would figure this out the way they had figured everything out over the years and they would emerge from this bad place in tact. Stronger, wiser, with some definite walls to climb, but in tact.

When all the presents were opened, and Amy had cleaned up all of the wrapping paper, Jack went to the kitchen to make the traditional Hanlon Christmas-Morning Breakfast, ham and eggs with his Grandmother's recipe for pork-sausage and gravy on the side.

The boys busied themselves playing with their new toys in the front room while Jack cooked. He put on a pot of coffee and started scrambling the eggs. Amy came in with a garbage bag full of paper and boxes she put by the back door for Trevor to take to the alley later.

"Why didn't you want me to get the video camera out this year?" he asked her.

"Because Jack, this is not a Christmas any of us are going to want to remember."

"What does that mean?"

"I told you, we'll discuss this tomorrow."

He grabbed her arm and turned her to face him. "What do you mean this isn't a Christmas any of us will want to remember? The boys are fine. They don't seem the least bit phased by my not being here last night. If we don't make a big deal out of it, they'll forget all about it."

"They might, but I won't Jack. We'll talk about it tomorrow."

"What are you saying? You can't forgive me for yesterday? Honey it was..."

"Tomorrow Jack!" she caught herself then lowered her voice, "tomorrow." She turned from him and went from the room, careful to conceal the tears filling her eyes. She went straight to the bathroom and locked the door, where she had a good, solid cry.

Mrs. Kelly slept in Christmas morning. After Midnight Mass and her meeting with Father Kuzinski, she had a difficult time falling asleep.

She awoke around noon Christmas Day to a ringing phone. It was her son in Arizona calling to wish her a Merry Christmas. She knew what was coming, he'd put each of the grandkids on to tell her what they'd gotten from Santa, then ask how she was, what was new in the neighborhood, how was midnight Mass, what were her plans for Christmas? Then he'd tell her how much he really wished he could be there with her, but you know how expensive it is to fly the whole family and really they're all extremely busy, but it's been great talking with you Ma, and then they'd hang up and she'd wait for the next child to do the same. It was an annual tradition.

She ignored the phone. She'd call back later after she'd had her coffee. She sat at the kitchen table sipping coffee in silence until two o'clock when she finally returned all the unanswered calls from her children and grandchildren.

She spent her Christmas in her nightgown under an afghan listening to old Irish records Harold had bought for her, until the lights of passing cars swept across the room and she decided it was time to eat something.

As she dragged her tired bones to the kitchen to find a can to open, the doorbell rang. She'd been living a rather solitary life for the past few months, avoiding friends, neighbors, and family. As a result, it'd been quite a while since she'd had anyone at her door. The chimes rang like an old song from happier times and for a moment she recalled what life had felt like before that conman had committed his crimes.

The feeling was fleeting and she grumbled as she shuffled to the door, weary of who might be out there and what their intentions might be. She peered out the curtain on the door's window, pushing it aside ever so slightly as if something might jump out at her and devour her if she the motion of the curtain were detected from the outside. She couldn't get a good look. There was more than one; that she could tell. The bell rang again. Mrs. Kelly froze for a moment. Then she heard the cough.

It was the familiar cough of Annie Lynch and unmistakable brogue of Nora Hogan. "Irene Kelly, you open up in there you hear me? You'll not be spendin' this evenin' alone. We come bearing food and drink," Nora called.

"Irene," Annie pleaded, her voice the raspy-gurgly kind of the life-long smoker who perpetually must clear her throat, "it's damn cold out here. You gonna let us in or what?"

"Let us in," Nora called again, "we have pornography!"

"We do not! "

"We do. Gobs and gobs of pornographic pictures of sweaty firemen and that fella you like from the pictures... um... what the hell is the name of that one she thinks is so darling?"

"Jason Bateman," Annie said.

"Jason Bateman," Nora called through the door, then turned to Annie Lynch and said, "Really? Jason Bateman? Irene could do better." Calling through the door again she continued, "We have dirty pictures of Jason Bateman and

Sean Connery! You'll not be spendin' Christmas Night alone, you know. Open the door."

"Oh, shut up you old fool," Annie pushed Nora aside and stepped closer to the door to be heard, then yelled, "Irene, we don't have any of that, don't listen to her. We have beer, we have chips and dip, and we have a Tupperware fulla turkey and stuffing and potatas and what not, pictures of the grandkids, and plenty of gossip."

"We saw the curtain move Irene, we know you're there and we know you're gigglin'," Nora said.

Mrs. Kelly rolled her eyes and opened the door.

"Well it's about time, I'm freezing my tatas off out here," Annie stated stepping into the house.

"Oh that's just wishful thinkin'. If ya froze yer tatas off, you'd have nothin' ta wax da floors wit?" Nora chided Annie, and gave Mrs. Kelly a peck on the cheek and handed her the Tupperware of food, "Merry Christmas dear."

"Very funny. You're one to talk." turning to Mrs. Kelly, "Merry Christmas Irene, how have you been? Where have you been? We've been worried. You don't mind if I smoke, do you?" Annie's cigarette was lit before she'd finished the question.

"Come into the kitchen. I'll get you an ashtray Annie," Irene Kelly said leading her friends to the kitchen table.

Mrs. Kelly put the Tupperware in the fridge. Nora went to the cabinet where she knew the beer glasses were kept and grabbed one for each of them, then poured out three beers. Annie opened a bag of Jay's potato chips and a plastic container of onion soup mix stirred into sour cream.

"What a surprise," Mrs. Kelly stated still unsure of whether it was a pleasant surprise or not, "what brings you by?"

"We tought ya could use some compny," Nora started, "we haven't seen hide nor hair of ya in monts. Where ya bin hidin' out?"

"I've been here. I just haven't been feeling well. The cold, you know?"

Annie ashed her cigarette into the ashtray. "Bullshit. I've seen you trudge through a blizzard just to get a hot dog at Windy Ray's. Come on, come clean. What's really goin' on?"

"Nothing's going on. Just the winter blues I guess. Really I'm fine."

"The Irene Kelly I know doesn't get the blues. There's sometin' goin' on and we want ta know what it is."

"Nora, I'm telling you, there's nothing wrong. Got it? Now drop it!" Mrs. Kelly's eyes lit and her face flushed.

"Okay. Notin's goin' on. Got it."

"You ladies promised gossip and pornography," Mrs. Kelly said trying to lighten the mood, "now where are the dirty pictures of Jason Bateman?"

Annie coughed. "There are no dirty pictures of anybody. But have we got some gossip for you. Go on, tell her Nora."

"Well, do ya remember the ding-dong twins?"

"The sisters who used to walk down the street waddling side to side like bell clappers?"

"Yes, dem. Well... and you didn't hear dis from me... I heard from Mary Roarke dat da shorter one of da two, da one with a face like a frying pan..."

"They both had a face like a frying pan," Annie interrupted, "they were twins."

"Alright, the short one, the one with the kinda lazy eye."

"Oh, that one. Yeah, I know which one now. We used to call her sideways Sally," Annie stated.

"I don't think her name was Sally," Nora said.

"No. I don't know what her name was. It might have been Donna, but we called her sideways Sally because that sounded better than sideways Donna, what with the crossed eye and all. Anyhow, go on."

"Well, I heard that after her sister past away... they lived together ya know... well Mary told me that sideways Sally kept the other twin's corpse in da tub on ice so she could keep collectin' da social security checks. Did this for tree months, she did. Got away with it too til the neighbors complained about the foul odor."

"You'll love this next part Irene, wait 'til you hear this," Annie interrupted, "Go on tell her Nora."

"The stink wasn't from the corpse, ya know, it was from Sally! With her dead sister on ice in the tub, she had nowhere to bathe."

"I knew those girls were creepy when we were kids." Annie crushed out her cigarette and reached into her purse. "I have pictures Irene. Lisa came by last night after dinner with the kids... oh they're getting so big... they're living down in St. Hubert's parish now, it used to be the dumps over there, remember, but apparently it's an up and coming area now. He's a analyst or something, I don't know <cough> but he makes good money... anyhow, her oldest, Kathleen..." Annie reached down and pulled her Buick of a purse off the floor, plopped it on her lap and began digging through it. "... is singing in the church choir and they put the picture of the whole choir on the front page of the Weekly Bulletin. I have it here somewhere."

"While she's lookin' fer dat, take a look at my little granddaughter. Made her first communion in November at St. Juliana's, ya know." Nora slapped a snapshot on the table in front of Mrs. Kelly. "Isn't she darlin'?"

Mrs. Kelly held the picture up and gave it an adequate appraisal. "Very nice," she said, "pretty dress."

"And me other daughter's youngest met da Cardinal." Nora slapped another snapshot on the table. "They're down on da south side at St. Turibius, ya know, and they got to go down to Holy Name and meet His Eminence."

"Found it! Here, look at this," Annie unfolded a weekly bulletin from St. Hubert Catholic Church of Chicago that she'd dug out of a side pocket of her giant purse and handed it to Mrs. Kelly. On the cover of the bulletin was a black and white photo of a group of fifteen people of varying ages from fourteen to seventy. Annie, with a shaky aged finger, pointed to a beautiful young woman of about sixteen or so. "That there's my Kathleen. Isn't she pretty? And you should hear her sing..."

Annie went on bragging about her granddaughter and Mrs. Kelly gave an obligatory look, nodding along but not really listening. Her eyes scanned the faces on the grainy picture so as not to offend her friend. Annie's granddaughter was quite pretty, with 'the map of Ireland' on her face as they say. Much brighter than many of the dull faces that made up the rest of the choir. Frumpy old women and balding middle-aged men, and... the blood flooded from Mrs. Kelly's face. "Irene are you okay? You're white as a ghost." Annie asked.

Mrs. Kelly didn't answer. She was stunned. There, two rows behind and three people to the right of Annie's granddaughter was... him.

Mrs. Kelly took the reading glasses from her nose and wiped them with her shirt and looked through them again moving the picture closer then farther then closer again, trying to get the right view, testing her vision. It couldn't be. It couldn't possibly be him. But it was. She was sure of it. More sure than she'd ever been of anything in her life. But then again, less than twenty-four hours ago she'd made a fool of herself because she was so sure she'd seen him, hadn't she? She would have sworn on the Holy Bible last night that Mr. Sicci was the conman, and yet she knew now how wrong she had been. But this man, this man in the picture was identical to the mental image she had of the man on her porch that summer day. This had to be him!

There were no names identifying the choir members in the picture. She scanned the article about the group, but the only person named specifically was the choir director, Sister Maryanne.

"Who is this?" Mrs. Kelly asked Annie.

"I don't know. Why? Do you know him?"

"I think he worked on my roof once," Mrs. Kelly replied.

Mrs. Kelly lay in bed that night, the smell of Annie's cigarette smoke still hanging in the air and the image of that picture hanging in her mind. She tried to get Annie to let her keep the Bulletin, but Annie said it was her only copy and it was going back up on the fridge as soon as she got home.

152

Mrs. Kelly wasn't sure exactly what she was going to do, but she was sure of one thing, she'd be going to Mass at St. Hubert's in the morning, with a gun in her purse.

PART THREE

NEW MOONS, SABBATHS, & CONVOCATIONS

What is religion if not a set of beliefs that dictate your actions?

CHAPTER TWENTY-SIX

DECEMBER 26, 2010

Timmy gave Jack a big hug and a kiss on the cheek. "Bye Daddy," he said, then, bundled from head to toe to protect him from the unforgiving cold, he raced to catch up with his brothers who were already getting into Grandma Rosemary's car.

"I can have them home tomorrow afternoon, but if you need more time, let me know, they can stay as long as they want," Rosemary said. She gave a sidelong glance at Jack, whispered something to her daughter, then left. Jack thought he saw sympathy in that look from his mother-in-law, a woman who'd never cared for him before. It was surprising and worrisome. To elicit her sympathy must mean something was seriously wrong. It was a look nurses give terminal patients who have not yet been informed that death was imminent.

Amy paced through the front room, wringing her hands, collecting her thoughts, trying to remember the speech she'd rehearsed in her head a hundred times but was now evading her.

"Jack," she said at last, "I want you to leave."

"What? I thought we were going to talk about..."

"No. I want you to leave. Pack your things and leave."

"Leave leave? You don't mean..."

"Yes. I do..."

"Amy... "

"No. Enough is enough. It's not working."

"We hit one rough patch and you give up? What the hell Amy?"

"One rough patch? Jack living with you has been hell. I've tried. I honestly have tried. I have tried to talk to you, I have tried to seduce you, I have tried to ignore you, and it just isn't working. I'm so tired Jack. So tired of it all."

"Tired of what? I had one bad day..."

"One bad day? Are you kidding? It's been a string of bad day on top of bad day since this whole GS bullshit started. You're short tempered, you yell at the kids for no reason, you yell at me for no reason, you sit and sulk and brood, you're smoking like a chimney, you don't talk to me, you don't touch me, you don't have anything to do with the boys anymore. I'm tired. I'm tired of not being married to the man I fell in love with. It's like I'm sharing the house with a stranger."

"I'm going through a tough time. For better or worse, remember?"

"I remember. I remember very clearly. I remember the morning you proposed to me. I remember sitting on the Waveland Avenue rocks, the sun coming up over the lake, and you promising me that we'd have a happy home, not a fancy home, not a big bank account, not an expensive car, but a happy home. I believed you. And you came through; you gave us that happy home. But then you took it away. You stole it from us because someone else stole a gob of money from you."

"I fought for that gob of money for you and for the boys..."

"Well guess what, I don't want it. If you had listened to a word I've said over the past six months you'd already know that. It's not worth this. It's not worth what you've put us all through. It isn't Jack."

"How can you say that? Don't you see, that's what they want us to think? That's what they want us to do, to give up? To say 'it isn't worth it' and let them win? That money is ours, yours and mine and the boys'. I earned it. I did what they asked for the price they named and they owe it to me, to us. Don't you see that? Don't you care?"

"Yes! Yes I care Jack! I care more than you can imagine. I never asked you to drop the suit. I never said, 'Jack let them win'. Until I saw that they were taking from us more than just money. They were stealing you from us, and I was not willing to give *that* up, not for anything. But you couldn't see it. You still won't see it. The money, hell, that's on them, but their stealing you, that's on you. *You* let

156

that happen. You've been slipping away from us for months now and I honestly don't think you're ever coming back. The Jack I fell in love with is gone. You let them steal him. Shame on them for taking the money, but shame on you for letting them take you!"

"Amy, you don't understand, I'm still here. I love you. I love our family. I love our home. I love all we've built here together. Please don't give up on me."

"Jack, you gave up on us a long time ago. I can't have you living here with our boys any longer. It's not good for them. It's not good for me. I lost you. It breaks my heart. I cry myself to sleep every night over it, but I lost you. There's no getting you back. What happened Christmas Eve proves it. The man I married would never have done that. He might have thought about it, he may have wanted to, but he never would've done it. Not on Christmas Eve, not with his boys waiting for him. Not over some fat slob who had no worth anyhow."

"He ruined Trevor's Christmas! I told him I had to get to the bike store to get...

"Are you kidding? Did you see Trevor yesterday? He was thrilled with what was under the tree. You think his Christmas was ruined? He never even mentioned the bike. And his Christmas can continue another day when I take him to the store tomorrow to get the bike anyhow. How the hell was his Christmas ruined by Bugiardo? Huh? It wasn't at all. You lost your temper, that's what happened. You hated the job, you hated him, you hated taking his shit, and you hated that you ever had to go there to work in the first place and you took all your frustrations over GS and the car lot and the fat slob out on him by beating him to the point that he was hospitalized and you were arrested! You don't see the wrong in that? It had nothing to do with Trevor's Christmas or the bike. It had everything to do with you and GS and that goddamn money!"

"Well guess what Amy, that goddamn money is what pays our bills. Money is how I *give* you this 'happy home'. Money is how we eat and sleep with a roof over our heads and how we educate our kids. Money is what it is all about and if you can't see that..." he took her by the shoulders and shook her. She pushed against his chest and took three steps back.

"You don't think I know what it takes to put food on our table and a roof over our heads? Fuck you Jack. And the fact that you say 'money is what it's all about' tells me I'm right, you're lost. Money is how we pay for what we need, but it isn't what it's all about and it never has been, and that's what you've forgotten. You put that money and your pride and your hurt feelings ahead of us and then when things didn't go your way, you took your aggravation out on *us*. I won't stand for that anymore. I won't have my boys be your emotional punching bag anymore. Pack your bags, and get out of my house!"

CHAPTER TWENTY-SEVEN

The celebrations were over. The Holiday lights dimmed. Funny how the Christmas season begins in October but ends immediately after the gifts are opened and the turkey is eaten. Nothing left to sell it would seem. Jack sat alone in a motel room on Lincoln Avenue. The carpet was stained and the room smelled of must and decades of cigarette smoke to which Jack now added his own. The bed was lumpy, the blanket tattered, the sheets were stiff and he was afraid of what lay beneath them on the old mattress. The room had not been updated since the late 1970's, but the price was right.

In the room next door, through the thin walls, a woman cried out. Her moans hummed through the wall while the headboard banged an arrhythmic beat. Jack turned the volume up on the TV in a fruitless attempt to block out the sounds of sex. He assumed the woman making the noise was earning her pay. It was that kind of motel.

She had wanted him gone, so he left. He packed just the essentials and left the rest of his belongings behind with Amy. She'd offered him use of the car until he found a place, but he refused. He descended the steps of his home, their home, with an old duffle bag and a hundred dollars in his pocket, money he'd been saving to buy Amy a Christmas gift he never got around to getting.

He walked down the empty street to the bus stop and caught an eastbound bus to take him down to where the rooms were affordable and transportation accessible.

The wall pounded in an ever-increasing tempo until finally it stopped. There was a part of Jack that envied the man next door. Never in his life had Jack employed the services of a prostitute, but sitting alone in this empty sewer of a room, he felt the need for some human contact, some diversion from his troubles. He loved Amy still, and he hadn't been with another woman since they began dating in college, but now, for the first time, he felt the urge to share his bed with someone, anyone, just to numb the pain. Instead though, he polished off the last of a six-pack and faded off into a restless sleep. By week's end, all that would change.

Sunday morning, Mrs. Kelly woke at four. She dressed for church, took two buses, and arrived at St. Hubert's in time for 6:30 Mass.

She searched the small crowd for the man, but came up empty. She stayed for every Mass that day: the 6:30, the 8:30, the 10:30 and the noon. She watched the faithful file in, take their seats, and begin the rituals. When the noon Mass ended, she was confident that she'd not missed a single person coming through the doors of the church, and the thief was not among them. She took the buses back home. She'd try again next week. It occurred to her that perhaps, he might attend the Saturday evening Mass, and so next week, she would attend that Mass too.

CHAPTER TWENTY-EIGHT

Jack spent Monday looking for work to no avail. Stores were laying off seasonal help, car dealerships weren't hiring, and corporations were manned by low-level employees who'd not yet earned the right to take time off during the Holidays and were unauthorized to do any hiring.

Jack walked the streets. Families passed him on Michigan Avenue and he thought of his own. Couples walked along the Ohio Street and he thought of Amy. Some kid would yell "Dad" and he would instinctively turn to respond.

When Jack thought back on that day after Christmas, what he remembered most was the fear he saw in Amy's eyes. She feared him. He'd disappointed her before. They'd had their share of arguments over the years like any couple, but she'd never been afraid of him before. Did she really think he had the capacity to hurt her or the boys?

Jack had always felt that trust, beyond anything else, was at the heart of any good marriage. Not just the trust of sexual fidelity, but a deeper trust, the trust that the other person has your best interests at heart... the trust that in the arms and company of your partner, you are safe - physically, emotionally, and otherwise. Trust that even when you're sick and looking your worst, the love is there. Even when you look foolish, you are among a friend. Even when your imperfections show, which they are bound to do, you are safe from ridicule, safe from harsh judgment, safe from the tortures of gossip. It's what makes sex with your spouse so good, the trust; the trust to get naked, expose yourself to the person, flaws and all, and give yourself over completely without fear. To open yourself up to the risk of getting hurt knowing it is no risk at all. Trust.

To see fear in his wife's eyes, fear of him, meant that trust was broken. Somehow he'd broken it. Somehow it was gone. He couldn't for the life of him think of why. Sure, he'd beaten the fat man and beaten him good, but that was the fat man, the fat man deserved it. The fat man was the fat man, a mean, selfish, arrogant, glutinous prick. He was practically a stranger; he wasn't Amy. He'd never lay a hand on her. So why was she afraid? Why had that trust that had been there from the very beginning been broken?

A homeless man stepped out from a doorway and asked Jack for money. Jack pulled his pockets inside out to indicate he was broke himself and walked past. He kept what little money he had left safely tucked in a zippered pocket of his winter coat.

He walked west to the Red Line subway, transferred from the subway to the Brown Line 'L', then to a bus, then walked the remainder of the way back to his motel. He passed four prostitutes on the stairwell as he made his way to his room.

Once inside, he turned on all of the lights so the roaches would scatter, peeled off his clothes and took a hot shower. As he showered, he thought of excuses he could use to place a call to Amy. He decided to call on the pretense of 'just checking on the boys'. That wasn't entirely false, he wanted to know how they were doing, but, of course, he knew they'd be okay in their mother's care. What he really wanted was to hear her voice. To make another plea to her to let him come home where he belonged.

With just a towel wrapped around his waist and still dripping from the shower, he sat on the bed, picked up the phone and dialed his house.

Amy loaded the dishwasher with dinner plates. Her mother had offered to keep the boys for the week, but Amy declined. Without them to distract her, she'd go out of her mind. She needed the reminder of why she'd kicked the love of her life from their home. It was for the boys' sake.

She still loved Jack, but she was, for the first time since she'd met him, afraid of him. She was afraid of what he was capable of doing. In all the years they'd been together, he'd never once been in a fight except for the day they met, and then only because Dan had tried to hit her. He was always a levelheaded, gentle man. Bigger and stronger than most, and more than able to beat the living daylights out of just about anyone who crossed him, but he never did. He never let his strength and his size and his ability to fight turn him into a bully. He was kind. He helped people weaker than him rather than intimidate them. It's what she loved most about him. He was a gentle soul. But that changed. She'd seen it coming long before he beat the living shit out of the fat man.

From an outsider's perspective, one might think he'd just had enough and needed to put Bugiardo in his place, but Amy knew better. She knew this beating was more than simply letting out frustration; it was a fundamental change in who Jack Hanlon was and what he was willing and capable of doing. It was hard to explain to others. To her mother's questions she could only respond, "I know him, he's mine, and he's changed." Her mother never liked Jack before, but stood up for him now.

"Men go through things. They have their own way of dealing with things. If he beat this man so good, maybe he had a good reason," she'd said. "Men accuse us women of being emotional, but in reality, we are the more rational gender. Sometimes they have to fight each other in order to figure things out. That's no reason for you to be afraid of your husband. If anything, you should be proud. He did what he did for you and your boys. If I'd have thrown your father out for every time he got into a fistfight, you'd probably never been born. It's just what men do, dear."

But Amy knew that this wasn't just a fistfight, not just a manly show of dominance. It was only a matter of time before he exploded for real, and one way or another that explosion would make casualties of their sons. That was something she was not willing to let happen.

Still she'd been fighting the urge to call him home. She longed for him. She longed for his touch, his caress, and those shared moments only they knew. She longed for her best friend. She longed for the person she could confide in, the person she could lean on when she was afraid. She longed for her husband – her love.

But what she saw in him the past week: the hatred, the anger, the violence just simmering there in those once gentle brown eyes that had, at one time, put her at ease,

162

disturbed her. That's when she decided he had to go. The Jack she'd known was replaced by someone else, someone she couldn't predict, someone she no longer trusted.

As she loaded the last of the dishes into the dishwasher, the phone rang. She closed the door of the dishwasher and picked up the receiver on the kitchen wall-phone that she'd re-hung inches away from the hole Jack had punched in the drywall the night he'd been fired. The voice on the other end was Jack's.

"Amy? Hello?" Jack waited for a response but got none. "Hello? Amy, are you there? It's Jack."

"I know who it is," she said at last.

"I... ah... I was just calling to see how the boys are. To make sure you're all alright."

"We're fine."

"Amy..."

"What?"

"Amy, please. We can work through this. I don't want to lose you. I don't want to lose them. I want to come home."

Silence on the other end.

"Do you hate me that much? Can't you at least say something? Anything?"

"Jack, we've been through this. You've changed. Maybe you can't see it. Maybe you don't realize it, but you have. You've changed in a way I can't deal with."

"I haven't Amy. I haven't changed. I'm still the same guy I always was. Please take me back."

Amy held the phone to her ear with one hand, and wiped away her flowing tears with the other, but she held her voice steady. "I can't Jack. Not now. Maybe it's me. Maybe I'm just not strong enough for this fight you're in, but I can't let you back in this house the way you are. I can't. I'm sorry." She hung up the phone, put her face in her hands and slid her back down the wall until she was sitting on the kitchen floor sobbing. She put her head between her knees and cried.

Outside, the snow began to swirl in the wind. The weatherman on channel nine was calling for near blizzard conditions.

The line went dead and Jack gently placed the receiver down. Above the steel dresser on the opposite wall of the bed in the tiny motel room hung a mirror. Jack stared at himself in that mirror for an eternity. His marriage, his life, was over. In his worst nightmares he never imagined this was possible.

Naked except for the towel around his waist, Jack stared at his own reflection. He stared deep into his own eyes and saw, for the first time, what Amy had seen, what she had seen that frightened her to the point that she'd sent him packing. He saw it and he smiled. A sad smile. The kind of smile you give an old friend as you bid him a final farewell. He smiled and then he swung. With a twist of his hips and his body behind it, he swung with no regard for the wall behind the mirror. No hesitation. No holding back. He swung and he connected hitting his reflection square in the jaw, shattering his reflection, the mirror, and his fist.

The towel fell from his waist and he stood there naked.

The mirror splintered into sharp slivers of glass, remnants, pieces of what once formed a shimmering, useful tool now lie in small useless daggers. Sharp, angry shards that now glistened with the intent to cut and stab and draw blood. Injurious and fatal in their brokenness. Like that poor egg who'd fallen victim to the forces of a high brick wall and the unforgiving pull of gravity, never to be put back together again.

His broken hand throbbed. The pounding from the room next door slowed to a stop. The ringing in Jack's ears did not. With his good hand, he dug into the pockets of the jeans he'd tossed across the bed and pulled out a sodden ball of money, twenty dollars in all. He dropped the money on a table, dressed, and went out the door.

Traffic rushed by on Lincoln Avenue as he leaned on the rusted metal railing covered with a thick coat of turquoise paint under a thin layer of ice. Jack laid his throbbing hand on the frozen rail for relief. Snow swirled through the air. Chicago was ripe for a winter storm. After five minutes of standing on the balcony, the door to the next room opened.

He saw her then, for the first time, the woman responsible for the banging, the moaning, the squeaking of the bed in the room next to his. He watched her walk away from him, turn left at the end of the balcony, then he saw her emerge at the bottom of the stairs and into the parking lot below him. She walked towards Lincoln Avenue, and stood on the corner. Jack leaned on the metal railing, watching her from above, for the better part of half an hour. Eventually, a black Lexus stopped along the curb beside where she was standing. The passenger side window rolled down and she leaned in. After a moment or two, she opened the door and slid in. The car sped away. Jack put out his cigarette, went back into his room, and drank.

Through blurry vision, Jack gazed at the television. A pretty blonde sat at the desk talking into the camera. A graphic hung above her head that caught Jack's attention.

'Illinois College Savings Plan Bust,' it read.

Jack turned up the volume.

"The State of Illinois' Brilliant Beginnings College Savings Plan is in less than brilliant shape. It was announced today by the watchdog group Citizens for Clear Government, that mismanagement of the fund has lead to over $200 million in losses, more than double what Treasurer Michael Fogarty previously disclosed at a news conference last week."

"Families who have placed their college savings in the mutual fund, attracted by tax incentives and the promise of a safe tool of growth will recoup a fraction of their initial investment. Doug Farnsworth, spokesperson for the watchdog group had this to say, "People put their faith in their government on the promise that this was a safe investing option, and now, they'll be lucky to get back half of what they put into it. The real shame here though, is that this didn't have to happen. The monies were handed over to a firm run by Mr. Fogarty's good friend Alex Green. Green and his firm made millions on administrative fees, and Mr.

Fogarty's office recently purchased a $50,000 luxury car for the Treasurer to use as his state vehicle. All of that money came from the public fund. Someone should go to jail for this," he added."

"When questioned, the Treasurer denied any wrongdoing stating, "The fund lost money, as have many funds, both private and public, in the past couple of years due to the downturn in the economy and the recession. When the economy recovers, so will the fund," he said. But our Economic Analyst Mary Durkin disagrees. "It's true that the recession has hit many areas of investment, however, mismanagement and outrageous fees are the major causes of the Brilliant Beginnings' troubles."

When asked if there'd be a criminal investigation into the Brilliant Beginnings Fund, Attorney General Clarissa Sheehan said there would not. Sheehan's uncle, the powerful House Speaker Tom Albrecht is also Treasurer Fogarty's brother-in-law. We'll be back with sports after this..."

And there it was, the nail in the coffin. The life savings Jack had put into the Brilliant Beginnings College Fund for his boys' future was half-gone in just a matter of a few months. Thieves were everywhere. The chips were stacked against Jack and guys like him. But what was there to do? 'Fight back,' he thought, 'fight back.'

The alcohol took over and Jack fell asleep.

CHAPTER TWENTY-NINE

Amy spent New Year's Eve at a friend's party. She insisted she did not want to go, but it was clear that Cassie Smolneki was not going to take no for an answer. Once Amy's mother, by nosing through the mail, had gotten wind of the invite, it was a certainty that the boys would be staying at their grandmother's house that night. Also one to never take no for an answer, Rosemary Shea told her daughter, "You need to get out of the house, be around people who don't watch cartoons morning till night. It'll give you some perspective, or at the very least, you'll forget your troubles for a few

166

hours, have a few drinks, a few laughs and a slight hangover the next day. That always seemed to help your father think things through. I'm taking the boys. That's settled. If you want to waste the night sitting at home in your jammies crying in your milk, well that's your decision, but you'll have no one to blame but yourself."

Amy knew that if she didn't go to that party, she'd never hear the end of it from neither her mom nor Cassie, so she resigned herself to go.

She dressed in a sparking little silver number that Jack had given her to wear to a General Systems Holiday Party years before when they still had holiday parties. She was stunning in it and Jack had told her so. Even she had to admit, she looked damn good in that dress. But when she checked herself in the full-length mirror, she began to sob uncontrollably. She sat down on the bed and wept. She couldn't wear it. She was already a half hour late for the party and now her make-up was ruined from the crying and she had to find something else to wear. She settled on a simple black dress she'd picked up on sale at Express five or six years ago, fixed her make-up and rushed out the door before she could change her mind.

Amy and Cassie had met on Amy's first day of work at Big-Box Bullseye. They were fast friends. Cassie was a petite woman, about six inches shorter than Amy, with dirty blonde hair she dyed a different color every few weeks it seemed. This night, it was a bright bleached blonde and cut in a short straight bob.

Cassie answered the door with her usual brilliant smile. "Amy Hanlon get in here." She was holding a glass of red wine that sloshed about in the glass as she grabbed Amy's elbow and led her into the house. "I was beginning to think you'd chickened out. Where have you been?"

"Last minute wardrobe change." Amy knocked the snow from her shoes onto the mat at the front door.

"Oh, I know how that goes. Come on in, I'll introduce you around. First, what are you drinking?"

"Do you have Vodka?"

"Honey, I like the sound of that. Yes we have Vodka, plenty of it, and good stuff too."

"Well if you have it, I'll have a Vodka-Sprite."

"Follow me to the drink table."

Amy followed the perky little woman through the house. Cassie Smolneki had decorated her home with taste and style. She had a good eye for such things and chose furnishings and decorative details that appeared more expensive than they really were.

Cassie fixed Amy a drink, heavy on the Vodka. "Fruit?"

"A lemon if you've got them."

Cassie dropped a lemon wedge into Amy's drink and handed it to her. "Come on, I'm excited to introduce you to everyone."

First they came to a round man and his haggard, rail-thin wife. The man was balding on top, but not on the sides, and his cheeks were perpetually flushed. His wife was not only much thinner, but much taller than he. She had a tired look in her eyes, but smiled politely when Cassie introduced them.

"Amy, this is Kent and Berta Jarlsen. Kent works with Kevin."

"Kevin work?" Kent Jarlsen let out a boisterous laugh, "Cassie, I haven't seen your husband work a day in his life." Again he laughed. Berta seemed utterly horrified.

"Kent, stop it."

"What? She knows I'm only joking. I kid. Your Kevin is a great guy, if you like that type." Amy knew now why Mrs. Jarlsen looked so haggard.

"It was nice to meet you both," she said and walked away, Cassie at her side.

"He's an ass, but Kevin insisted on inviting them. Why, I don't know," Cassie whispered too loudly.

Next they came to a couple closer to Amy and Cassie's age. He was tall, good looking, and well dressed. She was average height, obviously exercised regularly, strawberry blonde with a giant rock on her ring finger. Cassie introduced them as Finn and Marney Dickenson. Finn went to high school with Kevin, then moved on to the University of Illinois, then John Marshal Law School. Marney was his legal aide at his first firm. They had money, and they wanted you to know it.

After the Dickenson's, Amy met a few more couples, one of whom reminded her very much of Jack and herself, and it was they she wanted to flee more than any other. She'd happily spend the night listening to Kent Jarlsen crack himself up than spend a second more with the friendly, happy couple that resembled how she and Jack had been just a few months back.

After a few more short introductions and the exchange of a few more pleasantries, they found themselves back at the drink table where, to Amy's surprise, stood Bill Tallman.

"Of course, you know Bill," Cassie pertly announced.

"Yes, of course I know Bill. Hi Bill, how are you?"

"I'm doing just fine Amy, much better in fact now that you two gorgeous ladies happened by."

"Oh Bill, you're such a kidder," Cassie stated while checking the level of ice in the ice bucket. "Hey, since you two know each other, I'll leave you here Amy, I have a few things to do in the kitchen."

"I'll help Cass..."

"Nonsense, you're my guest. Stay here and chat with the boss-man. Maybe if you're charming enough, you'll get a raise. I'll be right back."

Cassie disappeared through the crowd. Amy looked up at Bill for a second then back into her drink. She found her straw and surveyed the room as she spoke to him.

"So, where is Mrs. Tallman tonight Bill?"

"At home with the kids. We couldn't find a sitter, and no sense in both of us being stuck at home, so she stayed and I came out."

"Wouldn't you rather stay home and spend New Year's Eve with her?"

"What fun would that be?" His eyes narrowed while he smiled and sipped his drink; glaring at her over the rim of his glass.

"Yeah, I suppose."

"And where is Mr. Hanlon this evening? Did I miss him coming in? I saw you, but you seemed to be alone."

"No, no you didn't miss him. I'm here alone. Jack had ... something to do tonight."

"You know Amy, if there's trouble at home, you can always come talk to me. I want you to count me as a friend, not just as your boss."

"Gee, Bill, that's awfully nice of you to offer, but everything at home is fine, just fine. Thank you though."

"Honestly Amy, you haven't seemed yourself lately. I suspected something was wrong on the old homestead a while ago. If you say it's fine, I believe you, but the offer stands, if you ever need to talk or need a friend to lean on, I'm here for you." He placed his hand on her wrist.

"Thank you Bill, but really, everything is fine." She gently pulled her arm away from his touch and dropped it to her side.

"Okay, if you say so. Hey can I freshen up that drink?"

"Sure, that would be great. Thank you. Vodka and Sprite please."

"You got it. Vodka and Sprite coming up."

Tallman mixed the drink, making sure to be heavy handed on the vodka; then mixed one for himself.

"Thank you Bill. You know, I think I'm going to mingle a little bit. I'll see you in a little while."

"I'll be looking forward to it." He watched her walk away, paying particular attention to her shapely legs and the way her cute, tight backside moved beneath the little black dress.

Once away, Amy breathed a sigh of relief. Bill had obviously been drinking. The little flirtations at work were harmless, but tonight he seemed wolf-like, predatory. It was a side of him she hadn't seen before, and she didn't like it.

He was an attractive man, good-looking, friendly, nice when he wasn't so obviously on the prowl. Their personalities clicked. That happens. Had she met him before she was married, she could see the two of them dating. But he was a married man, and he knew she was a married woman. He had no way of knowing that she'd recently sent her husband out the door. She knew Cassie wouldn't have told him, and the only other person who knew was her mother. Besides, what did he expect? For the two of them to just sneak away since the spouses weren't in attendance and fuck in the backseat of his car like two teenagers? Did he think that little of her? Or was he that observant? She approached the Dickensons who were engaged in a discussion with another couple she'd met, the Klazuras, and inserted herself into their conversation.

Cassie returned and Amy eventually met Cassie's husband Kevin. A sheet-metal worker by trade, Kevin Smolneki was a happy guy with thick shoulders and arms, rough hands, and a warm smile. By the time Amy had gotten to meet him, he'd consumed his share of Old Style beer and was feeling no pain.

The night wore on and Amy found herself actually having a pretty good time. She commiserated with the other mothers and laughed quite a bit as they traded poop stories, and broken bone stories, and fighting sibling stories. She talked shop with some of the folks from 'the Bullseye'. She met a woman who'd grown up in the same neighborhood as she had, though the woman was much older. They spent a lot of time talking about the places that were still there and the ones that were gone and some others Amy had never heard of because they were gone before she was born. Some of the teachers were the same. Catholic school doesn't change much over the decades and so they had had similar experiences. It was a good conversation and Amy had forgotten her troubles for at least a little while, just as her mother had said she would, when midnight rolled around.

Just as the countdown to the New Year was about to begin, she found herself standing shoulder to shoulder in the compressed group with Bill Tallman. At this point, Amy had had more than her share of Vodka-Sprites and was feeling happy and giddy and carefree.

Cassie turned the television to Channel 7, and the televised countdown at the parties in downtown Chicago were underway. The crowd at the party gathered in front of the TV and counted along with the rolling numbers on the screen... 10... 9... 8... 7...6 ...5 ...4... 3... 2... 1… and the party erupted into a collective cry of Happy New Year. Streamers flowed from little string-pop toys and noisemakers blew. Auld Lange Sine blared from the TV. Amy felt Bill's hand rest on her lower back, warm and strong. She looked up at him. He held her hand in his, for how long she didn't know, his other hand still on her back easing her to him. He peered down at her with a dazzling smile and she peered back up at him and before she knew it they were locked in a kiss.

She felt his strong arms around her, and could feel the gentle sweep of his hair on her fingers as she held the back of his head. His chest, strong and muscular, pressed against her and their hips met close and tight, pulling in towards each other. The room was ringing loud around her with celebratory cheers and laughter, but her eyes were shut tight and her mouth pressed tight against Bill's. Their tongues performed a seductive dance, warm and wet and tinged with alcohol.

As the revelry around them settled into a noisy stir, they released their kiss and stared smiling into each other's eyes. Then, as if suddenly aware of themselves and the others, they let go of each other and awkwardness set in. Still, he stood close beside her, his arm lightly brushing against hers. She excused herself and retreated to the washroom to fix her smeared lipstick.

As one o'clock approached, the crowd was thinning. Amy was sitting on a love seat sipping a cup of coffee. Bill Tallman hadn't left her side since their midnight encounter.

Bill checked is watch, "So Amy, what do you think? Time to call it a night? I'll give you a ride home. Jack won't mind will he?"

She was annoyed. "Why do you keep doing that?"

"Doing what?"

"Talking about my husband like that? Like there's something wrong with him."

"Amy, less than one hour ago, you had your tongue down my throat. Obviously, there is something wrong with

172

your husband. If you were my wife, I would never let you out of my sight."

"And where *is* your wife tonight Bill? Are you sure she's home with the kids? You sure she's not out playing tonsil-hockey with some good-looking stud?"

"Thank you for the complement. I'm a good-looking stud, huh?"

"That's not what I meant. You are conceited aren't you? For your information, there is nothing wrong with my husband, not that it's any of your business."

"So then why were you pressed so hard against me that you could feel everything you couldn't see through my jeans?"

"I don't know."

"I do; because you want me as much as I want you. Okay, so there's nothing wrong with your husband. Sometimes people are just attracted to each other. You can't change that. You can't fight it. It just is. So why don't you forget Jack for a night and let me take you somewhere we can both get what we both want. Who will know? And if no one knows, who will care? I'm very attracted to you Amy, as you might have already guessed. You had to feel that. And I know you are attracted to me, so what's there to think about? Life is short. Let's go. It'll be fun. And when you get home, nothing will have changed. I'm not looking for you to leave your husband and run away with me, but we're both adults and we both want each other, so let's forget our troubles for a little while and enjoy life. Like I said, life is short."

Amy listened to him talk and she saw him for exactly what he was. The temptation had been there. She'd given in to it long enough to have that kiss at midnight. But the temptation was gone now. He was ugly to her, and with each word he became uglier. He was slimy and untrustworthy... like a... like a... like a 'used car salesman'.

Amy got up from the love seat while Bill was still talking, went to the kitchen where Cassie was loading the dishwasher with champagne glasses, thanked her for a wonderful time, found her coat and her purse by the front door and walked out into the driving snow.

When she got home, she slipped out of her little black dress and into a flannel nightshirt, crawled beneath the covers and cried herself to sleep.

The next morning, she called her mother and asked if the boys could stay with her a few more days. Her mother said, 'of course', and Amy cuddled up beneath a warm blanket with a hot cup of tea and her wedding album. She paged through the photos of friends and family, some already passed, some she hadn't seen in years, and on the last page she came to a picture of Jack and her, cheek-to-cheek, and madly in love.

She went through every photo album in the house, crying intermittently. Then she moved on to the home videos.

The next day, Sunday, January second, she called Seth Levine's office and left a message requesting a meeting with him as soon as possible. She spent the rest of that day working around the house. She found she did her best thinking when she was busy and so she kept busy, tossing out old toys, bagging up clothes that no longer fit the boys or were too ragged for them to wear, dusting cobwebs from the ceilings, mopping the floors, polishing the woodwork, reorganizing the silverware drawers, the cabinets, the junk drawer, the DVD drawer, the nightstand drawer, then she bundled up and shoveled the snow, came back in and scrubbed the toilets, the tub and the shower. When she was finished, she was exhausted, but her mind was clear. She had worked through much of what had been bothering her, and she thought she might have come up with a plan of action moving forward. She'd have to wait until after her meeting with Seth to be sure, but she had high hopes that things were going to work out after all.

She microwaved a frozen dinner, turned on a Billy Joel CD, closed her eyes and slept until morning. It was the best sleep she'd had in weeks.

CHAPTER THIRTY

She was pale and wore a short leather skirt. Beneath a thin leather jacket, a mesh half-shirt revealed a black bra. Her hair was red and done up high, her make-up heavy around the eyes. She was young, but her face showed the age of a much older woman.

When she emerged from the room, she caught Jack's eye and smiled. It was a knowing, shameless smile. She turned and walked toward the staircase, just as she had done the night he broke his hand on the mirror.

"Hey," Jack called to her.

She turned on her heels and sauntered to him with the seductive smile of a professional. She came up to him until her breasts pressed against his chest. Her fingers played with his hair. "Was there something I can do for you cowboy?"

"There's a lot you can do for me, but twenty bucks worth will have to do."

She stuck out her lower lip in a pouty way a child does when she's told there's no more candy. "Twenty doesn't get you much. For a little bit more, you get a whole lot more." She positioned herself so that she straddled his left leg. Jack could feel the sensual warmth of her on his thigh through his jeans.

"If I had more, I'd give you more, but I have twenty. Take it or leave it."

She considered this for a moment.

"Look," he told her, "unless you have an appointment right now, which I figure you don't since you stopped and came back to me, then you're gonna go stand on the street corner in the cold and two feet of snow until some john comes by. That could be right away, that could be an hour from now. I have twenty bucks and a warm room and I'm right here. You don't have to stand around waiting for me. You come in, make a quick twenty, and go on your way with easy money you weren't expecting. Or you can go stand out in the snow in your bra and wait for some dude to come by."

"Fine," she said. "Make it quick. I'm not gonna be workin' up a sweat to get you off pal. And I want the twenty up front."

"I ain't lookin' for romance or a big production. You've got somethin' I want to rent for a few minutes, that's all. Come on in sweetheart."

The blizzard raged outside.

He led her into his room.

"What the fuck happened in here?"

Jack had refused to let the maid in, and the broken shards of mirror still lay about the floor. He'd only cut himself a couple of times in the days since he'd broken it.

"The mirror fell. I'll be contacting the concierge in the morning about that."

"That explains the purple hand you got there," she said, "should probably see a doctor about that, man."

He dropped the twenty bucks in her hand, she put it in her purse, and before she could set her purse back down, he was stripping her.

It was efficient but rough. Animalistic and raw. He mounted her and drove himself into her. He thrust like a beast, grunting and growling and scowling. Sweat poured from his forehead and dripped on her face as she made little high-pitched whinnies. With each thrust, he tried to drive deeper into her. The veins in his neck swelled. His hips thrust madly as he scowled at her. She played her part, though unconvincingly. He didn't notice. His eyes were clenched shut and his adrenaline had taken over his body. It was angry sex, forceful and rough. He took her as if she were nothing but a vessel, a depository for his dark emotions. He pushed and pushed until finally he unleashed his pent-up anger, releasing a stream of hate and frustration flowing into her. He grunted and pushed a couple of more times until he felt he'd sufficiently completed the act. Then he pulled out of her, a part of him dripping from her onto the sheets, and he dropped on the bed.

"What the fuck? Angry much? You're supposed to wear a rubber asshole. You better not be positive."

Jack was out of breath and his throat was raw. "No need to worry about that. You're the only woman I've been with other than... you know what, just get dressed and go."

"Jeez, relax. It's warm in here. Got a smoke?"

With his good hand, Jack lifted his pants from the floor beside the bed, dug his cigarettes from the pocket and tapped out one for her and another for himself. He lit them both and handed her one. She dressed as she smoked. There was still half a cigarette left dangling from her mouth when she was ready to go.

"You work here every night?"

"Not for twenty bucks I don't." And she was gone.

Jack took a deep breath and wiped sweat from his forehead. He took a satisfying drag from his cigarette and blew the smoke out in a long stream of white and blue. The immediate frustration was gone, but the rage still burned a slow and steady ember inside him. He lay naked on the bed smoking. Never in his life had he paid for sex. Never had he been unfaithful to Amy. Never had he broken his marriage vows. But that was all different now, wasn't it? Everything had changed. He lay now in a shit-bag motel, with no wife, no kids, and the thick stink of hooker perfume stuck to his pillow.

On January third, Gerald Fitzsimmons returned from lunch at the Fifth Avenue Deli to his office and the red blinking light on his phone. He had a voicemail message. Sheila was still on vacation.

He listened to the message and returned the call.

"How was your holiday Rhonda?"

"Fabulous Gerald, just fabulous."

"Where did you go?"

"Italy. We had a fantastic time. We rented a villa in Tuscany and simply ate wonderful food and drank fabulous wine for two weeks straight. I can't say enough about it."

"Ah, a vacation revolving around wine, I should have guessed."

"Not just wine, *Fabulous* wine. Eric wanted to spend the holidays in Connecticut with his children, but I needed, *needed* to get way. I love New York, but sometimes..."

"... you need Tuscany," Gerald said finishing her sentence.

"Exactly. How about you, what did you do Gerald, dear? Spend a whole two weeks with the wifey or did you have some fun as well."

"Oh, a little of both I suppose. I can't leave the children on Christmas, that just doesn't seem right, but I told Kathy that I had to fly to California on business, so I left on the 26th and flew into LAX, rented a car, picked up a friend of mine, and went to a place I rented in Newport Beach."

"Do you have any sun to show for it?"

"Not much. But it was a great time. Exactly what I needed."

"I'm sure. I'm sure your 'friend' was young and pretty too."

"Anyhow," he replied, "you asked me to call. What did you need?"

"I was talking to Riggleman, he's worried about this Hanlon shit. He thinks we might have jumped the gun in firing him and that may give him sympathy in the eyes of the court, and might also allow him to not only collect on the bonus money, but also on a wrongful termination suit."

"Riggleman's an asshole. He needs to stick to his own area of expertise; he's no lawyer. What the fuck does he know about wrongful termination suits," Fitzsimmons was livid. His smallish face turned beat red. It had been *his* idea to fire Hanlon. If they were going to claim Hanlon had broken company policy, which was the only way he could see of getting around paying the man that awful commission, Gerald had to terminate him. He'd been building this case against Hanlon for months now, and some idiot from finance was going to second guess him?

"Oh, I agree with you completely Gerald, I just wanted to let you know what Ross was thinking. This isn't going to bite us in the ass is it? I'm hearing there are more layoffs coming, and the bottom of the food chain around here has been sliced as thin as it can get, which means, they're moving up. Looking for cuts among management. If we don't win this Hanlon case or make it go away quickly and quietly, we are all going to attract attention and not the good kind."

"Relax Rhonda. Ross has you all worked up. Hanlon is not getting a payday. He's not getting a wrongful termination settlement from us. We have him backed into a corner, and we're going to win, plain and simple. The case against him is solid. Okay?"

"Okay. I just..."

"You just listened to someone who has no idea what he's talking about. No idea what we're doing over here. If you're so concerned about your job, stop listening to uninformed people and stop panicking. It is all going to work out just fine and a month from now, it will all be over. Goodbye, Rhonda." He hung up the phone before he could hear her farewell response.

Gerald Fitzsimmons thought about Jack Hanlon and cursed him. The truth was, he too was worried about the entire affair. Though he was confident they would win the case before a judge, or force Jack into backing out of the suit due to financial constraints, there were a lot of shake-ups going on at GS, just as there were in a lot of companies these days. He had only six years until he could retire with a large pension and profit sharing. If he were to lose his job now, he would get very little in the way of a departure package and that is money he would never get back; plus where would he go? He was in his late fifties and commanded a large salary. Who would hire him in this economy? He himself had let go experienced, well-compensated attorneys and replaced them with kids just out of law school who would work for a fraction of the salary of those they replaced. The other companies were doing the same, and the old-timers who held on, held on for dear life. He had to win the Hanlon case or make it go away completely. He was not going to let some small salesman knock his ass off the hill he'd worked so hard to climb. Besides, he'd refinanced the house to put on the addition, and he had two girls in college. Life is expensive. There is no room for mercy.

To take his mind off of Hanlon for a moment, Gerald Fitzsimmons leaned back in his office chair and thought about his trip to L.A. and the perky little brunette he'd taken for a tour of the General Systems/Five Star Studios movie sets and back-lots. They'd stumbled on the set of a Mark Wahlberg movie and she begged him to introduce her to the star.

Gerald Fitzsimmons was a petite man who'd never lifted anything heavier than a briefcase in his life, and whose hair was now thinning and more grey than brown, his facial features soft, pink, and unimpressive, almost feminine. An impressive title, money, and access could garner a man like Fitzsimmons a fresh, buxom cutie for the week, but not if he started shoving her in the face of movie stars with fame, money, and abs.

He ushered her from the studios under the guise that Mr. Wahlberg and his 'unbearable' director could not be bothered while on set. Though he *could* introduce them, because after all he and Mark go way back, it would be in bad taste to interrupt them at such a pivotal moment of filming - none of which was true. In truth, he would've had to ask a favor from Riggleman or one of his friends on the studio side to gain access to the star and he wasn't in the habit of asking for favors if he didn't have to.

She bought the story and went along with him, looking over her shoulder at the shirtless Mark Wahlberg going over lines with his director and the leading lady.

From there, he'd taken her to the home of a friend who'd gone on vacation to New Zealand and offered him use of the house after Fitzsimmons basically begged for the invite. There, they spent the week dining on steak and fresh seafood, fresh fruit, and drinking vats of wine. At night, they'd lie in the enormous pillowed bed and he'd run his hands over her naked body. She was half his age and well out of his league, but she had a glamorous house in Newport for the week and played her part well. To get through the dull, uncomfortable writhing of the soft-bodied, Viagradependent man who had the rhythm and coordination of a spastic epileptic having a seizure combined with the tact and charm of a fourteen year-old boy, she closed her eyes and envisioned the half-naked movie star she'd almost met, and in doing so came close enough to satisfaction as to make it believable. And that is how they spent their week. From the day after Christmas until the day before New Year's Eve when the soft pink man with the fat wallet drove her back to Los Angeles and headed off to his plane bound for New York and from there Connecticut and his wife and kids and that life as an aging man in Manhattan.

The night of January second, Jack drank a bottle of cheap wine he'd bought the night before and puffed on a cigarette from an almost empty pack. Things were getting tight. He'd extended his stay at the shit-bag motel with his credit card. Amy had yet to take him off the account. The credit card was good. It would help establish places and times as he wanted, but he was in desperate need of cash, untraceable cash for those moments when he'd need to be off the grid. His mission depended upon his having both.

A blustering wind smashed ice pellets and snowflakes against the drafty window. The snow piled up. City plows could barely keep up with the driving blizzard. Jack lay naked in bed thinking through what he was going to do. The blizzard provided a good excuse to not leave the comfort of the motel bed, which was beginning to feel less filthy and more and more like home. There he made his plans while the TV flashed ignorable crap. He flipped around some and settled on twin midgets selling real estate advise. The little people offered dreams of riches with little work and Jack went back to plotting his revenge.

After cash, the next thing he would need was a gun.

CHAPTER THIRTY-ONE

Jack stood in the blistering wind watching his former home from the bus stop at the corner. He wore his hat down low, and a scarf around his mouth and nose. His coat collar was turned up. It was Monday, January third.

He had arrived at approximately 7:00am at the bus stop a few doors down from the redbrick bungalow where lived his wife and his children. He'd been standing there for two hours when Amy stepped out of the house, locked the door, brushed the snow off the windshield of her car, shoveled it out of the parking spot where the city plows had buried it, and let the engine idle for a few minutes to get the fluids warmed up and fluid again.

Jack shook the impulse to run up and help Amy free her car from the snowed-in curbside spot and, instead, waited patiently for her to drive off.

Jack then hustled from the corner to his house, unlocked the door and let himself in.

He stood at the doorway and took a good look around. The place was at once familiar and foreign to him. Nothing in the home had changed. Every piece of furniture was exactly where it had been a week before when he'd left, the walls the same colors, the pictures hanging from those walls the same, even the smell of the place was exactly as it had been, and yet, it all looked different to him. The house hadn't changed, but he had.

He shut the door behind him, kicked the snow off his shoes, and went directly to the basement.

When Amy and Jack first moved into the home, closet space was at a premium. As a result, Jack had to store most of his belongings in boxes in the basement storage room. He soon realized that most of what he'd held onto over the years, was junk, but important junk, important to him at least: souvenirs of his life too sentimentally valuable for him to throw away, but too trivial to keep out. He hadn't opened the boxes since moving in.

Most of it was junk, yes. But the night before, laying there naked in his motel room and plotting his revenge, he remembered there were a few items in those boxes with some real value, not just nostalgia, but real cash value.

Jack dug through the remnants of his past life. One box contained his old Scout uniform and a sash displaying all the badges he'd earned on his road to Eagle. Another held his high school year books, his letterman jacket, his class ring, his wrestling singlet, and several medals he'd won at various tournaments through his high school and collegiate wrestling careers, including one from high school that read 'Second in State'. He tossed both those boxes aside.

The next box contained mementoes of his time dating Amy. Letters and cards and gifts she'd given him over the years. He resisted the urge to dig through that box, to re-read every letter, to re-live every memory hidden there and tucked away for oh so long. All those little trinkets and gifts and photographs and love notes sent from one young heart to another as they slowly got to know each other and fall in love so many years ago. To go through all of those would simply break his heart. He put that box aside as well.

The next box held what he was looking for. He sliced through the packing tape and unfolded the cardboard flaps. Therein lay the funding for his mission. He closed the box up, stuck it under his arm, and headed back towards the basement stairs. Halfway to the staircase, he stopped and went back to the box that contained the mementos of his love affair with Amy, grabbed from it a small novelty coin they'd gotten at a carnival that first year, and, for the last time, left the house he used to call home locking the door behind him.

Once on the bus, he opened his palm and looked at the coin. In the center was a shape of a four-leaf clover and around the edge, like the word 'Liberty' at the top of a quarter, pressed into the soft metal wrapping, were three simple words: AMY LOVES JACK.

Amy arrived at Seth Levine's office at a quarter to ten. She was nervous. Though they'd spoken briefly on the phone over the past year, usually simple pleasantries when he'd call for Jack and she happened to answer, this was the first time she'd been to Seth Levine's offices. She felt guilty about that. All this time, she'd let Jack fight this battle on his own. She never once offered to accompany him to Seth's office. Maybe if she had come along with him, even if just to listen, she'd understand better what he was up against and what he was going through. Maybe she could have helped. At the very least, maybe Jack wouldn't have felt so alone. Maybe he would have felt that they were fighting it together, as a team. Isn't that what they were supposed to be after all, a team? That might have been enough to keep him on solid ground.

But she didn't. She didn't ask him questions, she didn't try to understand it, she had left it all in Jack's hands, and look what had happened. She wasn't sure if she could undo all the mistakes they'd both made, but she was here now and she was ready to ask questions, to finally understand exactly what it was that had driven her husband over the edge, and to see if there were any possible way of bringing him back.

CHAPTER THIRTY-TWO

Jack sat on the unmade bed of his motel room. Around him were scattered relics from his former life. Some of these treasures came from his childhood, when he'd lived with his parents and relied upon them for everything from the basic necessities of life to a BMX bike and an Atari 2600. Those were happy times. Some of the treasures came from his young adulthood, his days in late high school and early college years, he referred to these days in his mind as the 'pre-Amy' years. There were some good times then too, but mostly, and without knowing it at the time though it seemed so clear now looking back, those were the years he was simply waiting to meet her, not knowing whom 'she' would turn out to be, but waiting for 'the one', and she turned out to be Amy. The rest were things he'd collected in the years since (the 'with-Amy' years). He rummaged through them now, seeking out things of value, things he could sell off and turn into cash.

These days, now, were the 'post-Amy' years and they were in their infancy.

He picked up an old baseball autographed by Mr. Cub, Ernie Banks. Jack held it in his right hand then shifted it to his left when his busted right hand began to throb and ache, the warmth returning to it after having been so long in the cold.

Jack was twelve years old when his father had given him that baseball. Jack and his friends had ridden their bikes down to Wrigley Field that day to catch a Cubs-Pirates game. It was 1984 and the Cubs were on fire that year, on fire for the first time since the black-cat-cursed-1969-season, and they were undoubtedly headed to the World Series for the first time in thirty-nine years. After the game, Jack and his friends stood at the chain link fence along the players' parking lot waiting for their hero, Ryne Sandberg, to emerge from the ballpark to get to his car. Jack had caught a foul ball that day and he wanted desperately for Ryno to sign it. For young Jack it wasn't a matter of financial value, of re-sale possibilities, it simply would be totally awesome to have a baseball he'd caught at Wrigley Field signed by his hero from this World Series destined team.

A hefty crowd had gathered around the fence, all looking to get an autograph from the star second baseman. Then there he was. Changed from his pinstripe uniform into a smart button down shirt and blue jeans. He walked with purpose from the bricks of the old ballpark out into the open of the parking lot. Jack jumped up and stuck his toes through the diamond shaped holes between the links of the fence so he could reach over the top. He held his ball out with one hand and held tight to the top of the fence with the other, and yelled as loudly as he could, "Mr. Sandberg! Mr. Sandberg!" he yelled. "Ryno! Ryno! Mr. Sandberg, may I have your autograph please! Mr. Sandberg... Rynoooooooooo!"

Sandberg made his way toward the fence behind which, and in some cases upon which, stood the shouting crowd. He smiled as he took a scorecard from an old lady in a Cubs floppy hat bedazzled with various Cub pins and buttons she'd acquired over the years. He scribbled his name on the scorecard and handed it back to the woman and moved down the line to the next person.

Jack waited patiently, his toes planted securely in the web of the chain link, his belly resting on the top cross pole, the top links digging into his gut, his arms stretched out, ball in hand. Sandberg handed an autographed napkin back to a kid a couple of people over from Jack. People were pushing and shouting behind him, but Jack had a great spot and knew he'd get his ball signed.

He was almost next. Two more people stood between him and his baseball hero. One scorecard, one cap, and then his. He was giddy inside, and nervous too. Ryno stepped up to the kid next to Jack, grabbed the boy's Cubs hat and looked down as he signed his name on the green cloth under the cap's bill. Jack was next, seconds away from meeting his idol.

Jack felt a hand grab the back of his collar, and before he knew what had happened, he was down from the fence and staring at the back of a pink Ralph Lauren Polo shirt, the collar turned up. A man in his early thirties, sandy hair neatly feathered and gelled, was shoving a ball out to Ryno.

"So, Ryno, are the Cubbies really going to move out to Schaumburg if they don't get lights in Wrigley? I sure hope so. Right in my backyard. I'll never miss a weekend game."

The second baseman smiled at the man, handed him back his ball and moved down the line to the next person.

Jack couldn't believe it; he'd been ripped off. Some dude actually yanked him off the fence and stole his place in line. Sandberg didn't notice because he was looking down at the cap he was signing when Jack was yanked from the fence. Ryno didn't see any of it or he would've leapt to Jack's defense; Jack was sure of it.

The man in the pink shirt turned and pushed his way through the crowd, staring at the autographed baseball in his hands. Jack glared at him. He wanted to yell. He wanted to scream and he wanted to kick that walking Jordache commercial square in his nuts. But he didn't. He did, however, manage to stick his leg out enough to make the man stumbled a little. Jack wanted him to fall flat on his face.

"Hey, watch it kid," the preppy douche-bag scolded as he brushed past the little boy he'd yanked down from the fence. Then he was gone. Jack scrambled back to his place on the fence and got up above the crowd just in time to see Sandberg slide into his car and wave as he drove away.

Jack was heartbroken. When he got home, he went directly to his room. The events of the afternoon played over and over in the twelve year old brain. Had it been another kid, hell, he wouldn't have been surprised, but a grown up? A grown-man? Jack beat on his pillow, the angry tears flooding to the surface but not falling.

The door to the bedroom opened. "Hey, you don't even say hi? What gives? How was the game?" his father asked. Jack's face was beat red, his hair a tumbled mess. His eyes watering and pink.

Jack sat on his twin-sized bed, a Cubs comforter tucked neatly beneath him, and told his Dad what had happened after the game. His father seemed to understand. "Wait here a second," his Dad told him.

When his Dad returned, he sat next to Jack and put his arm around him, then handed him a baseball. Jack looked at it. Turned it over in his hands, and there between the red stitching on the yellowing leather was the signature of Ernie Banks. Though Mr. Cub had retired before Jack was born, every young kid in Chicago knew the name Ernie Banks, even the Sox fans.

"Is this real?"

"Hell yeah it's real. I got it in 1959 when I was just a little younger than you are now. It's yours if you want it."

"Really Dad? It's mine?"

"If you want it, it's yours."

"But, it's Ernie Banks, Dad. Are you sure you wanna give it to me?"

"Of course I want to give it to you. You're my guy. What happened to you today should never happen to a kid.

That piece of shit is lucky I wasn't there with you or he'd be breathing through his ass-crack right now." Jack smiled at the thought of that. His father continued, "But, lesson learned. There are good people and bad people everywhere and you can't tell just by looking at them which they are. Hey, there'll be other ballgames and other chances to get Ryno's autograph on that ball. I don't think he's going anywhere anytime soon."

"As for the suburbanite in the pink shirt, think about it like this, you'll never have to see that guy again in your life, but for the rest of *his* life he's got to live with himself knowing he's a guy who bullies little kids and wears pink collared shirts to the ballpark. I'll bet he puts ketchup on hotdogs and gets his period once a month too. "

Jack and his Dad shared a laugh over that, and he was feeling better. He thanked his dad with a hug. Then put the special Ernie Banks ball in his underwear drawer for safekeeping. He saved up his money that summer and bought a display case to protect it and keep it from further yellowing. The Cubs never made it to the World Series that year, and Jack never did get his foul ball signed by Ryno, but he had his father's Ernie Banks ball, and there was no price he could put on that.

But that was then. Now, sitting on the rumpled bed of a filthy motel room, he wondered just how much cash he could get for that baseball with Mr. Cub's name scribbled across it.

There were other things in the box too: a watch his grandfather had given him, an old metal 7-Up sign he'd found in an alley behind a corner grocery store, a pair of gold cufflinks, a Spuds McKenzie/Bud Light aluminum beer tray, an original Ren and Stimpy lithograph, two Spiderman comic books from the 1980's, some Star Wars action figures, a yellow protest button that read "No Lights in Wrigley Field", a 1990 issue of TV Guide featuring the Simpsons on the cover, and three political buttons, one that read "Reagan for President" from his 1984 slaughter of Walter Mondale, one that read "Daley for Mayor" from the younger Daley's first mayoral election, one that read "Harold Washington for

188

Mayor" from the 1983 election that gave Chicago its first African-American Mayor, and another that read "Ditka for Mayor" from 1985.

These were the things Jack figured he could sell. The rest was just junk. He collected the things of value and walked down Lincoln Avenue to the nearest pawnshop where he sold his various treasures for a grand total of $789.35, with the vintage 7-Up sign and the comic books bringing in the most money and the Daley for Mayor button bringing in the least.

He sold his treasured Ernie Banks baseball from his father to the broker for thirty bucks.

Next Jack walked down to the local branch of the Chicago Public Library and reserved a computer. He sent out a few e-mails from his personal account, booked a hotel room in Virginia Beach, Virginia, purchased a pass to the Southeastern Medical Technology Convention, logged off his e-mail, browsed the fiction section, checked out a Travis McGee novel at the front desk, and trudged through the snow back to his motel room.

Upon returning to his room, he used his cell phone to call his house. He knew Amy wasn't there, and that was preferable. He couldn't listen to her voice. She was in the past. He had to move on. His mission now was the final thing he had to do before striking out to make a new life somewhere far away.

He left this message on the voicemail at the house:

"Amy, it's Jack. I know you probably don't want to hear from me, but I have to ask you a favor. I'm staying in a horrible place here. I need to get back on my feet. I'm no good to you or the boys or myself like this. I'm going to Virginia Beach, to a Medical Convention down there, hoping to find a job. I sent out some e-mails and hope to have some interviews or at least some meetings set up before I get there. Anyhow, what I need is for you to please keep me on the credit cards long enough for me to rent a car and a hotel room so I can get a decent job again. It seems I've burned all my bridges here. I thought maybe a change of scenery would change my luck. Anyhow, I won't stick you with the bills, no matter how this trip turns out. I'll make good on them, I promise. Anyhow, I hope you're doin' good and tell the boys hello for me and that I love them. I love you too. I don't know if I should be saying that, but I do. Okay. So if you could do me that favor... oh, and keep my cell phone paid up so I can connect with these people while I'm in Virginia. If nothing comes of it, you can cut it off then, but if something does, I'll be able to pay you back for everything. Thanks. Okay. Take care. Bye."

He didn't think Amy hated him so much as to ignore that and purposely cut him off the credit accounts. Besides, it was in her best interest financially for him to get a good job so he could pay her alimony and child support. She could never raise three boys and pay the mortgage and all the bills on what she made as a cashier. He needed a good job and she needed him to get a good job. That should be enough to keep the credit lines open. He turned off his cell phone. If she called back to tell him to go to hell, he didn't want to hear it.

He lay back in the bed, grabbed his book, 'The Green Ripper', and began to read. He fell asleep with the book on his chest, a cigarette burning in the ashtray, and the sounds of hooker-sex pounding against the wall from the room next door.

Amy returned home from her meeting with Seth feeling optimistic and hopeful. She understood now why Jack was so upset about the whole sordid thing. Why he felt so betrayed. She didn't excuse his behavior, but she admitted she could've handled it better. It wasn't too late, though. She understood now. She was informed now. She knew what was going on and what she had to do to make it right.

Seth told her the trial date had been set, gave her the rundown of what they had against General Systems, briefed her on some of the past cases they've had filed against them for similar actions and some for harassment, both sexual and non-sexual leveled at some of the key players in the decision to cut Jack out of his earnings.

His investigator had found plenty of dirt on several of the GS executives. He had that in his back pocket if he needed it. Just like with Bugiardo, it's funny how things can go away when certain things may be revealed during the course of the trial that would be of particular interest to the spouse. The fight in them tends to subside and they see dollar signs flying out of their wallets and realize that maybe they had been mistaken after all.

On top of that, like every other major corporation in America, General Systems was in desperate need to cut expenses. The loan arm of the corporation had over-extended itself on bad loans. It had bet on the subprime housing market and had gotten caught with its pants around its ankles. It had a ton of bad debt on the books. Problem was, it affected the whole corporation, not just the loan arm. They needed to stop bleeding cash. As a result, the usual cuts at the bottom weren't enough. They'd have to consolidate at the executive level. Suddenly a lot of very secure wealthy people were no longer very secure and they wanted to remain wealthy. No one was going to fall on any swords for anyone. And so, to appease the board of directors, and to save their own asses, the top executives of the corporation sent their minions away from the factories and the sales departments and toward the managerial suites to see where the fat could be cut there. This had everyone worried, but no one more than Ross Riggleman.

Riggleman was no dummy. He had his finger firmly on the pulse of General Systems. He knew which way the wind was blowing. He also knew that drawn out lawsuits by former employees, especially ones with a decent wrongful termination suit, was not going to be looked upon favorably from above. Maybe a few years ago, they would've agreed with Fitzsimmons, but times had changed. Politics had changed. The very business of business had changed. It was a matter of time before the papers picked up on this case, and after having been raked through the coals by the likes of CNN for having received substantial Federal tax breaks to the point that they actually paid $0 in taxes for the previous year while also garnering government contracts, laying off a record number of employees, shipping jobs overseas, and still bringing in profits in the billions of dollars, General Systems could not afford any more bad press. Especially since it was very possible that they would have to rely on the Federal Reserve to bail them out of all these bad loans. A bailout which would be paid for by the taxpayers of the United States, among which, through clever accounting, General Systems was not. What General Systems needed most of all was to keep its nose clean and its name out of the papers.

Having seen the writing on the wall, Riggleman had placed a call to Seth Levine just after Christmas. "What's happening to your client is wrong. This is off the record of course. I've said from the beginning that we should pay him what the contract says he is owed. Contracts are the glue that holds this economy together, if we can't rely on a signed contract, what do we have? But there are others who disagree with me. I will do everything in my power to convince the others that we should pay Jack what he's owed and simply forget the whole thing, but I want something in exchange."

"And what is that," Seth replied.

"I want you to keep me out of this as much as possible. If you go to court and lose, when you appeal, I want it on record that I said all along that Jack should be paid what he's owed, and that you and I had tried diligently to hash out a mutually beneficial agreement, but were stymied by the efforts of Fitzsimmons and others. Unless of course, I tell you otherwise. The wind changes here often."

"So you're covering your ass with both hands. What do I get if you aren't able to convince your colleagues that doing the right thing is the right thing to do?"

"E-mails."

"E-mails?"

"E-mails. E-mails of internal correspondences between all those involved. Trust me, with those, you'll win your case hands down."

"Won't that be traced directly back at you?"

"No. There are at least three other people who work for me who could have access to those if I play it right, which I have."

"Those won't be admissible in court if they were obtained illegally, even if someone at GS handed them to me."

"Well, considering they're e-mails concerning your client, it wouldn't be out of the ordinary for someone to 'accidentally' forward said e-mails to Jack Hanlon having seen his name in the subject line."

"Okay, you have yourself a deal. I'll be looking for those e-mails to come through in the next twenty-four hours. If I don't get them, the deal's off and this entire conversation is fair game."

"I'll send them myself from another computer tonight. You'll have them when you come in in the morning."

They were turning against each other, mutiny in the ranks; the first signs of an army about to lose the war.

Levine called Amy and relayed the gist of the conversation he'd had with Riggleman. She hoped that if Jack could see the system beginning to work in his favor, it might be enough to bring him back to the point that they could start repairing their broken marriage.

For the first time in a very long time, she smiled as she opened the door to the little brick bungalow on Mobile Street. As she closed the door behind her, she caught the tail end of Jack leaving a message on their digital machine. She raced to the phone, but didn't catch it in time. She dialed his cell number, but immediately got his voicemail. He'd shut it off. She listened to the message he'd left, and tried calling him again. She left a lengthy message begging him to come home and meet her. There was a lot to talk about and most of it was great news. She sat by the phone awaiting his call, but it never came. She gave up and went to bed just after one in the morning, with the phone cradled close to her breast.

CHAPTER THIRTY-THREE

Little black faces peered out of old windows from drafty apartments. Jack walked in the streets to avoid trudging through the snow on the neglected sidewalks. He had stepped off the 'L' at the 63rd Street station and stepped into Englewood, a notorious neighborhood that often made the national news for its gun violence. "What better place to buy a gun," Jack thought.

On the surface, Englewood didn't look much different from his own neighborhood on the northwest side of the city. The houses were all in the same styles, brick bungalows of red or yellow, small frame houses, narrow redbrick two-flats and, on the corners, four-flats. The only difference was, here everything was broken. From the windows on the houses to the bottles in the streets to the porch pickets and the chain link fences, everything was broken. Windows broken. Front doors broken. Snow-covered toys on the porches, frozen and broken. The rows of houses were interrupted here and there with vacant lots making the whole block look like a busted smile.

The older residents remembered how the neighborhood used to be and longed for those days when violence didn't ring out so readily. There were those who wanted out of the neighborhood, to raise their families in a part of the city where teenage funerals weren't so common. And then there were those who had figured out how to make the neighborhood work for them. They were the people who learned how to mine gold from the broken streets. They ran the corners and the vacant lots and the schoolyards and the parks. They had garnered power and fortune not through election but through cunning and survival. They were mostly young; the mortality rate in their occupation was extremely high. They were the people most in the neighborhood tried to avoid; yet they were the people Jack had come to see.

He had $780.00 tucked under his foot in his boot, and the remaining nine dollars and thirty-five cents in his pocket.

He passed a young man about nineteen years old walking alone in the opposite direction as Jack. The man's hands were in his pockets and he buried himself deep into his puffy winter coat, like a turtle barely peeking from his shell. They made eye contact but did not acknowledge each other. His eyes were dark in the middle and yellow where they should have been white. There was something missing there in those dark eyes, a blankness where hope should live. The young man looked into Jack's eyes and saw the same.

Even the eyes of the children that he'd see looking through the glass held a skeptical gaze beneath which laid anxiousness, restlessness, and rage. Indoors, they looked no warmer than he was out there in the snow and cold.

Jack shared something with those restless, anxious eyes. He was one lost soul powerless against a brutal machine of money and influence. He heard the same voice, the voice that rang out in his heart and in his head that said, "you can not win at their game, it's rigged. The dice are weighted and the cards are marked. There is only one way to beat them. There is only one way to even the score. There is only one way to get what you have coming to you, and that one way is through blood."

That high-voltage voice hummed through Jack's mind. "The world is a brutal place, but *they* made the rules. Not me, *them*. *They* set the game up to be every man for himself, then *they* tilted the rules in *their* favor. But that doesn't have to be the last word. That doesn't have to be all there is. I'm not layin' down to be somebody's beaten mutt! And that's what we are to them, all of us, white, black it doesn't matter. If you aren't in the executive suite, if you don't have the law degree from the right school, if you don't make it high enough on the food chain, you're just a dirty dog. A tool. A cog in the wheel. They'd pay us nothing if they could get away with it. We are simply their property, 'the help', working the trenches to fatten their stock portfolios. They've figured out how to make slaves of us all by giving us just enough to think we are free. Just enough of the good life to make us so terrified of losing it, that we sell our souls to them."

"They're no different than the kingpins who run the street-corners here in Englewood, only on a much larger scale. These men, they run Wall Street, and Main Street, and Pennsylvania Avenue. They run the companies that hold our money, that get rich off of our work, that set the prices for our food and our clothes, and then they use that money, our money, to buy our politicians and our judges to use against us. And then they make us piss in a bottle and test it for drugs with no probable cause. Even the police can't do that, but Corporate America can. They make the man who mops the floor piss in a bottle, but they run the whole fucking company fueled by cocaine and greed and no one is checking their piss. The guy mopping the floor can be high as a kite and still get the floor mopped, but the guy making all the decisions needs to have his head on straight, yet the mopper gets checked and the bossman doesn't. Why? Because they own the plantation, and we're all of us, just workin' their fields. Well fuck them. I'd rather be a mad dog snarling and foaming at the mouth than a cowering beaten mutt. If I can't beat them at *their* game, I'll beat them at *my* game. But one way or another I will win. They will pay. They will learn what it means to lose. The world *is* a brutal place; that's what they came up with, those were their rules. It's time to teach them how brutal it can be. It's time Chicago justice hit the quiet rural roads of upstate New York and Connecticut."

Jack walked as far East as Parnell when he finally stumbled across what he was looking for. A group of four men stood in front of the charred remains of what had once been an apartment building. Kitty-corner to that was a brick four-flat with a black Escalade parked in front of it and three other men standing near the side door of the building.

A string of cars were lined up along the curb in front of the charred building like they were waiting in line at the McDonald's Drive-Thru. Jack was no longer the solitary white man on the block. White people occupied every one of those cars, Toyotas and Nissans and Hondas, sedans and mini-vans. Not one of the cars had a Chicago City sticker in the window. They'd come from the suburbs, from Hinsdale and Elmhurst and Naperville. From Tinley Park and Mokena and Oak Brook. There were Businessmen in Brooks

Brothers suits and soccer moms in Gucci shades. Twenty-something's sporting Fuel jeans and Marmot jackets.

One of the four men working the corner would lean toward the driver's window. He'd listen for a second then make a hand gesture to signal one of the three men across the street in front of the other building. One of those men would then disappear into the side door, be gone for a minute or two, and emerge from the building with his hands in his pockets. He'd walk casually over to the car, pull a small baggie from his pocket, collect cash from the driver, hand him the baggie and walk back over to where he'd been standing before. This went on and on, car after car, from afternoon until the small hours of the morning.

Jack was on foot. He approached the four men in front of the charred building. He stood close enough to be heard, but out of arm's reach.

One of the men nodded his way. "Whatcha need playa?"

"I need a gun. Something small and clean that I can throw away."

The man signaled something toward the corner building. Waited. Got a return signal and turned back to Jack. "Gonna cost ya a nickel."

"Does that include the ammo?"

"Nah, that extra. Now we talkin' closer to six. Say, five eighty. Clean ammo, clean piece. Twenty-two or three eighty, your choice."

"When can I get it?"

"Now if ya got the Benjamins."

Jack wasn't about to pull seven hundred dollars from his boot like he was buying a pack of gum. This was their turf. They made the rules here. He decided neutral ground would be better.

"I didn't bring the money with me. I need to get it. There's a Dollar Store on 63rd next to the Currency Exchange. I'll meet ya in the parking lot. My guys'll be watchin'," Jack lied, "Ya know, to ensure customer satisfaction if ya catch my drift."

The dealer laughed. "Yeah, okay Dude. I feel ya. You bring the money and don't fuck with us, everything'll run smooth. That location ain't gonna work. There a Blockbuster two blocks up, be there in ten."

"Bring the twenty-two. That's what I want."

Ten minutes later, Jack was standing in the parking lot of the Blockbuster Video on 63rd Street. He was alone. If the deal went sour, there was no recourse.

He'd gone into the bathroom stall of a Burger King and removed the small roll of money from his boot. He counted out five hundred eighty and put the remaining two hundred back in his boot. He curled his left fist around the bills and plunged that fist in his jacket pocket where it stayed until the Escalade he'd seen on Parnell pull into the lot.

Chances were, he was either going to walk away from this about six hundred dollars lighter but with a gun in his pocket, or he wasn't going to walk away from it at all. The window of the Caddy slid down and Jack approached with trepidation, the roll of money clenched tight in his fist.

CHAPTER THIRTY-FOUR

Amy was getting worried. She'd been trying Jack's cell phone all day, and each time it had gone directly to voicemail. She hoped he hadn't yet left for Virginia.

She paced the floor searching for a way to track him down. She played his message again, the one he was leaving just as she'd walked in the door.

Jack's digital voice sounded hollow. *"Anyhow, what I need is for you to please keep me on the credit cards long enough for me to rent a car and a hotel room so I can get a decent job again. It seems I've burned all my bridges here..."*

Amy dug her card from her wallet and called the number on the back. She listened to the computer announce her options. She pressed zero for an operator. She waited impatiently on hold for someone to come on the line. They were all busy assisting other customers. Her foot tapped.

She chewed her nails. She paced the floor. She wanted to run, to just bolt out the door and run as fast as she could. Run to Jack and bring him back home. But before she could do that, she needed to find out where to run, so she waited listening to insufferable versions of some of her least favorite songs, interrupted every thirty seconds by the voice telling her to 'remain on the line, all customer service representatives were busy assisting other customers'. She heard that message so often she wanted to scream.

Jack arrived back at his motel room and packed his belongings. The small caliber pistol was zipped up in the pocket of his winter coat, the ammunition he stuffed in his duffle bag. The remainder of his cash was still hidden safely in his boot. The transaction on 63rd street had transpired without a hitch.

The man in the Escalade had taken Jack's money, and then directed him to a black Impala five cars over.

"Check the top of the rear passenger-side tire," Jack was told. He did, and resting there on the tire was the .22. The serial numbers on the gun had been filed off. There was now no way to identify where it had come from or to whom it once belonged. Jack slid it into is pocket and headed toward the 'L' bound for the north side.

He checked out of the motel. He had thought about keeping the room, how it would look if anyone were to investigate. He thought about the message he'd left Amy. He was going to "see if he could start a new life in Virginia", he'd told her. Keeping the motel room in Chicago would seem contrary to that story. Also, he didn't know what was going to happen if he went through with his plan. He may not be able to return right away. Having a motel room lay vacant for too long would raise a red flag. He decided it was best to check out. If he did return from Virginia, he could always rent another room then.

He asked the man at the front desk if there were any rental car places in the area. The man was a foreigner. Jack didn't know from which country exactly. Jack guessed he was from somewhere in the Middle East. He had a blue tooth in his ear and was speaking rapidly in Arabic, or something like it. Without stopping his conversation and with no acknowledgement he'd heard Jack's question, he slid a brochure across the counter to him.

According to the brochure, there was a General Rent-a-Car lot two miles west on Foster. "How poetic," Jack thought, "General Rent-a-Car, subsidiary of General Systems, Inc." He headed out the door toward Foster Avenue. Took a right on Foster, and started walking west.

The blizzard had finally stopped and the arterial roads were clear. Amy raced eastbound on Foster Avenue toward Lincoln Avenue and the Tisiphone Motel, one of the last vestiges of Motel Row, and one of the most unsavory. She couldn't believe that's where Jack had spent the remainder of the Holidays and she hated herself for it.

She caught every red light it seemed, and she cursed at the busses to get out of her way. She weaved around slower traffic, narrowly missed pedestrians, and angered more than a few other drivers when she cut them off.

She was so determined to get to her destination, she didn't notice the man walking along the sidewalk westbound on Foster, his hands stuffed deep into his pockets, his head held low, a duffle bag slung over his shoulder, and wearing the winter coat she'd bought him for Christmas the year before.

CHAPTER THIRTY-FIVE

Mrs. Kelly lay in bed with a fever. The sneezing and coughing started late Sunday afternoon after she'd returned from her hunting expedition. By Monday morning, the cold had taken full hold of her. Then the chills began. She couldn't get warm enough. She bundled herself under blankets and quilts to stop the shivering. Her throat was raw from coughing and her nose ran like a faucet. She ate very little.

Her bones ached. Her head pounded. She buried herself beneath the blankets, only to kick them off as her weary body alternated between icy shivers and burning sweats.

She slept a lot.

When she slept, she dreamt. Her dreams focused mainly on the thief, although sometimes Harold would make a cameo, and she'd cry out for him. She'd cry out in shame for letting him down. She'd reach out for him, but he was always just out of arm's reach. Each time he appeared, Harold wore a look of disapproval. She interpreted this as meaning she had indeed let him down by allowing herself to be swindled out of their money. In her dreams, Harold would shake his head, turn his back to her, and fade away.

Jack rented a midsize sedan, nothing flashy, paid for it with his credit card. Told the man at the counter that he'd be driving it to Virginia and may return it back here in Chicago, or if things were to go well down there, would return the vehicle to a General Rent-a-Car location in Virginia. He got in, set the GPS for Virginia Beach, plugged his dead cell phone into the car charger, ignored the no-smoking sign, lit up, and drove off.

He paid the toll at the Chicago Skyway, and again in Indiana, and again at the Ohio Turnpike. By the time he reached Toledo, it was well past dark. He found a Super 8 just off the Turnpike, checked into a room, took a hot shower, and slid naked between the sheets. He read four pages of The Green Ripper before the slow blinks took over and he drifted off into a deep and dreamless sleep. His now fully charged cell lay in the cup holder of the sedan, still off from having died earlier. With no one to call, and expecting no calls, Jack had forgotten all about it.

Amy arrived at the Tisiphone Motel not ten minutes after Jack had checked out. The clerk was still rattling on in his native tongue when Amy rushed through the doors and asked him for the room number of Jack Hanlon. The man rambled on ignoring the crazed, hectic woman. As he turned away from her, he exposed the ear with the blue tooth in it. She reached out, grabbed the device from his ear, took two big steps back from the counter and held the earpiece above her head.

"What the fuck lady," he demanded.

"Oh, you do speak English. Good. Direct me to the room of Jack Hanlon and you get your phone call back."

"Bitch, give me my blue tooth," his accent was thick, but his English was good. "I cannot give out the information of our guests."

"Oh, because you're a stickler for the rules around here? I saw three hookers in the thirty seconds I was in your parking lot. Tell me the room number or I crush your ear piece under my boot."

"Okay, okay. He's not here anyway. Checked out a little while ago."

"How long ago."

"I don't know, ten maybe fifteen minutes."

"Which direction did he go?"

"He was going to a car rental place just west of here on Foster."

She tossed the blue tooth back to him and darted to the door.

He replaced it in his ear and proceeded to call her all sorts of profane names in his native tongue to the person on the other end.

To say Ross Riggleman had his finger on the pulse of General Systems was an understatement. Less than one week after his phone call to Jack Hanlon's attorney, Levine, there was a new CEO in place, and the shit was rolling both down hill and up.

In the months since Jack Hanlon had filed his lawsuit against the company, three more suits were filed by both existing and former employees; all three were within the Medical Devices Division.

One was filed by a young woman who worked in the Tampa office accusing her manager of sexual harassment and the claim went on to state that when brought to the attention of Human Resources and Legal Affairs, neither department took her matter seriously. The manager was still employed by General Systems and her requests for transfer were ignored. As a result, she not only still had to work for the bastard, she'd been retaliated against for having spoken up for herself.

The other was filed by a researcher claiming General Systems had stolen his copy-written material, created a full year before his employment at GS, and passed it off as their own and profited from it.

The third was from another salesman, this one from Philadelphia, who claimed that the company had shorted him twenty-five thousand dollars in commissions.

Complaints were streaming in from other departments as well. Unions were coming after the company for breaking collective bargaining agreements, vendors were suing for late payment and non-payment, and customers were suing over deceptive business practices and broken contracts.

Each one of these complaints could, one way or another, be traced back directly to Gerald Fitzsimmons' office. Riggleman was smart to remove himself from Gerald as much as he could, and took opposing positions wherever possible.

Beyond all of this, General Systems was in much bigger trouble than anyone imagined. The problems in the loan arm of the corporation were coming to a rapid boil, with the lid rattling off the pot.

As one of the world's largest corporations, many other businesses worldwide depended on the financial health of GS. Since every facet of GS was posting record profits, no one seemed worried. But there was that one division that was flying under the radar and it was becoming more and more difficult to keep it a secret. As major banks and investment firms were either collapsing or being rescued by the U.S. Government, nervous investors and Wall Street insiders were starting to wonder publicly about the economic stability of General Systems Finance division.

Buy a GS appliance, GS would loan you the money, with interest of course. Need a car, GS would give you a loan. But that's not all GS Finance was into. They also took heavy risks in the subprime mortgage market and all its derivatives. They were heavily exposed to bad loans on top of bad loans on top of bad loans. They'd been able to keep that information internal, but it was only a matter of time before stockholders and Wall Street in general found out. And when that happened, the health of the other departments of GS would not be enough to keep the company's shares from plummeting amid fears that GS might turn out to be the next Lehman Brothers.

Everyone at GS was nervous. There were going to be some major changes occurring. It wasn't a matter of if, but when, the shit would hit the fan. Shakeups were in the wind and Riggleman was determined to ride out the storm.

A new CEO often meant new blood at the top. Sometimes this would take some time as the new leader settled in and got his bearings. But this was a time of crisis, and there was no time for settling in. The new man was brought in to right the ship. A new crew would be in order.

Riggleman knew though, that good men were hard to come by, and experience matters. It helps the new captain to keep some of the people who are familiar with the ship aboard it, especially if they are clearly not involved in what has set the old girl leaning in the first place. Getting himself away from the Hanlon case and the other lawsuits was absolutely necessary for survival.

He sent out an e-mail that morning urging Fitzsimmons to settle the suits that would ultimately cost GS the most in terms of bad publicity and large pay-outs if they were to lose in court. At the top of that list were the sexual harassment claim and the Hanlon case. "Reaching a mutually beneficial resolution while successfully getting the complainants to sign a non-disclosure agreement would be the best possible route at this juncture," he wrote, "to do otherwise would expose the company to serious expenditures to the aggrieved parties, create uncertainty and fear among shareholders, as well as giving the media the ability to paint the company in a bad light at a time when such bad press

204

could really do damage, not only to our corporate public image, but to our price per share as well."

Before sending his mail flying out into the stratosphere to be bounced back down to Fitzsimmons' computer in New York, he copied Lloyd Sheldon, Rhonda Royce, Carrie Miller, Bruce Chung, and Brad Tennenbaum, the President of General Systems Medical Device division.

Fitzsimmons kept Tennenbaum in the dark on virtually everything. To include him on this dispatch would be tantamount to setting off a stick of dynamite in the lap of your comrade. The lines of war had clearly been drawn and Riggleman had fired the first shot.

CHAPTER THIRTY-SIX

Amy had no choice but to go home. She'd missed Jack at the motel by ten minutes, and at the rental car place by just a few. She'd tried driving around in hopes of finding him, but the streets were too crowded and she had no idea which route he'd taken. After half an hour, she'd given up. Every attempt to reach his cell phone connected directly to his voicemail.

She picked the kids up from her mother's, and drove them home in silence. Children can sense when something is wrong despite the best efforts to conceal it from them.

Once inside, they did just as they were told and went straight upstairs, brushed teeth, washed faces, and got into bed.

Amy tucked each of them in and kissed them goodnight. As she reached the door and was about to turn off the light, Sean's voice broke the silence. "Mommy?"

"Yes Sean?"

"Are you and Daddy getting a divorce?"

"Seany!" Trevor scolded, though he was desperate to hear her answer too.

Amy walked back into the room and sat on Sean's bed and held his hand.

"Well, I won't lie to you. Daddy and I have been having some trouble lately. But, we're trying to fix it. I made some mistakes, he made some mistakes, and, well it's kind of complicated grown-up stuff, but I'm working on putting things back together, okay? I can't promise anything right now other than I'm... we're working on it. But I can tell you this, no matter what happens between me and your father, I will always love you and *he* will always love you. I'll always be Mommy and he'll always be Daddy, and you three will always be the most important things in our lives. Okay? And none of this is your fault. It is all my fault and your Daddy's fault and it has nothing to do with any of you. You're great boys and I couldn't be prouder of you and I know your Dad feels the same."

Sean broke down into tears. Timmy did too. Trevor wiped his tears away quietly.

"I don't want you to get a divorce Mommy!" Timmy cried out.

"Oh honey," Amy moved to his bed, "I don't want to get a divorce either. And I don't think Daddy does. We just have to talk some things out, okay?" She hugged him close. The other boys ran over to her and the four of them sat there in a huddled hug, weeping, each of them afraid and confused and unsure of what the future held.

Mrs. Kelly's cough had worsened. She began coughing up green globs of mucus. She couldn't catch her breath. She called to ask Amy if she could run to the drug store for her and pick up some cough syrup. She couldn't get through the sentence without stopping to catch her breath or breaking into a coughing fit. Amy was alarmed by the sound of the old woman's barking cough. Her long day was about to get longer.

The doorbell rang moments after Mrs. Kelly had hung up the phone with Amy. Mrs. Kelly shuffled to the door and let Amy in. It looked as if the pretty young neighbor had been crying. "Guess I'm not the only one with problems," the old woman thought.

"Mrs. Kelly, you sound horrible," Amy stated.

"I feel worse," Mrs. Kelly replied.

"I brought you some cough syrup we had in the house, but you really should go to the doctor. I can take you over to Our Lady's now."

"I appreciate that, but no."

"Mrs. Kelly, you need go to the hospital. The boys are asleep and Trevor is fine babysitting if his brothers need anything. It really is no trouble for me to take you there. I'd sleep better tonight myself if we got you checked out right away."

Mrs. Kelly thought about it. She needed to be better by Saturday so she could get to 5:30 Mass at St. Hubert's. There was no time to be sick, she had a crook to catch. If she were to go to the doctor now, she'd get some antibiotics and be back on her feet by the weekend.

"Okay Amy," she said, "you win. If it'll make you feel better, you can take me to the doctor."

"Thank you Mrs. Kelly. I think we'll both feel better. Why don't you put something warm on while I run home and grab my keys and phone and tell Trevor I'm leaving. I'll warm up the car and come back for you in a few minutes, okay?"

"Okay Amy."

In the night traffic, it only took ten minutes to get to Our Lady of Victory Hospital. The quiet of the still, frigid night was broken when Amy and Mrs. Kelly stepped through the sliding doors into the ER. The brightness hurt their eyes and the room was bustling. Germ-ridden people coughing up various forms of mucus and fluid occupied almost every seat. Babies were wailing and an old man moaned in pain. A little boy held his arm and sobbed as his father tried to soothe him. A middle-aged woman with reddened eyes tried to console her elderly mother.

Amy was afraid to touch anything for fear of catching some awful bug that would bring her straight back to this place in a few days, joining the ranks of the ill.

"There's an empty chair there against the wall Mrs. Kelly, why don't you go sit down and rest," Amy told her, content to stand, arms folded, breathing shallow breaths through her nose as if that strategy might protect her from the germs.

Mrs. Kelly took her seat among the other sick and broken people. 'If there's a hell,' Amy thought, 'this must be what it looks like.'

For the next two hours, Amy watched as people came and went through the doors of the Emergency Room at Our Lady of Victory Hospital. Each time someone came through the doors, either aided by a relative, or wheeled on a stretcher by paramedics, she was struck by the fragility of the human body and life itself. "We are, any of us, just one car accident, one super-bug, one nasty fall away from disaster," she thought. "None of these people woke up this morning thinking they'd be ending their day like this, and yet, here they are: fractured bones, bruised organs, bloody wounds, labored breathing, constant vomiting, failing hearts - all sudden. One second everything is fine, the next you're calling an ambulance, or racing to the hospital in the car; the day has turned to shit in an instant, the adrenaline is flowing, the heart is racing, worry envelopes you. The race is on, the race against time and the reaper. The goal: to cheat death. The sooner the ailing or injured get to the fix-it shop, the better the chances they'll still be with us tomorrow." She thought of her boys, safe at home, for now at least, but what will tomorrow bring? Fear and worry of the mother set in. "It is all so sudden. It's all so fragile. We take so much of it for granted."

"Irene Kelly," the station nurse called.

Amy helped Mrs. Kelly out of the chair and walked with her to the nurse's desk.

"Are you a relative?" the nurse asked Amy.

"No, I'm a neighbor."

"You'll have to wait here then," the nurse told her.

Mrs. Kelly shuffled toward the open door leading to the examination rooms. Amy watched her go. The woman who had always been so vibrant, so energetic and so full of life now looked so frail, so old. Spring didn't seem all that long ago, and yet, look how much had changed since then. "It's all so fragile," she thought again, "so very fragile."

208

CHAPTER THIRTY-SEVEN

Virginia Beach was about an eleven-hour drive from Toledo. Twelve if you included bathroom stops and a lunch break. Jack was on the road by four o'clock Tuesday morning. He wanted to be in Virginia Beach before the used car lots closed.

He gassed up in Toledo and stopped for something to eat in Pennsylvania. While he was eating in a Waffle House just off the interstate, his cell phone rang. He'd left the phone in his car and missed the call.

He gassed up again in Maryland, and stopped one more time in Richmond for some coffee and a snack. Each time he stopped, he used his credit card. In Richmond, he also hit an ATM, checked the balance in his joint checking account, and withdrew $300.00. That left Amy with enough for groceries and essentials. Maybe a couple of utility bills would have to be paid late.

Once he was headed south, he'd driven well over the speed limit with no fear of being pulled over. In fact, a speeding ticket would actually be a good thing for establishing time and place. The further south he was, the better it would be. He eventually started trying to get pulled over, but as luck would have it, when you want a speeding ticket, there's not a cop in sight.

When he arrived in Virginia Beach, it was just after 3:30pm.

On the plus side, there was plenty of time to cruise around and case the town for a used car lot that met his needs. He found the seediest looking one, the one that most resembled Bugiardo's joint back home. It was about three miles from his hotel. He went back to the hotel, checked in, and went for a three-mile walk.

"Mommy... Mom... Mom, wake up," Trevor gave his mother's shoulder a delicate shake.

Amy opened one slow, sleepy eye. "What is it Trevor?" she croaked.

"Mom, did you forget, we have school today?"

"You what?" Amy fought to shake the fog of sleep.

"We have school today, it's Tuesday. Christmas break is over."

Amy sprung upright in her bed. "You have school today?"

"Yes Mom. We got out the Tuesday before Christmas and now it's been two weeks and we have to go back. Break is over."

Trevor was dressed in the Blackhawks sweater Grandma Rosemary had bought him for Christmas.

Amy grabbed the clock from the nightstand. "Oh my God, you have school today! Tell your brothers to get dressed; I'll go make breakfast. Hurry up or you're gonna be late!" Amy bolted from the bed and grabbed her robe from the door hook.

"Mom..."

"Not now honey, just get your brothers up, I have to make breakfast and lunches and..."

"Mom, that's what I'm trying to tell you, the boys are up and they're dressed. I already told them to. I got them Apple Jacks for breakfast, and made them take their vitamins. We're ready to go. Ham sandwiches in our bags for lunch, I made them myself, it's easy. They're getting their snowsuits on now."

Amy soaked up the moment. She was frazzled and still in a sleepy shock. She looked at her eldest son and smiled.

"I just wanted to say good-bye so you weren't wondering where we were."

"Come here." She wrapped her arms around him, pulled him close to her and squeezed. She kissed his head and cradled his face in her hands. "You're getting so tall. When did you grow up, huh? It was just yesterday you were my little boy, and now, you're ... I'm so proud of you. Thank you for doing this today."

The boy pulled away from her, as any boy his age would. "No problem, Mom. I know you were late at the hospital with Mrs. Kelly. I figured I'd let you sleep."

210

That was true. Amy hadn't gotten home from the hospital until close to one in the morning. She'd been so wrapped up in herself and Jack that she'd completely forgotten that school was starting back up. She felt guilty.

She kissed the boys good-bye and watched as they trudged off to school, bundled up from head to toe, through the snow and the cold. Children are resilient. They bounce. They can weather the storm so long as they know that they are not alone and that one day, the sun will shine again.

Amy wiped a lone tear from her eye, and hurried to the phone to dial Jack's cell again.

When Irene Kelly awoke, a nurse was hanging a bag of clear liquid on a tall stand next to her bed.

"Hello Mrs. Kelly, how are you feeling?"

"I'm in the hospital. I ain't feelin' real hot, sweetie," Mrs. Kelly replied then went into a coughing fit.

"The doctor has you on some strong antibiotics and a saline drip to help rehydrate you. It's a good thing you came in last night, you're very sick."

"If you know that, why the hell did you ask me how I was feeling?"

"Now just take it easy. I wanted to know if there'd been any improvement over last night."

"I'm still very congested. And I'm very tired. When can I get out of here?"

The nurse chuckled. "You're very congested and very tired, and you want to know when you can get out of here? I understand hospitals aren't the nicest places to be in, but you have an upper respiratory infection and walking pneumonia. The doctor is also concerned about your heart. He's ordered some tests for later this afternoon."

"There's nothing wrong with my heart. Let him run his tests if he wants. Just keep the antibiotics flowin', I gotta be outta here by Saturday afternoon."

"Mrs. Kelly, I don't think that's possible."

"We'll see sweetie. You'll be surprised how quick an old broad can heal when she puts her mind to it."

211

Gerald Fitzsimmons paced back and forth in his office, his face red with anger, trying to get his emotions under control and return to rational thought. "How dare that motherfucker send out an e-mail like that to everyone?" he barked aloud to himself. "If that's the game he wants to play, fine. I can outplay him any day. He has no fucking idea who he's fooling with!"

Gerald had been in a pretty good mood when he arrived at the office that Tuesday morning. The shake-ups at GS weren't all bad. The great thing about new blood is they are easily manipulated because they have no history. They're like blank slates. They've never had opposing opinions, they've never been let down by a mistake you've made, they've never seen you at your best, but they've never seen you at your worst either, and so you can reinvent yourself for the new men to fit what they're looking for in a V.P.

But here comes this fucking Riggleman, the same goddamn day the new CEO takes over, sending out this fucking e-mail. Everything he said was in direct contrast to what they'd discussed over the phone. Of course, the whole idea of discussing matters over the phone was to eliminate those pesky e-mail trails that could one day come back to haunt you. But damn if Gerald didn't wish he'd had an e-mail trail now. Sure, it might hang him, but Riggleman would hang with him. Instead, the bastard was coming out smelling like roses with Fitzsimmons as the manure.

"And now, all these kiss-ass, spineless morons were stepping into line with Riggleman. It's funny how morons are morons until it comes to saving their own ass, then all of a sudden they're geniuses. Conniving little cocksuckers, that's all they are." Fitzsimmons said, speaking aloud again to the empty room.

Gerald put out a demand for a phone conference to all parties involved for ten o'clock eastern time. If that meant Riggleman in L.A. couldn't have his morning fuck. Well too damn bad!

Gerald Fitzsimmons didn't get to where he was by being outplayed by some glorified numbers cruncher. It was nine o'clock. He had an hour to figure out his strategy.

212

Voicemail again. Amy left another pleading message for Jack to call her back. She was feeling desperate now. The further he got away, the less likely it seemed that she could fix this.

At first, she wasn't worried so much about Jack taking this trip. What's a few days in Virginia? She'd get in touch with him, they'd talk a little, and after the convention, he'd come back home where they could meet and get to work on rebuilding their family. But that was assuming she'd get to talk to him. It never occurred to her that he might not answer her calls, that he would ignore her messages. She knew she'd hurt him, but she also knew he loved her and his boys and she believed that love would get him to at least call her back. Up until now though, it seemed she was wrong.

She put the phone down, sat on the couch and chewed her nails, trying to think of what to do next.

"Gerald, I don't know why you're so upset. I told you from the beginning that we should pay Hanlon what he was owed. The amount of man-hours it's already taken up, not to mention if this thing goes to court, which it looks like it will. If we lose..."

"What the fuck do you mean 'if we lose'? We're not going to lose Ross. We have him dead to rights. He violated company policy. He traded a favor for a sale. That's illegal. The man should be in jail."

"And when they get that old man Hornsby to testify that they'd never met before their encounter in the parking lot, and that Hanlon had no idea who he was until after the flat was fixed, then what? Hornsby's reputation is impeccable. It was a great bluff, but they called it. There's no way it'll stand up in court. The judge will see right through it. It's time to cash in the chips, call the man's lawyer and see what we can work out. Besides that, we've got a sexual harassment suit that is going to go to court unless we shell out a shit-load of money to that woman, and two other suits that are pending. We have got to make some of this shit go away, or we'll all be out on our asses. I have a pension I'm working towards and so do you. If you lose your job here, who do you think is going to hire you? You're old. No one is going to pay you a large salary when there are a thousand young eager law school grads sitting in daddy's basement waiting for a job to open up. They'll do what you do for half the pay and no parking spot. It's time to start bailing the water before the entire ship goes down. Hanlon made the sale. You and I set the bonus levels. That we can survive. Fighting against a contract and losing, we cannot survive, not with this new regime. We can always blame the former bosses for our past mistakes; we can't blame them for the ones we make now. Let's just settle with the man and move on before anyone gets wind of this and it goes from something that happened under the old leadership, to something we're responsible for. Think about it Gerald and get back to me. Good-bye."

With that, Ross Riggleman left the conference call. Rhonda, Carrie, Jacob, and Bruce all voiced their concurrence and left the call one by one. Fitzsimmons was left on the line alone having lost the battle before he'd begun to fight. He set the receiver down on its cradle and sat back in his chair thinking about what Riggleman had said.

He picked up his GS coffee mug, downed the last swallow and threw the mug across the office. It shattered against the wall.

His office phone rang with one long ring indicating an internal call. Without looking at the caller ID, he hit the speakerphone button. "What?" he bellowed.

"Mr. Fitzsimmons, this is Lucy Ramirez. Mr. Tennanbaum would like to see you in his office right away." Ramirez was Tennanbaum's personal assistant. Had Gerald bothered to look at the caller ID, he could have avoided the call; postponing the confrontation until he'd developed a new strategy. Now he had no time to compile any files or evidence to present in his defense. He straightened his tie and tidied up his shirttails, took a deep breath, and ventured out to fight for his reputation, and possibly for his job.

214

The sun had set by the time Jack reached the used car lot. He stopped along the way at an ATM to take a five hundred dollar advance on his credit card.

The lights above the lot were dim. Jack knew the game. He saw the salesman, a guy not unlike him, before the salesman noticed him. He was peering into the window of a Mustang when the salesman approached.

"Hi fella, what can I help ya'll with tonight? Like this Mustang?"

Jack offered his hand to the man and they shook. "Conrad, Joe Conrad. Nice to meet you," Jack said as an introduction.

"Johnny Finn, nice to meet you Joe. So, what do ya say we take this baby fer a spin?"

"Actually no. What have you got in the way of a cargo van?"

The salesman was unlike Jack in one way, he was a hustler. He was ready, willing, and able to put the screws to his own mother if it meant a sale and money in his pocket. Jack was counting on that.

"We don't have many cargo vans, but I have some beautiful mini-vans over here. That's really what ya want, Joe. The rear seats fold flat, the middle seats come out, you can transport anything ya want in these and then when work is done, the seats snap back in and you can take the family out wherever they need to go. You married?"

"Nope. Single and I'm not looking for a passenger van, just a simple cargo van." There were three shiny new cargo vans lined up, but the one that caught his eye was a beat up old Chevy parked in the back corner of the lot. Rust had started to eat at the bottom of the doors.

"What about that one there?"

"That? I could show you that, but there are others that..."

"No, that's the one I want to see. How much is it?"

"That's a '97 Chevy. Got a little over a hundred thousand miles on it. But it's a great vehicle. It'll run forever. Detroit doesn't make them like that anymore."

"Detroit hasn't made them at all since you and me were kids pal. That's a '97, it was built in either Mexico or Canada."

"Yeah, well anyhow wherever it was built, it's a solid vehicle, but I have others with less miles on them and no rust for just a few thousand more."

"I'm not lookin' to spend a few thousand more. Would you take nine hundred cash for it?"

"Sorry Joe, it lists for fifteen hunert. I'd have to ask my boss. I don't think he's gonna go fer nine hundred to be honest with ya. You'll have to come up from there. The scrap value alone is worth more than that."

"To be honest with you, I used to sell these damn things myself until just recently. Save your time and energy walking into the trailer to bullshit me over the price. Seriously, what can you let it go for?"

"Okay, I knew I was dealing with a smart business man. But if you used to sell these things, then you know I can't let it go for nine hundred. Thirteen is about as low as I can go. Seriously. That's the bottom. Obviously, you want this van. You gonna let it get away from you over few hunert dollars?"

"You know what, you're right. That's stupid. I have the cash, I like the vehicle. Thirteen is close to fair. But I want to drive it first."

"Of course, I'll get the keys and we can go for a test drive right now."

"No, I don't want to drive it around the block. This is an old car. I want to take it to my mechanic, have him take a look at it. I want to give it a good test. Keep it for a day or so. Make sure she runs the way she should. If she passes the test, I'll come back and sign the papers, if not, we're no worse off than we are now."

"I can't let you just take it. It's sold as is. If you want to bring your mechanic by here tomorrow, you're more than welcome..."

"Look, my mechanic can't leave his shop to come over here to look at an old van. I'll tell you what," Jack pulled eight hundred dollars cash from his pocket, "here's eight hundred dollars, I'll leave this with you as collateral, if I don't return the van, you can report it stolen, get the insurance money, and still keep the eight hundred. I'm not looking to go to jail or lose my money. I'll be back with the van and my decision. If I buy it, you get the remaining five hundred and the deal is done, if I decide I don't want it, give me back my money but you keep three hundred for yourself for your service. What do you say?"

The prospect of making three hundred cash for doing nothing was tempting. Johnny Finn didn't own the lot, but he did do a lot of the buying for his boss, who these days seemed to put in fewer and fewer hours while Johnny was putting in more and more, with no raise. This particular van, Johnny had bought at auction for seven hundred. He seriously doubted the boss would notice the van missing. He wasn't even sure the asshole knew the van was there in the first place. He was sticking his neck out some, but not too much, not for three hundred cash in his pocket. As long as the van made it back before the lot by the week's end, no harm no foul. And if this dude didn't come back, he was personally eight hundred bucks richer and the boss could file a police report and collect from the insurance company to recoup the seven for the stolen van. Johnny knew the guy had an angle, but he didn't understand what the angle could be.

From where he sat, he was in a position to make money on this deal one-way or the other. He considered the offer for few moments, trying to find how he could lose, but in the end he decided he was taking very little risk, and could only win in the end.

"Okay Mr. Conrad, you've got yourself a deal. My boss ain't gonna like this, but okay. I'll git the keys." More bullshit. The boss was never going to know about this little side deal.

When Finn returned with the keys, Jack handed him the eight hundred.

"You want a receipt for this pal?"
"No, I trust you. I'll be back."

217

Jack drove off in the direction of his hotel. He parked the van on a residential street about three blocks away from the rear of the hotel and walked back. There was still plenty of work to be done. He wanted desperately to sleep, but there'd be no time for that, for at least the next twenty-four hours.

He hurried back to his room to prepare for the next step of his plan. He hadn't looked at his phone since he'd left Chicago.

Gerald Fitzsimmons returned from his usual lunch at the Fifth Avenue Deli in a sullen mood. It had been years since he'd been taken to task by a superior. Tennanbaum held nothing back. Gerald felt cheated and betrayed by his colleagues. Worst of all, he felt that self-awareness that is the badge of the loser. It felt as if everyone he passed on the street could see it and know he'd lost. He hated losing. He hated having to admit he'd lost. Like it or not, he was going to have to swallow his pride and place a phone call to Seth Levine and wave the white flag. It was the general's orders.

Seth Levine was reviewing the financial records of a pinball manufacturing company that shut its doors on its workers without notice two years prior. One of the suddenly unemployed contacted Levine about a lawsuit and Levine had turned that into a potentially very lucrative class-action suit against Liberty Games Inc.

It seemed that the owner, no longer wanting to run a union shop, secretly shipped machinery and siphoned all of the company's assets to a non-union company in Kentucky. He then bought that company. When he closed the doors in his Chicago factory, he told the employees they would not receive their final paychecks, nor would they receive compensation for unused vacation days because the company was bankrupt and shutting its doors forever. Not even thanking them for the two-weeks free labor they unknowingly put in for him. Then he moved to Kentucky and went on with business as usual under the new name. Levine was excited to get moving forward on this one.

218

He was about to get up to stretch his legs and refill his coffee cup when his phone rang. He sat back down and waited for Suzy to announce the name of the caller.

She usually used the phone, but this time she stuck her head in his office. With a larger than usual grin and a hushed tone she announced, "A Mr. Gerald Fitzsimmons from General Systems is calling."

"I think I'll take the call Suzy, thank you," Seth returned the grin, "I believe they've come to the realization that they are holding a busted hand."

Seth cracked his neck, loosened his tie, put his feet up on his desk and picked up the phone. "Gerald, my good man, how *are* you this fine afternoon?"

"Just fine, Seth. Just fine," the tone of his voice said otherwise.

"Great. Glad to hear. What can I do for you Gerald?"

"After much consideration," Fitzsimmons took a deep breath, swallowed hard and continued, "General Systems has decided it is in everyone's best interest to come to a mutually beneficial settlement without involving the courts. We're prepared to put a new offer on the table."

"I'm listening. Go on."

"We are prepared to offer Mr. Hanlon the full amount of the disputed commission and bonuses totaling $363,072.55, if Mr. Hanlon agrees not to continue pursuing this matter in either civil or criminal court, he agrees that this settlement terminates his employment with General Systems and any of its subsidiaries, signs a non-disclosure agreement, and understands that this settlement is in no way an admission of guilt or any wrong-doing by General Systems and Technologies Incorporated, it subsidiaries, its agents, representatives, etc."

Seth could not contain his smile. This was not what he was expecting at all. He had figured that GS would want to settle before going to court, even before Riggleman's phone call. But he didn't anticipate a full amount settlement. He assumed they'd offer a low-ball amount and it would take weeks of negotiating to bring them to a point where they would go no higher and he'd have to convince Jack to take the deal. But this! This was a slam-dunk. He got himself under control and did what any good lawyer would do - he asked for more.

"I'm glad to see that you're starting to see the light over there, Gerald. It's a tempting offer, but honestly, my client has been through hell and back because of this. The amount you just offered is what he should have received years ago. He has since lost his career, been separated from his wife and children, experienced incalculable pain and suffering, and has spent what little you left him with on legal fees and costs. I'm sorry, but your figure doesn't take into account any of those factors, nor does it factor in the interest lost on that money over all the time it's been kept from my client."

Fitzsimmons groaned. His brow furrowed and he thought for a moment he might vomit. He hated doing this. He was under strict orders though to make this go away.

"I understand. What did you have in mind?"

"Well, let me ask you this, did Advanta renew their contract with General Systems and is there still a relationship between the two companies?"

"Yes," it was all Fitzsimmons could get out. He was choking on every word.

"Well then, I think my client is responsible for that and I believe you owe him for that lucrative relationship. Have you lost any customers since you summarily dismissed my client?"

"Yes."

"And did any of those customers site Mr. Hanlon's absence, or the ineffectual performance of his replacement as the reason for their leaving?"

"Yes."

Seth had done his homework. A lawyer never asks a question to which he doesn't already know the answer. "So one could argue that my client was a valuable resource for General Systems, no?"

"Seth..."

"And, did my client have unused vacation time, sick days, personal days, etcetera when you let him go?"

"Yes."

"As a fellow attorney, I'm sure you can estimate the number of man-hours my staff and I have put in," Seth was going for the jugular now, "not to mention my investigator's time, travel to and from New York, and his per-diem."

"Seth, really. An investigator? Nobody here has complained about someone going around asking questions. Let's stick to the reality of the situation here."

"No, Gerald, I had an investigator. A good one at that. I use him all the time. If you don't believe me, I have his receipts right here. Let me see," Levine pretended to shuffle through the investigator's receipts. He knew what to say, and he knew it would be the nail in the coffin. From here on out, Jack would get whatever he wanted. "Yes, here it is, plane ticket from New York to Los Angeles the day after Christmas. Rental car in L.A, hotel, meals, gas to Newport Beach, photo processing, you get the picture."

"This is blackmail Levine. Pure and simple!" Fitzsimmons was on his feet. His tie was loose. He was sweating.

"No, it's not. It's not blackmail Gerald. It is legitimate costs that my client incurred in the process of fighting for the money he rightfully earned but you refused to pay him. My investigator didn't know what you were going to California for until he followed you and saw for himself. We both assumed it was a business trip. It wasn't. Regardless, he bought the ticket, took the trip, did the work. Around here, when someone does their job, we pay them. Time you learned that lesson."

"Just give me the final figure," Fitzsimmons sounded like a man defeated.

"Final figure? So soon? We haven't even gotten to the pain and suffering and the broken marriage yet. Get comfortable Gerald, this is going to take a while. Oh and by the way, the meter is running."

At six thirty that night, the Hanlon's phone rang. Amy raced to it hoping it was Jack. It wasn't. It was Seth Levine, but what he told her was enough, she thought, to get Jack to call her back. When Seth was done laying out the details of the settlement, Amy hung up the phone, her hands shaking, and dialed Jack again.

"Jack honey, you've got to call me. You won Jack! You won! It's all over now. Please call me back. And if you don't want to speak to me, at least call Seth. He's looking for you too. Please call."

That night, Jack Hanlon was bellied up to the hotel bar. He was surrounded by fellow conventioneers, and was fully engaged in the next step of his plan. His cell phone lay unattended on the dresser in his room, red message light blinking.

CHAPTER THIRTY-NINE

A gaggle of middle aged men filled the hotel bar. Some of them dressed in the latest style of the day, others in the style of previous decades, unaware that time had passed them by.

Also in attendance were a few outnumbered female conventioneers, many of whom, in any other circumstance, wouldn't get a second look but were now basking in the attention of the hounds on the loose. Shiny, baldheads bounced around the room in search of a free taste of what they usually had to pay for back home. No wives, no husbands, hotel upstairs, and plenty of liquor. The rules were different here. Attractiveness didn't matter as much. Consequences weren't considered.

The night was young, but the men were already talking too loud and too close. The women were getting very flirty. The liquor flowed freely, and men jockeyed for position at the bar.

They exchanged stories of big sales, big bonuses, and shitty bosses. They traded business cards and cell phone numbers. They talked sports as if they were experts, and discussed politics as if they were insiders.

The bar was getting loud, and Jack had disappeared in the crowd, which was not what he wanted. So he downed his drink, stood on the rail of his stool and hollered, "My name is Jack Hanlon and I'm buying every woman in this bar a drink!"

The women applauded. One man yelled from the back of the room, "Make those drinks strong, big spender!" Jack slipped from the rail of the stool, fumbled through his wallet for his credit card, found it, dropped it while handing it to the bartender, and raised his nearly empty glass to the crowd. "I love conventions!" he announced. Downed what little was left in his glass, slammed it on the bar and ordered another.

A few women approached him to thank him for their drinks. Jack met them with drooping eyes. He toasted them, and gulped his drink.

The man next to him elbowed him in the arm and said, "Pal, you're making us all look bad. Don't do that again. I was just making headway with that blonde until you pulled your little stunt. Now she's back in the corner with her friends and the drink you bought her. Lay off will ya?"

Jack nodded at the man through heavy eyes and turned away. Then he stood on his stool rail again to make another announcement. "I have just been informed that I am an asshole. That was not my intention. This time, I am buying a round for every man in here whom I have offended by buying a round for every woman."

Of course, when put that way, most men did not take him up on his offer. A few did, but they were the men who more concerned with getting drunk than getting lucky.

Jack decided it was time to work the crowd. He stumbled off his stool and made his way through the throng, making sure to bump shoulders and trip into several people, spilling his drink on them along the way. He stopped at the group of young women huddled in the corner that the man at the bar had pointed out.

"Are you ladies having a good time?" he slurred, throwing his arm around the shoulder of the nearest woman.

"We are," the prettiest one answered, "thank you for the drink."

"You're very welcome. My father always told me that a beautiful woman should never buy herself a drink," he responded.

"I think you're drunk Mr..."

"Jack. Call me Jack. Jack Hanlon. Nice to meetchya. Yeah, I've had a little bit to drink, but isn't that what conventions are all about. Gotta let loose while you can, ya know?"

"Oh, I know," she placated him. "Are you sure you have enough money to cover all the drinks you've bought tonight?"

"I sure do. I made a big sale to the Advanta Group and it's just a matter of time before I see a big payday. I could buy a drink for everyone in here and still have plenty left, but why should I buy drinks for my competition?"

"Competition? Competition for what?"

"For you, I guess. You know, you're very pretty."

"Thank you Jack. You know you're very drunk?"

"Ah, bullshit. I would think you were pretty drunk or sober."

"Well thank you, but I'm a married woman," she held her ring finger up for Jack to see. The diamond was impressive.

"I apologize. I didn't know. I'm sorry. Is your husband here?"

"No. He's in Pennsylvania with our kids."

"Well then. You need a date. You should not be wandering around unaccompanied. Some of these guys are wolves. They may get the wrong impression and think you are free."

"That's kind of you to offer Jack, but I don't think that'll be necessary. You should probably get to bed. The conferences start early tomorrow."

"Gettin' to bed is what I'm tryin' to do. Wanna take a walk? It's a lovely night."

"It's fucking cold outside. No, I don't want to take a walk, and you're drunk. Good-bye Jack, it was nice to meet you, but you should go now." She removed his arm from her as if it were a wet sock.

"Oh, come on. What's your name?" He reached to put his arm around her again. She ducked it.

"Never mind my name, it doesn't matter."

"I'm Jack. Jack Hanlon."

"I know Jack. You told me already. Time for you to say bye-bye."

"Okay, fine. If you're not interested, I understand. Sorry if I bothered you. I've been drinking a little bit."

"Really? I hadn't noticed. Bye Jack."

Jack stumbled away from the beautiful blonde and sauntered up to another group of women and tried the same routine. Before long, everyone in the place knew Jack 'the drunk guy' Hanlon.

Jack kept this up all night long. At one point, he'd approached a cute little redhead who was talking to the biggest guy in the bar. Jack slid his arm around her waist and whispered something incoherent in her ear. This did not sit well with the big guy, who grabbed Jack by the collar and lifted him off the floor.

The room fell silent as everyone turned to see the fight that was brewing.

"It's time for you to go to bed, dude."

"Hi, I'm Jack Hanlon, nice to meet ya," Jack responded without malice, as if there were no contention between he and the man who was choking him.

"Well Jack Hanlon, if you know what is good for you, you'll get the fuck away from me, pronto, understand?" The man squeezed Jack's throat harder.

"I understand," Jack squeaked out.

The man released him and Jack lost his balance and fell to the floor. He stumbled a few times getting up, but eventually found his footing and made his way to the bar.

"Another whiskey and water," he demanded.

The bartender approached him and, leaning in so as not to make a scene, told Jack he'd had enough. He was cut off. Jack argued the point.

"I am not drunk!" he yelled. Again all eyes were on him. "I want another drink. You don't know who the fuck I yam. I'm Jack Hanlon goddamnit, and I demand another whiskey and water, pronto, mudderfucker."

"Sir, if you don't leave now, I'm going to have to call security and have you removed from here. Please. You've had enough to drink for tonight. Go back to your room on your own or I'll have you escorted out of the hotel."

"Really? You have me estorted fom da hotel? You know what I bought tanight? D'joo know what my bill is? I bought drins for eberyone in here. Ya owe me. D'joo know who da fuck Iyam?"

"Yes sir, you're Jack Hanlon. You were generous enough to buy drinks for all the ladies in here and some of the men, but you've had enough to drink and it's time for you to go Mr. Hanlon."

"Ju wan me ta go?"

"Yes sir I do."

"Fine. Fine. No probem chief. Gott'n lame here anywhoo. But I gumma call ju mamma ta come suck my dick. Ha ha ha!" Jack stumbled through the crowd. They made room for him to get by like the parting of the Red Sea. He tried twice to hit the 'up' button on the elevator, but missed. He gave up, and stumbled out the sliding glass doors of the hotel and out into the cold. When he was gone, the bar erupted in cheers.

"Good-bye Jack Hanlon and good riddance," one man announced and the crowd applauded again. "Hate to be him in the morning," another guy added, "Jack Hanlon is going to feel like Jack Dog-Shit tomorrow." The crowd laughed and the party continued.

Jack turned around, stumbled back into the hotel lobby, dropped onto a couch, and closed his eyes. This annoyed the night manager who tried to rouse Jack, but Jack wouldn't move. A couple made their way through the lobby from the bar towards their room.

"Excuse me," the night manager called, "you're coming from the bar, do you happen to know this gentleman?"

"That's Jack Hanlon and he's an asshole," the man announced then continued on his way.

The manager looked up Jack's room number in the computer, got a security guard to help him, and they carried Jack to his room, laid him out on the bed and shut the door behind them when they left.

"That gentleman is going to be in some serious pain tomorrow," the security guard noted.

"My head hurts just thinking about it," the manager agreed.

Jack lay in the dark waiting for the door to click shut. He knew what he was going to do next, but he couldn't risk being spotted. His plan was contingent on his playing the part of a drunken loud mouth convincingly. It seemed as if he had achieved that goal. He certainly smelled the part. The next goal was to get out of his first floor window and to the van without being seen.

Once he was sure he was alone in the room, he got up from the bed and crouched beside the window. He peered out between the thick curtains to the parking lot. He'd specifically requested a first floor room.

There were a couple of men smoking cigarettes in the lot just a few rooms away under the canopy by the rear door. He prepared the hotel room for his exit while he waited for the men to extinguish their smokes. When they were gone and he felt he'd prepared for any contingency, Jack slipped out the sliding window. He landed on landscape pebbles and cursed at the noise they made under his feet. Staying low, he slid the window to his room almost, but not completely, closed. Then he moved stealthily through the cold night and the desolate neighborhood until he was at the van.

It started on the first crank. The tank was full. The night was dark. The streets were empty. Jack pulled out of Virginia Beach and headed north towards New York. Toll change in one pocket, a steel gun in the other.

CHAPTER FORTY

Like before, Amy called the credit card company to locate Jack's hotel. It was late on the east coast, so she was confident she'd catch Jack in his room. He may be asleep, but what better news to wake up to.

The night manager answered the phone on the fourth ring.

"Hi, could you connect me to the room of Jack Hanlon please. This is his wife."

"Mrs. Hanlon, this is Jim Beekman. I'm the night manager here. Listen, Mrs. Hanlon, I can connect you to your husband's room, but I don't think he's going to answer."

"Is there something wrong?"

"No, I wouldn't necessarily say that, but about a half-hour ago, one of my security staff and myself had to assist your husband back to his room after, well, let's just say he had just a little too much fun tonight. He was out cold when we laid him on the bed."

"That doesn't sound like Jack."

"Well, ma'am, I've been working here a while now, and when men get to these conventions, they tend to over indulge a little. It happens all the time. This is nothing unique to your husband. He'll be feeling rough in the morning, but he'll be fine. If you call back then, I'm sure you'll have a much better conversation with him than you would now. But I seriously doubt he'll even hear the phone ring tonight."

"It's important that I speak with him. Could you send someone to his room to wake him up?"

"I'll send my man up, but like I said, it may be next to impossible to wake him. He didn't even notice we were dragging him to his room. If you'd like to wait on hold, I'll see what we can do."

"Thank you. I'll wait."

Jack smiled when he thought about his performance back at the hotel bar. It was too easy to transform himself

228

into an obnoxious drunk. He'd run into enough of them at weddings and corporate parties to know exactly how to behave. He was impressed with his acting abilities.

It may not be the best plan, but it was the best he could come up with. He made sure everyone in the place knew his name and his face and the extent of his 'extreme inebriation'. This would be his alibi. Everyone who'd been in the bar that night would know the name Jack Hanlon and assume his absence meant he was in his room nursing one hell of a hangover. A check of his phone records would show that his cell phone never left the area of the hotel. The rental car's GPS, as well as the mileage on the odometer, would indicate the car never traveled beyond Virginia Beach. Credit card transactions would all trace a route from Chicago to Virginia Beach and nowhere else. His name wouldn't appear on the manifest of any plane, train, or bus. There would be no report of him hitchhiking. He'd left only cash at the car lot where he'd used an alias. As far as Jack could tell, a thorough investigation into his movements would show he'd never left Virginia Beach. This of course depended upon one very important thing, that he make it to New York, do what he needed to do, and got back from New York without anyone finding out he'd left.

He drove on through the night.

The security guard banged on Jack's door twice then used his master key to get in.
The room smelled of stale whiskey and beer. The drunken man was no longer sprawled out on the bed. The guard's eyes had yet to adjust to the darkness of the room, but a sliver of light from the parking lot shone through where the two halves of curtains almost met. There was a mound on the bed draped in a blanket. The red light from the man's cell phone blinked from the dresser.

The guard approached the bed, the room door closing behind him. As he reached for the light switch, he banged his shin on the edge of a desk and let out a yell. He found the light switch and illuminated a floor lamp in a far corner away from the bed, rubbing his shin and cursing.

The bed was still mostly in shadow and the mound of drunken man never moved.

"This is fucking stupid," the guard mumbled to himself. He braced himself on the desk top with one hand while he stood on one leg, the other leg bent so he could rub the sore shin. "Hey pal!" he called out. "Mr. Hanlon, yo!"

The mound didn't move. "HEY! Wake up!" Nothing. "What the fuck am I doing here? If he ain't gonna wake up from that, he ain't gonna wake up. I hate being a babysitter for these drunks. This guy couldn't carry on a conversation anyway. He'd forget even having talked to the broad by morning." He limped to the door, leaving the light on. "Get some sleep pal. You're gonna be dealing with one angry-ass wife come morning."

He let the door slam behind him as he left.

Amy grew impatient listening to on-hold music once again. It had been three days of jumping through hoops just to try to get Jack on the goddamn telephone. This wasn't fair of him to do. Despite the problems they were having, despite what she'd said and what she'd done, there was no excuse for him to ignore her like this. What if one of the boys were hurt or sick and she needed to get in touch with him? This was just wrong.

When the night manager came back on the line he told her his suspicions were correct, the security guard was unable to rouse her husband. He promised to leave an urgent message to call home, but suggested she try back in the morning.

Amy was reaching the end of her rope. There wasn't much she could do now, but wait. She couldn't just up and fly to Virginia. She stopped for a minute and thought about that. Her mother would certainly watch the boys for her, and though they were stretched thin right now, they were about to get a windfall settlement from General Systems. To facilitate and expedite that as well as the rebuilding of their marriage and family was certainly worth airfare to Virginia. She got on the computer and started looking up flights. If

230

she could get an early enough departure, she could be in Virginia before noon the following day.

Seth Levine went home and poured himself a celebratory tumbler of single malt scotch. He didn't often dip into the really good stuff, but this had been an exceptional day. What had started out with tedious paperwork and eye-straining examinations of financial records, had ended with him taking a client from the brink of financial disaster to a two million dollar settlement from one of the world's largest corporations.

It had been much easier than he thought it would be. Fitzsimmons must have been told by the higher ups to make the thing go away. Why they would be so desperate to do that, he didn't know. The key point, he assumed, was the non-disclosure agreement. There must be bad news coming down the pike from GS and they didn't want any more bad press if they could avoid it. He made a mental note to call his broker and dump his shares of General Systems in the morning.

He'd gotten Jack his money and then some. The fact that he and Amy had split helped push the dollar amount up. Jack wouldn't have to worry about Seth's fee anymore, as Seth would take a percentage of the settlement as his fee, and there would still be plenty left for Jack and Amy to either split, or use to piece their lives back together.

"You've got a second chance Jackie-boy, don't fuck it up this time," he said aloud to the empty room, raised his glass in a toast, and sipped his scotch.

CHAPTER FORTY-ONE

WEDNESDAY, JANUARY 5, 2011

The sun had yet to rise when Jack arrived in New York. He parked the van on a residential street in Bensonhurst. The winter wind whipped through the dark streets. Jack put on a change of clothing in the back of the van to conceal his identity. With cameras everywhere these days, he was grateful for cold weather giving him the ability to hide beneath layers, a scarf, and a hat. He locked the van, walked to the subway, and took the D train into the city.

By the time he got off the subway in Manhattan, the sun had risen and the world had come to life. Taxicabs and delivery trucks and cars of every type clogged the streets.

There are two ways to get lost: in seclusion, and in the anonymity of a crowd, and the bigger the crowd, the better. Jack thought Midtown Manhattan would provide one hell of a big crowd, but when he stood on Fifth Avenue in front of General Systems Tower, the sidewalk wasn't near as crowed as he'd thought it would be. He was fairly certain pedestrian traffic would pick up by midday.

Jack walked up to the Fifth Avenue Deli. He ordered a corned beef sandwich for breakfast and sat down to eat.

He stared out the window at the bustling city; devouring his enormous sandwich and thinking about the last time he visited New York City and the Fifth Avenue Deli.

Early in their relationship, maybe the third or fourth date, Amy mentioned to Jack how she had always wanted to see a real Broadway show. She lit up when she talked about it. Her eyes filled with a dreamer's romanticism and she smiled the most beautiful smile as she described to him what she dreamt it would be like. Her face beamed. In that moment she was so pretty, so alive, that Jack never forgot it. So, years later, when he surprised her with a trip to New York and tickets to see The Producers on Broadway for their anniversary, she nearly broke down in tears, touched that he'd remembered such a seemingly insignificant detail from a casual conversation so very long ago.

They gave the little ones over to Amy's mother, and flew out of O'Hare into LaGuardia. He'd booked a room at the Plaza and they took a limo there from the airport. He didn't dare tell Amy what he'd spent or it would have ruined it for her.

They arrived on a Friday morning and Amy couldn't wait to get out and explore the city. They walked for miles and, by noon, they were starving. They happened upon the Fifth Avenue Deli and went in for a bite.

They got their sandwiches and were walking to their table when Jack almost bumped into a man coming through the door. He was dressed in a well-tailored, navy blue suit. Thinning hair was combed in a conservative style that masked the approaching baldness as best as possible. The soft, doughy face was flush and you could almost seen tiny red veins through the pale skin. Jack looked at the man. He knew him, but couldn't place the face. Then it hit him.

"Mr. Fitzsimmons?" Jack asked.

The man shot him a confused look. "Do I know you?"

"Well, sort of. My name is Jack Hanlon, I work for General Systems in Chicago. You visited our offices a few months ago to discuss the fine points of the new contract proposal for sales associates in the Medical Devices Division."

"Yes, of course. Nice to see you again, Mister … ?"

"Hanlon, Jack Hanlon."

"Hanlon, that's right. What brings you to New York, Jack?"

"My wife and I are here for our anniversary. Going to see The Producers on Broadway, get away from the kids for a weekend. Would you like to join us for lunch?"

"No, thank you, I don't want to intrude."

"It would be no intrusion, but I don't want to disrupt your lunch break. How's the food here? Do you come here a lot?"

"The food is beyond excellent. I come here everyday. Have for years. It is my one treat, my one respite in the day. I eat my sandwich and soup and think about anything but work. I find it recharges my mind."

"Well then, I'll let you get to it. I'm sure your lunch is short and your afternoon is busy. It was nice to see you again. Enjoy your lunch."

"I will and thank you. Enjoy your time in New York; it's a wonderful place. And while you're here, try the soup, it's superb."

"Everyday," he'd said, "for years." Jack's entire plan hinged upon the hope that Gerald Fitzsimmons, like most people, was a creature of habit and that the one treat he allowed himself hadn't changed. He'd said as much in Chicago during their initial meeting after the Advanta sale.

Jack wore a navy blue knitted hat, a U.S. Army jacket he'd picked up at a surplus store before leaving Chicago, a scarf that wrapped around his mouth and neck covering his face from just above the tip of his nose to well below his chin, the rest of his face was covered by a dark pair of sunglasses. He wore a pair of work boots that he'd intentionally gotten two sizes too big, and a pair of old Levi's blue jeans. He had a van in Bensonhurst, a gun in his pocket, a haphazard plan in his head, and three hours to wait. The only question now was, what to do until noon.

He slurped his soup as he pondered the possibilities. Gerald Fitzsimmons was right about one thing, it was damn good soup.

Amy found a flight departing O'Hare International Airport at noon, Central Standard Time, arriving in Norfolk, Virginia at just past three Eastern Standard Time, a two-hour flight. From Norfolk, it would be a twenty-minute drive to Virginia Beach. She hoped to arrive at Jack's hotel no later than four o'clock Virginia time.

She hustled the kids off to school, arranged for her mother to pick them up and stay with them for the weekend, packed a small carry-on bag of only essentials, and rushed to the airport on the off-chance she might be able to catch an earlier flight. She didn't.

She sat in the United Terminal of O'Hare, watching as other travelers rushed by, only to get to their gate and sit and wait as well. Winter brings plenty of delays, both into and out of O'Hare. Gates change at a moment's notice, connections are missed, and passengers are left stranded, sometimes for hours, sometimes for days. Amy prayed her flight would leave on time.

Sidewalk traffic on Fifth Avenue had picked up some for the lunch hour. Businessmen and women in well-tailored suits swung out the revolving doors of General Systems Tower while Jack Hanlon lay in wait. In the distance, church bells tolled the noon hour.

Like a hunter waiting for a twelve-point buck, he let the fawns and does and smaller bucks pass by unscathed. They strolled right past the would-be-gunman, the hunter, the half-cocked man with a taste for blood. Their heads buried in their smartphones, their ears glued to their Bluetooth and iPods, their minds everywhere but here and now, he let them pass, let them carry on to text another day. He knew his target and he wasn't going to take aim until he spotted him.

Then, like a pinball shot from the plunger, the prey was through the revolving door and out onto the sidewalk heading north toward the Deli; walking the same route, taking the same steps he had everyday for the past seventeen years, only this day would be different. On this day, there was going to be a detour, an eternal detour that would keep him from ever reaching his daily destination again. The man of course was unaware of what was about to happen to him, he was lost in his worries of office politics and the Hanlon affair. So much so, that he hadn't noticed the hunter, and for the hunted, that is always a deadly mistake.

There was street construction at the corner of Fifth Avenue and Thirty-third Street. The heavy machines roared as asphalt and concrete were busted. The workmen, having started their day earlier than the office workers, had already had their lunch and were well into their afternoon.

The businessman - the twelve-point buck - wove his way through the sidewalk traffic, the man in the Army jacket stalking from behind. Up ahead, the 'Don't Walk' signal flashed. The businessman quickened his pace in hopes of making it across the street before the light changed. The hunter thought at that point that he might miss his opportunity. They were approaching Thirty-third Street and that was where it was to happen.

The orange hand flashed on then off then on then off. The businessman approaching the intersection quickened his steps. The hunter did as well. Streams of pedestrians had now crowded the sidewalk creating obstacles to be navigated. The hunter wove through the crowd never losing sight of his prize.

The businessman took a step into the street when the light changed and a taxicab blocked his way. The once flashing orange hand of the "Don't Walk" sign now held steady as cross traffic flowed in front of him. He stepped back up onto the curb and waited.

The Church bells stopped ringing. The heavy machinery kept on pumping and busting, progress baby progress. The hunter caught up with his prey. A crowd stood at the curb waiting for the light to change so they could step off into the crosswalk and hurry on their way.

The light changed. Traffic stopped. A jackhammer roared. A generator whined. Cabs honked. The crowd stepped off the curb and into the street. A businessman in a wool overcoat, followed closely by a mummy in Army drab, hurried on his way.

The hunter felt his weapon in his pocket, held it tight. His senses were keen. He was alert. The timing was right. He approached the prey, awkward left-hand clenching the weapon, the right hand having been broken. He was about to pull the gun from his pocket when a dark figure came up from behind in his peripheral. He turned to look. Immediately he shoved the gun deep into the pocket again. Beside him strolled a large man bedecked in the navy blue uniform of the New York City police. The hunter changed his attention from hunting to camouflage so as not become hunted himself. He melted into the crowd and watched as the cop, having just crossed Thirty-third Street alongside him, stopped at the curb to wait for the light to change to cross Fifth Avenue.

With the cop left behind, the hunt resumed. The prey entered the Fifth Avenue Deli. The hunter followed.

236

Fitzsimmons placed his order and got his number: forty-two. He made his way to the back of the dining area and down a narrow hallway to the men's room. Jack got up from where he was sitting at the back of the restaurant and followed.

The men's room was small, one stall, one urinal, and a sink. Above the urinal there was one frosted-glass levered window that looked to have been painted shut with thick brown paint for half a century. It had burglar bars outside it and let in very little light. The floor was white and black ceramic tile, several of the tiles missing, tinged with the dirt and grime of decades of wear. A single bulb lit the room from behind a protective cage above an ancient porcelain chipped cast-iron sink.

When Jack walked in, Fitzsimmons was standing at the urinal, his back to the door. Jack could see the toilet stall was empty. There was no one else in the tiny room. The door was old and wooden and had a sliding bolt lock. Jack shut the door and slid the bolt in place, careful not to alert his prey. Then he waited.

Jack was still wrapped up in the scarf and sunglasses and hat and army jacket. He stood there motionless in front of the lone restroom door, his hands in his pockets, his left hand fondling the gun.

Fitzsimmons finished his business, zipped his fly and turned away from the urinal. The faceless man stood there, statue still, and Fitzsimmons jumped.

"Christ, you scared the shit out of me. I didn't hear you come in," Fitzsimmons was momentarily breathless and annoyed from being startled. "It's all yours now," he said to the stranger as he walked toward the sink.

Jack took a step to his right and blocked Fitzsimmons from getting to the sink.

"Excuse me, I need to wash my hands," Fitzsimmons had a slight unsteadiness to his voice and made a conscious effort to avoid eye contact with the shrouded man.

The two stood at an impasse for a moment, then, with sudden and violent force, Jack grabbed Fitzsimmons by the neck, squeezed as he lifted the short little man up to the point that only the tips of his toes touched the floor, and pushed him backwards until his skull met the plastered wall.

Fitzsimmons struggled to breath. He grasped Jack's hand with both of his, but he couldn't loosen the grip.

"Hello Gerald," Jack said in an overly friendly tone.

"What is this?" Fitzsimmons coughed out from his strained voice box.

"This is payback, that's what this is. This is karma. Do you believe in karma Gerald? I do. Of course, I'm not one to just sit around and wait for things to happen. If you want something to happen in this world, you've got to go out and make it happen. God helps those who help themselves, isn't that what the nuns used to say? Well, you helped yourself to my money, so I'm going to help myself to something of yours."

"Who are you?"

Jack laughed. For the first time since he'd arrived in New York State, he removed the scarf and shades. He did this with his free hand, the broken one, the one in which he could feel the beating of his heart, but he could feel no pain, the adrenaline having taken over and short-circuited the pain messages to the brain. His good hand continued to hold Fitzsimmons against the wall by his throat.

"Aw come on, don't you recognize me Gerald, it's your old friend Jack."

"Hanlon? What the fuck are you doing? Are you nuts?"

"No, I'm not nuts Gerald. I'm just pissed off and tired."

"Have you talked to your lawyer today?"

"No, the time for lawyers is over. I went that route. I tried to take the high road and where has it gotten me? Alone and broke and cast off by my wife; sent away from my kids. Homeless. That's where the high road took me, Gerald, to homelessness." Jack's voice rose and fell as the anger flared against the need to keep from being heard. Jack put his face alongside Fitzsimmons' so he could be heard without raising

238

his voice. Fitzsimmons could feel the heat of Jack's breath and rage on his neck and along his jugular.

"You should call him. Call Seth..." Fitzsimmons coughed out.

The strangle hold tightened cutting off the airway so that Fitzsimmons couldn't finish his sentence.

"Why? Why should I call Seth? So he can tell me of the new method you're using to try to steal from me? Uh-uh, ain't happenin'. Now it's between you and me. Right here, right now, this thing is getting settled."

Jack pulled back a bit so he could stare Fitzsimmons' dead in the eye.

"What I want to know most of all is why. Why did you choose me? Why did you decide I was the guy to fuck with? Was it simply because I was the one who brought in the big deal? Or was it because you could?- Huh? Answer me!"

A croak escaped from Fitzsimmons' throat, but Jack's grip was too tight for anything more than that to get out.

"I worked hard for you people. I really did. I know everyone says that and for some it's true and others it's not, but I really did. I *devoted* myself to GS." Jack had to struggle to keep his voice down. If anyone were to hear yelling, they'd come running. His anger hissed from him, like steam leaking from a pressurized pipe. "When I was at work, I *worked*. I didn't play solitaire on the computer, I didn't go see my kids' ballgames... I worked! I didn't manufacture receipts to add to my expense account. I came in, I did my job, I went home. I did what you paid me to do!" Jack's face reddened and spittle flew from his lips as he seethed. "I agreed to your stupid fucking contract knowing full well I'd never reach any bullshit incentives. Those were set high for a reason. Any asshole with half a brain could see that. That new contract was a veiled pay cut. But I signed it and stayed because I was comfortable there. I knew the machines. I liked selling the machines. I actually *believed* in the machines. I thought we were doing good! I liked helping doctors save lives. Hell Gerald, I was fuckin' *happy* there. Happy to be doing the job I was doing and happy to be working for GS. If you would have left me alone, I would've stayed until I either retired or dropped dead. But I'm no mutt either. A contract is a contract. It is legally binding. A deal's a deal. You do this, we pay you that. You don't do this, you're out on your ass. That's the deal. But you want it both ways. You want us to devote our lives to you. To see our co-workers and clients more than our families…"

There was a knock at the door.

"It's occupied!" Jack hollered. "I'm sick. You don't wanna come in here. Go next door!" Then he turned his attention back to Fitzsimmons whose eyes were bulging with fear.

"… you want us to do the work that brings in the money that pays *your* salary and *your* bonuses, but you don't have any devotion or even feel any responsibility toward us. It trickles down they say, ha! Trickle down, my ass! It all stays at the top. Well guess what, this time you took it too far. You wanted to take the fruits of my labor, renege on your end of the deal, and give me next to nothing. You wanted to throw me some crumbs and because I have a wife and family you figured I'd be *happy* for the crumbs. Well, I'll take your crumbs, but it's gonna cost you. I want something of yours. I want your last breath. I want to be there when you take it. I want to hear you exhale the last exhale you will ever let out on this earth. I want your life. You took mine, now I'm gonna take yours."

With his right hand, Jack reached across to his left coat pocket, pulled the gun out and pointed it at Fitzsimmons' head. Tears streamed from Fitzsimmons' dread-filled eyes. Adrenaline pumping through Jack's body concealed the pain of his broken hand.

Jack pulled Fitzsimmons by the throat off the wall, the gun still pointed at the man's head. He led him to the toilet stall and pushed him inside.

"It's nothing personal you know, just business," Jack went on ranting, "just crossing some t's and dotting some i's. You know how it goes."

"Jack wait," in the move to the toilet, Jack's grip had loosened enough so that Fitzsimmons could talk again,

240

though his voice was sore and rough. "Jack, it's all been settled, you won. I just got off the phone with Seth before I came here. You're rich. We caved."

Jack smiled. "Right. You really think I'm fuckin' stupid. I was born at night, but it wasn't last night. Save your breath, you don't have many left."

"Jack really and truly, don't do this! Don't! It's over, you won! I'm sorry! I'm so sorry!" Fitzsimmons broke down. Tears streamed from his eyes.

"Ashes to ashes my man. You sprung from shit and unto shit you shall return." Then Jack, dropping the gun into his pocket, spun Fitzsimmons around, grabbed him by his thinning hair and stuffed his head deep into the toilet. Fitzsimmons flailed and fought, but Jack was too strong for him. Fitzsimmons legs kicked helplessly with no traction from his loafers on the wet tile. The one arm that wasn't held behind his back by his attacker grabbed the porcelain bowl and struggled to push his head out of the water, but to no avail.

Jack pushed hard. He held the man's head down into the toilet water with all his might and kept it there as the toilet water splashed and bubbled, Fitzsimmons flailing for a breath, until finally the legs stopped kicking and the one free arm dropped from the bowl, the hand landing on the wet tile with a dead slap. The life slipped out of Gerald Fitzsimmons, toilet water filling his lungs, he drowned.

The body went limp. Jack held the lifeless head in the water for another minute. When he was sure Fitzsimmons was dead, he released his grasp.

Fitzsimmons' body lay motionless, head resting on the bottom of the toilet bowl, limp arms hanging off to the floor, legs spread out on the tile.

Jack stepped back from the scene and took it all in. It was done. It was finally done. He wouldn't see a dime, but he'd finally gotten justice. All that was left now was to escape without notice.

He replaced the scarf and sunglasses. He shook the water from his gloved hands. He pulled Fitzsimmons' head from the toilet and lifted his body, turned him, and sat him on the toilet as if he were there to do his duty. Make it look like he went out Elvis-style. Besides, he could sit there for hours before anyone dared open the door on the 'shitting' man. People would just assume he was taking a long dump. By the time the truth was realized, Jack would be out of Manhattan.

He shut the door to the toilet stall from the inside and turned the lock to the locked position. Then he climbed over the stall. He slipped when he landed on the wet tile and nearly took a header but caught his balance with his bad hand on the wall. It was throbbing again and the pain was slowly returning. He slid the bolt from the bathroom entrance door and walked out as if nothing had happened.

But something had happened. As he made his way through the crowded deli, he felt as if all the eyes in the place were on him. Something about the place had changed while he was in the bathroom exacting his revenge. The faces all seemed foreign to him now. He felt apart from the world they all lived in. It was as if he were an alien.

He walked directly to the front door and as he walked out into the cold and sunny streets of Manhattan he heard the man behind the counter bark, "Number forty-two! Forty-two, your order is ready!" That meal would never be claimed.

The van rumbled down the Interstate. Jack thought about Fitzsimmons' eyes. His eyes when he suddenly realized his fate. Those beady snake-like eyes looked right into him. Eye to eye. Mind to mind. Soul to soul.

Those eyes. That look of confusion and horror were burned into Jack's memory. He shook his head to shake the eyes away, but they remained. Emblazoned in the forefront of his mind.

He flipped the radio on and tuned it to an AM news station. A woman came on with a sultry voice to report the latest weather and traffic conditions, then a commercial for arthritis medicine.

"Murder in Manhattan," a male announcer declared, "details in two minutes."

Fitzsimmons was dead. The man who'd made Jack's life a living hell for the past year had breathed his last breath and now lay cold and blue on the coroner's table. Mission accomplished.

Jack had expected to feel some sense of victory. Some sense of closure. Some sense of justice. He felt none of that.

The announcer returned with the lead story. "An attorney for the General Systems Corporation was found dead in the toilet stall of a popular Manhattan eatery. Gerald Fitzsimmons had worked for the General Systems Corporation for eighteen years. He leaves behind a wife and two daughters. Cause of death is still undetermined but police, without giving exact details as to why, suspect foul play. They have no suspects at the moment and are asking the community for help. If you have any information, please contact the New York Police Department at 212..."

He'd always thought of Fitzsimmons as a harsh monster and evil businessman. He never considered that he too was a father. In a moment of rage, Jack had taken Daddy away from two children, brought violence and hatred to an unsuspecting family and forever damaged innocent people. Who was the monster now?

He turned off the radio and drove in silence.

Amy arrived in Norfolk on time. She rented a car with a GPS system to help her navigate to Virginia Beach. By the time she'd gotten from the gate to the rental counter to the car, it was three-thirty Virginia time. The display on the GPS told her that the estimated arrival time to her destination was 4:01pm.

She followed the directions to Virginia Beach, anxious and excited to reunite with her husband, to begin the process of healing, to make a new start on the old journey. She turned the radio to an FM pop station and sang along as Pink celebrated the power of female strength.

At 3:55 pm, Amy pulled into the parking lot of the hotel where Jack had booked a room. She'd driven faster than her GPS had anticipated.

At the front desk, the clerk checked her ID and her credit card, the same one Jack had used to book the room. Since the names and the credit card numbers matched, he gave her a key to room 122 and directed her how to get there.

The room was dark, the shades drawn. The air held the musty, sick smell of day-old booze. A figure lay beneath the blankets.

"Jack?" she called out, "Jack honey, are you awake? It's me Amy."

There was no answer from the bulk beneath the covers. As she approached the bed she could tell that the figure under the blankets was still as death. A sickness fell over her. She feared she'd find the dead body of her husband, his having choked on his vomit during the night or succumbing to alcohol poisoning, or worse - suicide. She approached the bed with apprehension.

Pulling back to blankets she revealed a pile of pillows made to look like a sleeping person under covers.

'Where had he gone?' she thought, 'Why would he try to trick someone into thinking he was asleep? Who was he expecting? Who was he trying to fool?'

At first, jealousy took hold of her. 'As far as Jack knew, the marriage was over,' she thought. 'Could he have given his key to a woman?' But that made no sense. A lover would certainly just climb in bed and find pillows instead of Jack.

She sat on the corner of the bed. From there she could see his cell phone sitting on the dresser, blinking. His suitcase lay on a chair beside the bed. He was coming back. The best thing, the only thing, to do was to wait until he returned.

She took the cell phone from the dresser, and, knowing his password, unlocked it. From what she could tell, he'd not listened to any of the voice messages she or Seth had left for him. He'd not read one text. He'd not opened one e-mail. He had no idea what was waiting for him at home. He'd no clue that Seth had been trying to track him down to give him the good news and get him to sign the papers. No clue that she'd had a change of heart and wanted to put their lives back together. No idea that all he'd hoped for and fought for was there, just waiting for him to reclaim it. He'd won the war and didn't know it. Everything Jack Hanlon wanted, was sitting there, just waiting for him, and he didn't know.

She searched through the history of calls on the phone, but found nothing of significance. His e-mail revealed nothing either. She lay back on the bed, thinking and waiting. She turned on the television and watched in horror as the news reported the death of Gerald Fitzsimmons, attorney at General Systems, in the bathroom of a Manhattan deli by an unknown assailant.

'Oh God Jack,' she thought, 'Please, God, that's not where he is. Please.'

Mrs. Kelly lay in her hospital bed coughing, but feeling better than she had when she was admitted. She watched the local news on WGN and saw a story about a New York businessman found dead on a deli toilet.

'The entire world has gone down the tubes,' she thought.

A nurse came in to check her vitals and change her IV bag.

"You're doing much better Mrs. Kelly," the nurse told her.

"Thank you. I feel much better. When the hell can I get out of here?"

"Oh, you're still very sick I'm afraid. We need to get you well before we can release you. I'm sure the doctor wants to keep you here resting for a couple of more days at least. Make sure your fever is down and you're properly hydrated."

"Couple of more days my ass. I'm outta here tomorrow, doctor's okay or no doctor's okay. I've got things to do."

"Well, you talk to the doctor about that Mrs. Kelly. I don't think you'll be ready to go home that soon, but talk to him about it. Try to get some rest now. The more you rest, the quicker you'll heal."

Mrs. Kelly turned up the volume on the TV and changed the channel to Wheel of Fortune. "Cookie sheet of paper you idiots," she yelled at the television. "Before and After! It's 'cookie sheet of paper'! Buy a goddamn vowel you moron."

Her strength was returning.

CHAPTER FORTY-THREE

Jack drove through the afternoon and into the night. His heart rate had long since slowed and the sweating had stopped. With the sun gone, the Eastern coast was bitter cold. He felt the chill in his bones and could not get warm despite having the van's heater on full blast.

Darkness blanketed him. Seeped into him. Passing headlights offered no relief from the black. It was in his heart now. In his soul.

This wasn't how it was supposed to feel. It was supposed to be a feeling of relief, of punitive justice having won. He was supposed to be enveloped in the comfort of revenge. But there was no comfort. No sanctified place in which to take refuge. Only darkness and cold and fear - and regret.

Fitzsimmon's eyes of pain and confusion flashed in his mind again and the gravity of what he'd done took hold. It weighed on him from his gut like a rusted anchor, pulling on him, dragging him down.

He thought about Amy and his sons. He longed to turn back the hands of time and be back in their happy home where money and lawyers, greed and treachery had no place.

He thought of his childhood and how his mother would hold him and stroke his hair when he would have a bad dream. Soothing him and kissing him and telling him everything was going to be all right. He wanted to crawl onto his mother's lap again now. He wanted to be that innocent child again. He wanted her to comfort him, make the badness go away and tell him everything was going to be okay. He wanted her to stroke his hair and make the stunned eyes of Gerald Fitzsimmons disappear like a bad dream.

That wouldn't happen though, of course. All he could do was pray that she would never find out, that no one would ever know what he'd done, not his mother, his father, not his children, not Amy.

But *he* knew. He would always know. There was no escaping that.

CHAPTER FORTY-FOUR

Jack arrived in Virginia Beach at a quarter to eight. Once he'd wiped the steering wheel, radio knobs, seat and seatbelt, driver's side door (inside and out), window and window crank with a rag soaked in a scent-free household cleaner, he returned the van to the used car lot, told Finn he didn't like the way it handled, but to go ahead and keep the three hundred he'd promised him.

Jack had thought about ditching the van, but that would've drawn attention. Finn would've had to report it stolen. Finn may have lied and said it was just taken off the lot, but then again, he may have told the truth, in which case the police would've had him describe the man who'd taken it for a test drive. That would arouse suspicion, and send people looking for him and the van. It was better to wipe it down and return it. Finn keeps three bills and his mouth shut. Jack leaves behind nothing that could identify him.

He walked a lonely walk down darkened side streets past quiet houses where blue light flickered through the windows from the television sets. In each of those homes was a family. Some content, others fighting their own battles.

Jack passed the homes and wondered what it was like inside. He couldn't help but feel he'd been tested, and had failed. He searched for that feeling of justice he'd longed for, but just felt a cold, hard emptiness.

When he reached the rear of the parking lot of the hotel, he crouched behind a parked car and listened. He couldn't hear anything but the distant roar of traffic on the main thoroughfare. He stood and looked around; he saw no one. He snuck through the cars in the parking lot, weaving between them, staying low to keep out of sight if anyone should happen by.

He was halfway across the lot when a beam of headlights swept around the corner of the building. He fell to his belly and rolled beneath a Honda. He waited. He heard the car swoop into a parking spot, saw the lights go out and heard the engine shut down. That was followed by the sound of slamming doors and a lady's laugh. He heard a male voice mumble something he didn't quite catch and heard their footfalls leading away from him.

When the lot was silent again, he rolled from beneath the Honda, crouched low and continued his serpentine trek between parked cars. The window to his room was within sight. It was still open a crack. Fifty more yards and he'd be inside. Once inside, he would shower and change and head out to face the crowd again, apologizing for his behavior the night before and in the process letting everyone know that he'd been nursing one hell of a hangover all day long and was just now able to get up and out and hoped his nighttime breakfast would stay down. Thus completing the final stage of the plan and solidifying the alibi.

A trace of his cell phone would prove it had never left his room. The army jacket, scarf, hat, and gun had been dumped with a heavy rock in a garbage bag from a bridge into the black of the oceanic waters where the Atlantic meets the Chesapeake Bay. The end of the nightmare day was in sight.

All that lay between then and now was twenty more feet. Once he was inside, there was no way for anyone to know he'd ever left. He made a sprint for it, reached the window, slid it open and jumped inside. He hit the floor, got back to his feet, shut the window and let out a deep breath.

"Hi Jack."

Startled, he jumped. His heart skipped beats and he momentarily lost his breath. A cry caught in his throat. He whirled around and saw Amy, his Amy, standing there.

248

Their eyes met and when they did, it was crushing. A head-on collision of reality meeting delusion. Reality won, and the wreckage was not pretty.

In her eyes he saw home. Home was never the little bungalow on Mobile Street. It was her. She was his home. And there he saw reflected back at him both the image of the man he once was, and the person he'd become. Not as he saw himself as he had in the mirror of that seedy motel, but as she saw him now. The love she felt for the man she married, and the sorrow she felt for the man standing before her. Those warm familiar eyes were grieving for him as he stood there. Grieving as if he'd been the one who died in that toilet in Manhattan that day. And in a very real sense, he was.

Tears flowed from his eyes. He thought for a moment he might vomit. His body trembled. Regret and sorrow filled the empty space.

"Jack," her voice quivered, "where were you? What did you do?"

Jack collapsed to his knees and sobbed.

THURSDAY, JANUARY 6, 2011

Mrs. Kelly unplugged the IV from her arm. She removed the medical tape and slid the needle from her hand. She took off her hospital gown, dressed in her own clothes, shut off the television and walked out of her hospital room.

"Ahem, Mrs. Kelly?" the nurse at the desk called to her, "where are you going?"

"Home," Mrs. Kelly answered.

"You've not been released yet. The doctor wants you to stay another couple of days at least."

"Well, tell the doctor you can't always get what you want."

"Mrs. Kelly, you can't just get up and walk out of here."

"Watch me."

"Okay, okay. Do me one favor, let me call Doctor Patel and inform him of your desire to check yourself out."

"You do that," Mrs. Kelly coughed. "You call Doctor Patel and thank him for his hospitality and his bedside manner. It's nothing personal, I just have things to do this..." she began coughing again, "... weekend and I can't just lay around in some hospital bed."

"Mrs. Kelly, listen to that cough. You are not well. I beg you, just give us a couple of more days."

"I can rest just as easily at home in my own bed. Better even. I won't have all these sick old people around me moaning all hours of the night. And I won't have you coming in to wake me up just so you can stick me with something and tell me to go back to sleep. I'll sleep better at home."

"Mrs. Kelly, I can't let you go."

"Am I a prisoner here? Am I being held hostage? Are you telling me I can not go, or I should not go?"

"I am telling you that you belong in a hospital."

"Can I leave if I want?"

"You can leave if you want, but I don't think..."

"I want to leave. Good-bye."

"Mrs. Kelly, if you're going to check yourself out against doctor's orders, you have to fill out some paperwork stating that you relieve this hospital and its agents of any responsibility for you once you leave here and that you are doing so of your own free will against the recommendations of your physician."

"Show me where to sign, I have a taxi waiting."

Mrs. Kelly signed herself out of the hospital 'against the recommendation of her physician', signed the paperwork necessary to do that, and shuffled down the long white corridor to the elevator. The desk nurse could hear her coughing until the downward elevator swept her away.

All the shades were drawn and blinds closed. Irene Kelly arrived back at her home from the hospital and entered a dark and empty house. She turned on a lamp and plopped herself in the recliner. Her breathing was heavy. She sat there until her heart slowed and she had caught her breath. She coughed a few times, harsh, gurgling coughs. She moved to the bedroom, undressed and put on a nightgown. She dropped into bed and fell into a deep, dreamless slumber.

CHAPTER FORTY-FIVE

A sliver of sunlight peered between the curtains and laid to rest across Jack's eyelids. He rolled over to get out of the sun's light and opened his eyes to an empty room.

She'd known. Even before he'd slid through the window, she'd known. When his sobbing had stopped, he'd tried to deny it, but it was no use, she knew. She relayed his day to him, minus some details, as if she had been there.

"You went up there didn't you? You waited for him, you followed him, and you killed him!" She was hysterical.

He denied it. He reached for her, but she pushed away.

"You have no idea what you've done Jack. No idea what you just threw away! What you lost! They caved Jack. They gave in."

Fitzsimmons had been telling the truth after all.

"Seth has the paperwork in his office just waiting for your signature," she explained as she sobbed. "You won. Two million dollars, Jack! That's what Seth got for you. That was your victory Jack! Not this. Did this make you feel like a winner? Did this make everything right? Even if we'd lost the case, would this have made it even? Do you feel vindicated?"

No. He didn't feel any of that. He thought he would, but he didn't.

"All this hell you've put yourself through, put your children through, and me, was it worth it?" Tears streamed from Amy's eyes. She walked in a small circle, wiping her cheeks then running her hand through her hair in disbelief and frustration. The crying had slowed. She caught her breath. She looked her husband in the eyes. "Why did you do it Jack? For what? Revenge? Is that what you were looking for? Revenge? Guess what Jack, there is no such thing. Revenge does not exist. We think it does, but it doesn't. The people you want to enact revenge on, don't make the connection. They don't see the cause and effect of it all. The message is lost on them, and so it is useless."

"And for the vengeful, well, they don't really come out of it any better, do they? Do you feel any better now than you did this morning? You allowed the same people who did you wrong to take control of your actions; you let them make you do things you never would have done. You relinquished control of your life to your enemy. You gave them power over you they never had before. That was your mistake Jack. That's where you went wrong."

He wanted to hold her, to pull her close to him, to find solace in her arms, the sanctuary he'd been searching for was right there all the time, it was her.

"I'm not going to turn you in, Jack. Maybe I'm wrong and selfish, but I won't do it. My children will not suffer any more than they already have. I won't put them through seeing their father tried as a murderer. But you killed a man over money, Jack. I can never love that."

She turned from the room and left. The door slammed closed behind her. Jack wept himself to sleep that night. He only awoke to remove himself from the sunlight.

CHAPTER FORTY-SIX

SATURDAY, JANUARY 8, 2011

Irene Kelly came to around eleven Saturday morning. She felt more energetic than she had in a week. Two full days of rest in her own bed had been good for her, and she felt she was on the mend. She walked to the kitchen, put on a pot of coffee, and switched to WGN on the little kitchen radio.

She made herself a hearty breakfast. Her appetite had returned, which was good, because she'd need plenty of fuel to get through the next twenty-four hours. Her cough was less persistent and drier than it had been the night before. Mrs. Kelly saw this as a good sign.

After breakfast, she showered and dressed in her prettiest dress. She sat on the back porch that afternoon, covered in a blanket and watching the sparrows play in the snow. Tiny wings and thin feathers and little thin bodies, and yet, they survived in the dead of winter. They not only survived, they thrived. These tiny little birds found a way to get through the cold, dark months so they could live to see another spring.

There was something to envy in that.

Mrs. Kelly dragged herself from her seat on the porch and went back in to ready herself for 5:30 Mass at St. Hubert's. She loaded her purse with lipstick, bus money, and her dead husband's gun.

She locked her front door and ventured out into the dreary dusk to hunt the thief.

Mrs. Kelly scanned the crowd. She took note of each and every person entering the church that evening.

She sat beside a young father and his three sons. As she scanned the crowd, she made eye contact with the young dad and nodded to him and he nodded back.

Mass began with a song from the choir and in the name of the Father, the Son, and the Holy Spirit.

Mrs. Kelly searched the pews for the face she knew she'd instantly recognize. She no longer found sanctity in the Catholic faith. Her new religion was the religion of revenge.

"Heaven and Earth are full of Your Glory, Hosanna in the Highest," the sound of the choir rang throughout the church. Mrs. Kelly turned, as did many of the churchgoers, to see the faces of the people who produced that glorious sound.

And there he was. Sitting up there above it all in the front row of the choir loft. The man she'd been looking for was hidden in plain sight among the beautiful voices. He was there after all.

An excitement overtook Mrs. Kelly. She'd found her prey. Found her thief. And this time, she was absolutely sure. Now that she saw him again in the flesh, she wondered how she had ever mistaken Dom Sicci for this man.

She was within reach of retribution. There would be no sloppy mistakes this time. She turned her attention back toward the altar and followed along with the Mass. Now that she knew where he was, he wouldn't be difficult to track and trap. She smiled for the first time in months. She held the songbook high and sang along with a smile on her face and murder in her heart.

CHAPTER FORTY-SEVEN

You may go now in peace, to love and serve the Lord.

With that, Mass at St. Hubert's ended. Father Denis Thadeus followed the altar boys in the closing procession down the long marble aisle of the church as the choir sang the Recsssional Hymn, *Adoramus Te, Christe.* The restless congregation was busy bundling up, gathering belongings, children and purses. Those closest to the altar were already filing out of the pews.

The hum of the ancient organ bounced off the ceiling from the choir loft to the marble walls, down to the floor, and around the church filling the air with vibrating notes that could be felt as well as heard. The choir sang large and strong. The Latin verses resting upon the pipe organ's notes to float and fill the vastness of the place with a full, loud sound.

Adoramus te, Christe,
(We adore Thee, O Christ)

The three altar boys approached the place where they would pass under the choir loft and next through the heavy wooden doors that led to the vestibule. Father Denis, lost in song, lagged several feet behind the rest of the procession.

et benedicimus tibi,
(and we bless Thee,)

The church was noisy now, not just with the reverberating music from the organ and choir, but from the congregation as they made their way from the pews to the exits, no longer whispering, but rather speaking loud enough to be heard over the music. Most of the crowd was still in the church, the exit stairwells too narrow to allow for a speedy disbursing.

No one seemed to notice the little old lady. Skeletal arms trembled, struggling to lift the old steel revolver. Blue and purple veins popped through celluloid skin. Shaking hands with frail fingers and rusted joints fought with the trigger to pull the heavy hammer back.

quia per sanctam crucem tuam redemisti mundum.
(who by Thy Holy Cross hast redeemed the world.)

A loud crack rang out, ricocheting off the marble. The sound loud enough to drown out the noise of the organ. A woman screamed. The music stopped. From the choir loft to the floor of the church, tumbled the large, limp body of a balding, beer-bellied man. He landed with a thud inches from the feet of a stunned Father Denis. The impact with the marble caused the front of the man's head to split with a horrifying sound. Skull against marble. The back of the skull was missing, having already been shattered by a bullet. The little bit of hair the man had left on his head had smoke rising from it. Brain matter crept from the broken head as blood seeped out of the wound and ran across the floor in a growing pool of crimson.

The sweet rancid smell of human grey matter mixed with the oily-smoky odor of gunfire.

In the seconds just following the scream, the massive church was overcome with a vast silence. The congregants had gotten low to the ground to duck behind pews or pillars. For a moment or two, not a soul moved, and all was still.

Above, in the choir loft, the paralyzed organist stared at a fragile old woman holding a heavy revolver in front of her as if still aiming at the vanished target; her eyes never moving from the spot where moments ago stood Marco Renny whose brains and blood now decorated the marble floor below.

The organist thought he should take cover or run, but he was afraid a sudden movement might draw the old lady's attention to him, so he sat still on his bench expecting she might turn the gun on him at any moment.

Domine, Domine, miserere nobis.
(O Lord, O Lord, have mercy on us.)

Instead, Mrs. Kelly simply said, in a calm and steady voice, "Got him."

CHAPTER FORTY-EIGHT

Amy Hanlon returned home to her children. She did her best to make home feel like home without Jack. Two weeks after her trip to Virginia Beach, she stepped out onto the porch to retrieve the mail, and there in her hands she found a large check made out to her from General Systems Corporation.

Jack had filled out the necessary paperwork and signed the money over to his soon-to-be ex-wife.

Amy held the check out in front of her. Behind it her sons played Lego Battle. She held the check to her breast and cried. Her reward for all she'd been through was something she'd never wanted in the first place.

Jack drove south.

He returned the rental car in a small Florida town and walked east along a desolate road. The sun, shrouded by the horizon, completed its descent in the western sky as day slipped into the dark of night.

The road stretched out before him with nothing in view but more road.

The air was thick. Jack stepped forward surrounded by the melody of the croaks and howls and buzzing of the predatory nightlife. Mosquitoes and gators and a dozen other various creatures poised to take a scrap of flesh if the opportunity were to present itself.

Jack Hanlon lit a cigarette and coughed. He disappeared into the growing darkness of the unforgiving wilderness of the Everglades.

Many thanks to Erin Dorgan, without your encouragement early on, I never would've gotten to this point.

Thank you also to Mary Anne Rooney for your critical eyes, your honesty, and your encouragement. You pushed me to get closer to my potential and you saved readers the torture of thousands of unnecessary words and paragraphs. Thanks also to the professional expertise of friends and family in sales and in law enforcement for your guidance and suggestions.

As always, thank you Mom and Dad for all the good advice you gave when this was still very much a work in progress and for your sacrifices, love, and support throughout my life. If not for you, I would truly have nothing.

Special thanks to: Carl Alaimo and Joe Carzoli for keeping me in a day job while I pursue this dream. Richard and Jerry for taking my writing education beyond the classroom. All my friends and family who helped spread the word on social media and beyond.

To Meg, for being my voice of reason, my grounding force, and my muse. I love you.

To Everyone who spent their precious time and money to read this book, I thank you and I hope it was worth your while.

Made in the USA
Lexington, KY
20 January 2015